LEGACY

OF THE BLOODBORN

Max Cooper

First Edition

C. Anderson Publishing

C. ANDERSON PUBLISHING

Published by C. Anderson Publishing

Printed in the United States

LEGACY OF THE BLOODBORN

C. Anderson Publishing Logo © C. Anderson Publishing 2013

Cover Pictures provided by Dream Times, Inc.

ISBN: 978-0615866529

10 9 8 7 6 5 4 3 2 1

For my Lord, Father, and King

To God, and his patience with me and for
blessing me always. To Ryan, Josh, Steph,
Don, and Brian for their ideas and input. And
to my wife, whose belief in me never wavers.

By blood things are made, and by blood they are undone. Thus there will be a time of great bloodletting when all the world will be unmade, and yet, it will be made anew.

The First Word
Summerset 1:6

The sun burned the vast prairie as dry grass danced in the warm wind. Faint screams of women and children echoed along the rolling hills as a pillar of smoke lifted past the horizon's edge. The earth quaked and rocks were jostled as two orcs raced over the hilltop and stumbled into the valley.

The elder of the two gasped for breath. The weight of his leather armor had become a burden – his mighty axe, an anchor. He slowed to a stop and fell to his knees. Sweat dripped from his face to the ground. The younger orc quickly turned and ran to his side.

"Urkog, we have to go," the orc pleaded.

"No," Urkog muttered fighting for breath. "They will track. We must split up. I will draw them till you escape."

"I won't leave you. We must go."

"I promised your father I would protect you. I fail by slowing you." Urkog pushed his ward away. "Go!"

The young orc reluctantly stepped away and fled up the next hill and out of sight. Urkog lifted himself up and tightened his grip on the old battle axe. He waited for his pursuers. He could hear them coming. Their loud metal armor clashed against itself. Their horses galloped across the soft earth. The knights darted into view; their black capes snapping like whips in the wind. Urkog drew in a deep breath before letting out a long roar and raising his axe to strike.

A spear flew under his arms and pierced into his chest. His axe fell from his grip. He stumbled to the dirt. For a moment, he found himself looking up at the clouds and the bright blue sky. The earth under him was soft and cool to his skin.

A gentle breeze tickled his face. The last rider grabbed the spear and ripped it out as he dashed by. Warm blood splashed Urkog's face.

The riders galloped over the hills. Mud flew from the horse's hooves. One of the knights spotted the fleeing orc in the distance. The knights quickened pace and closed on their prey. A massive man in dull iron armor led the pack.

A large scar across his aged face compounded his fierce gaze. He used his giant hammer to direct and command his men to flank the running orc.

A knight drew a rope from his saddlebag with stones tied to each end. He swirled it over his head before releasing it. The orc crashed to the ground as the rope wrapped around his legs. The knights encircled him, blocking his means of escape. The leader dismounted and approached carefully.

"I have to say, these beasts can run," the knight who threw the rope commented.

He was a young man with a wild expression and deep blue eyes. The meticulous detail on his armor portrayed his posh upbringing and highborn family. His cold gaze spoke of his ruthlessness.

"Not many animals craft such fine steel as orcs, Duke Erik Longcoast."

Erik shot an annoyed glance at his critic. "Well Stephen, any historian can tell you civilized nations are more than craft. I can understand how that would confuse you though, having no formal education."

Stephen chuckled at the rebuttal. He was middle-aged with unkempt brown hair and common features. The beginnings of a beard were on his chin and cheeks.

"Is it him, my lord Baron?" Stephen asked the leader.

Baron Umbra grabbed the young orc by the neck, "Are you Del'Caf, son of the Warchief of the Wazog tribe?"

The orc spat in Umbra's face. Umbra smacked the orc

across the cheek. Blood splattered the brown grass.

"My lord, tell us, is it him or did we burn that village for nothing?" James the Red asked fixing his bow to a more comfortable position.

Unlike his companions, he wore a simple leather vest and no helmet. His horse was smaller and his saddle simple. He could easily have been mistaken as a common hunter despite his high rank.

"It is not him," Erik stated flatly.

"It's him," Koll asserted, brushing his blonde hair from his face.

"No one asked you, Northerner," Erik barked. Koll clenched his teeth in distain.

"I was a Northerner once," Baron Umbra muttered, re-turning to his feet, "a lifetime ago."

"A different time and a different north," Erik defended himself.

"Is it him?" Stephen asked again.

"It is," Umbra concluded. "I saw the orc we killed with the Warchief at the meeting. He had to have been a guard. This is the son of the old Warchief, his only son. Koll, tie him to your saddle." Umbra said, beckoning the young North-erner to him.

Koll dismounted and wrapped the orc's wrists in thick ropes. The other rope end he tied to the saddle.

"You men in iron," the orc hissed as they tied him. "You have no honor. What kind of beast uses the Peace Place as a scouting ground? The Warchief will beat the drums and the tribes will come. Then your bodies will be stripped of their iron and left for the crows."

"I doubt the Warchief will risk his son by beating the drums." Umbra asserted climbing on his steed. "I think he will sing the Life Song and make peace."

"The Wazog will never sing the Life Song with you, invader," Del'Caf spat. The troop of knights laughed at the orc's defiance.

"We will see, young chief, we will see."

"My lord, it will be nightfall before we get back to camp," Sir Francis Drako said, "I doubt we want to be in open country at night."

Francis was young and handsome with a silent demeanor. The sides of his head were closely shaven to prevent any enemy from grabbing his black hair. His armor, though hardly as elaborate as Erik's, still showed his highborn status.

"We could make it at a gallop," Erik commented.

"The orc is no good to us if his body is left in a hundred pieces across the plains," Koll stated pulling the orc's rope to force him to follow.

"He may not be any good to us whole," Francis countered, "if the old Warchief refuses to deal."

"He will deal," Umbra asserted. "If there is one thing the orcs value, it is heritage. Without his son, the Warchief's life force will cease after he passes, and his tribe will splinter. The old Warchief will do anything to prevent that, even deal with us."

"You know nothing of my people!" Del'Caf protested, walking behind them.

"Silence, orc," Umbra barked back.

"I hope you are right, my lord," Stephen said, "else there will be a battle here unlike any of the current age."

"Good," Erik stated. "It's been ten years since the last real fight. Battles harden the ranks. How will we Broken Lances preserve our status if we are not sharpened by war?"

"It must be a trait of younger men to desire war," Umbra sighed fixing the iconic black cape on his back. The silver four-pointed star has been the symbol of the elite guild for twenty years. "We best get moving if we are to get back before the orc scouts find us."

"Yes, the Divines only know I have killed enough green skins for one day," Erik smirked.

> *To preserve man, the Divines made a*
> *compact with the ancient father Pertick. His*
> *line was pure of the black mark. From his*
> *linc came the first Prophet, whose name*
> *must never be spoken.*
>
> **The First Word**
> **Summerset 1:3**

The moon was high in the sky when Umbra saw the camp in the distance. Thousands of tents and fires covered the hillsides lighting up the horizon like sunrise. It was a most welcomed sight.

Head Prophet Philipus stood waiting for them at the edge of the encampment. He was a tall man with a slender figure and sunken face. The blue robes of his order swayed in the night wind.

Baron Umbra raised a hand in respect as he approached with his troop. The Head Prophet bowed in reply. Umbra slid off his horse and tied the steed to the water trough. The beast eagerly took to the water after its long day's work. Philipus looked through the group of knights and pointed a boney finger at the orc.

"Is that him?" Philipus asked.

"It is," Umbra asserted.

"Then you may have saved thousands of lives, my friend."

"That is my hope," Umbra replied petting his beast. "Koll, lock our guest away and bring him some food. We gain nothing by abusing him."

"Indeed not," Philipus agreed. "Umbra, may I have a word with you?"

"Of course, Head Prophet," Umbra said waving for his captains to take charge for his horse. He approached the slender man carefully; as one would a snake or a slippery cliff.

"Walk with me," Philipus requested. Umbra obliged with hidden animosity. Age was catching up to him and, as he walked into the camp with the Prophet, his thoughts drifted to a glass of wine and his soft bed. Philipus waited until they were away from Umbra's men before speaking.

"I understand you are the one who convinced the Guild King to seek a settlement with these demon worshipers," Philipus said.

"I wish, as does the Guild King, to avoid large scale conflict," Umbra stated.

"Our purpose here is righteous. The Divines ordain it. Why deal?"

"The orc tribes, if united, can field forty thousand hunters. We marched with barely half that. Only a fool would avoid a settlement."

"It is the Divines, not men, who win conflicts," Philipus corrected.

"And yet men carry the swords and bleed on the battlefields," Umbra replied.

"The Divines are in all wars, if you know how to see them."

"I admit I don't know the will of the Divines, nor do I pretend to, but war is one thing I believe I do know. For forty years, I have been a man-at-arms. I have seen four wars and countless battles. Many say the Prophets began the North Wars. They say you forced war by supporting the Guild King against the Lords. I know this war is part of your price for that support, but you have never seen a battle. A field of glory is a gruesome sight. You do not want the blood of tens of thousands on your head. A settlement is a much better way."

Philipus replied with a sly smile, "Your reputation as an

insightful, as well as powerful, man is well deserved. Yet heed this, man of war. I have seen the darkness gathering past the horizon. No matter what settlement you make, do not allow them their old ways. Burn every book; cut the tongues from every Shaman. Their masters are far worse a burden on my soul than dead men, no matter how numerous."

"Your support gives the guilds and the Guild King legitimacy," Umbra admitted soberly, coming to a stop. "So you have the right to make demands. I only hope you make them wisely."

Philipus bowed respectfully. Umbra offered no gesture in return. Both stood facing each other with an uneasy silence. Neither was willing to leave, and neither was interested in speaking further. The silence continued until a woman of distinct beauty exited a nearby tent.

"Ah, Lady Raven," Philipus called seeing his escape. "Umbra, please let me introduce you to Lady Raven of Eden. She is the daughter of Miss Edoweyhn, mayor of Mesmer City. She is our guest and most able advisor on the use of her mother's most gracious gifts."

"What gracious gifts?" Umbra asked.

"The cannon, of course," Raven answered approaching the two.

She was dressed in the elegant clothes of a Mesmer: a fine silk dress with long ribbons and a tight blouse exposing a firm bosom. Raven herself had long golden hair flowing down her back. Her face was lovely and well complemented by her kind smile.

"I rarely consider purchased cannons as gifts," Umbra stated bluntly.

Head Prophet Philipus chuckled awkwardly. "Lady Raven is also acting ambassador for her mother. She wanted to observe the campaign."

"And to learn your ways," Raven added. "The friendship between our people is vital to both our survival. It is my hope our bond will only grow stronger."

Raven presented her hand to be kissed, which custom dictates was Umbra's responsibility. Baron Umbra stared at her blankly not even acknowledging her hand. A few moments passed.

"My lord Baron," Stephen called out from down the line of tents. He walked briskly towards them with a scroll in his hand.

"My lord, the Guild King has called a council."

"This late in the night?" Philipus asked.

"An orc messenger arrived shortly before us," Stephen explained handing Umbra the scroll. Umbra opened and read the scroll to himself.

"Word reached the Warchief quickly," he commented while still reading.

"Yes, my lord," Stephen said. Umbra finished the scroll and turned his attention back to Raven.

"My lady," he excused himself without a customary bow.

"I best join them," Philipus decided. "Umm... Stephen, please entertain our guest."

"As you wish," Stephen said discreetly looking Raven over. Philipus gathered his robes in his arms and followed after Umbra.

"I suppose a warrior's life has hardened the Baron's heart to proper protocols," Raven commented, annoyed at Umbra's behavior.

"Don't mind him. He shows no respect to Mesmers, not just you."

"Why?" Raven asked. "Mesmer cannon aided the guilds in both the North Wars and the Vycesie Expedition."

"It is a personal matter and not a pleasant story. I doubt he would want me to tell it."

"Retelling a tale is all it takes to offend him?" Raven laughed turning away.

She pondered for a moment then said, "Did not Philipus instruct you to entertain me?" She said proud of her wit.

"It is not some play to amuse children!" Stephen snapped unexpectedly.

Raven drew back a few steps from his anger. Stephen recollected himself quickly and sighed.

"Apologies," he said lowering his head.

"No, I was being insensitive." Stephen looked Raven over again. She turned to the moon content with not getting her story. Stephen rubbed the back of his neck. Guilt lingered in his gut over his outburst.

"The Broken Lances were once called the Black Spears, many years ago," Stephen began. Raven returned her attention to him and listened politely. "Their first Guild Master was a young man-at-arms from Galsag. The first officer was a lowborn sergeant from Northrim who fled south after the Great War."

"Umbra, I am guessing," Raven interrupted.

"Yes. The guild found success, for a time. It was chaos then. No king or kingdom claimed us; just warring guilds looking for glory and hieratical lords desperate to keep their lands and titles. We lived as we pleased on our little plot of land.

"One of our rival Guild Masters feared our growing influence. He feared, however, open war with us more. Therefore, instead of violence, he chose cleverness and hired a Mesmer, a potion worker, to join the guild and become our friend. After he had our trust, he waited for a feast. While the nearly two thousand men ate and drank, he poured poison in every barrel of ale and ordered all mugs filled for a toast."

"That's terrible," Raven whispered touching Stephen's arm gently. He smiled and kindly removed her hand.

He sat down on a nearby stool and looked down into the mud, his gaze deep in memory. "I still remember the screams. You could hear them a mile away... It was over when we got there- pain frozen on their faces. Only a few of us are left. We were elsewhere for forgettable reasons."

"What happened after that?" Raven asked kneeling down before him.

"We scattered, for a time. Then our old Guild Master was approached by the Prophets and made the Guild King.

Why him, no one really knows. Umbra became a Baron and restarted the Black Spears, but he changed the name to Broken Lances in honor of the dead."

"Is this why Broken Lances don't join feasts?"

"Yes, that is why we don't feast."

"You cannot judge a whole people by one man," Raven stated rising back to her feet.

"Oh, I know that," Stephen chuckled returning to his feet as well. "I believe even Umbra knows that, somewhere in the deep parts of him. I do not blame the Mesmers for what happened. The men responsible are all long dead now, but he can't let it go. He is a man who clings to the old ways. In his heart, he is still a Northern man-at-arms charging into the fray. I think, sometimes, he would have been happier if he died in the Great War. Yet Umbra's curse has always been his longevity."

No man is born a king, regardless of what the lineage books say. A man is born a prince, but not all kings were first princes; and not all princes end as kings.

History of the Guilds
By Elder Lighours

The meeting tent was as vast as it was luxurious. A long purple carpet ran down the center to the decorative throne raised on a solitary platform. On each side of the carpet stood crowds of advisors, nobles, and guild captains mingling with prophets, scribes, and ladies. Large barrels of wine and long tables of cooked chicken and fresh fruit lined the sides of the tent. The whole scene struck Umbra as more of a royal court than an advance war camp.

Lord Beritor stood across the tent next to Lord Duke Herrion. Lord Beritor brushed his blonde hair out of his face and straightened the gold sigil around his neck. Lord Herrion wore a similar sigil, but his was far simpler and less expensive. Herrion's brown hair was chopped short for practicality and hygiene.

"So do you know what this council is about?" Lord Beritor asked while surveying all newcomers to see who decided to come and who decided to stay in bed.

"I do not," Herrion answered taking a drink from his cup and picking out several plump grapes from a tray.

Beritor laughed at his friend. "You came to a council without knowing what it is about?"

"I come to my king when called," Herrion explained.

"You are a much better man than I, then. I never do anything without first knowing why. Speaking of better men, there is Duke Johes. I hear his guild is the toast of the kingdom for their endless efforts to better the people's lot."

"Yes, what they leave out is him doubling taxes to pay for those endless efforts," Herrion mentioned. Lord Beritor laughed again.

"The clever omitting of facts is the foundation of politics," he stated. "Oh, and there is Umbra, Baron of Black

Shield: the ideal of a guildsmen, or so they say."

"Guildsmen raised this kingdom out of chaos," Herrion replied turning to see the great Umbra himself. He had to stand on his toes to view over the crowd's heads, but he managed.

"Yes," Beritor agreed, "but into what?"

Umbra wandered around the tent, uninterested in the many conversations around him. His eyes were caught by the countless trophies sitting as displays of art around the room. A full visual record of the Guild King's conquests was laid out for people who do not care about history.

Umbra walked around them, smiling occasionally at the memories they recalled. First, there were the horns of several Minotaur chiefs from back in the days of the Black Spears. Then there was a banner of a defeated lord next to the mantel of the Horsespear men. After that, there was the helmet of the King of Northrim, a symbol of his submission. Yet the true trophy of the North Wars was not an object, but was Koll. He was the much-loved son of old King Olfrie. He was the Guild King's hostage and their guarantee of peace.

The blue silk folds of the tent lifted and the Guild King entered. The whole assembly kneeled in respect. The Guild King was an older man with greying hair and a well-trimmed black beard. The gold crown on his head was shaped like dragon claws to match the fierce dragon designs on his armor's breastplate. His royal purple cloak draped over his shoulders with a gold four-pointed star similar to the Broken Lances' symbol.

The Guild King approached his raised throne and sat on its cushions. The members of the assembly rose, as was protocol. The tent was silent as they waited for the Guild King to speak first.

"I hear we are hosting a green guest," he said. The assembly laughed politely. "Where is Baron Umbra?" the Guild King asked.

"At your service, sire." Umbra stepped out onto the deep purple rug and approached the Guild King's throne.

"So your orc is well?"

"Well enough, sire."

"I hear there is a messenger from the Warchief here. How did word reach him so fast?"

"I don't know," Umbra admitted. "Perhaps they have more scouts than we thought."

"Or you let one live and he ran to his master," the King said in a deep tone.

"It is possible, sire."

The Guild King nodded his head slowly staring at the Baron. The Baron stood with his head bowed in respect.

"Send in the messenger," the King commanded.

Umbra stepped back into the crowd. An orc of impressive size entered. He walked in with the confidence and boldness of most orc hunters. He wore the traditional orcish mismatch of harden leather patches held together by straps. A fur of a strange beast covered his shoulders while many bones tied to his belt symbolized his kills. The orc stood defiant before the Guild King.

"Speak your message, orc."

The orc let out a snort then clenched his fists and closed his eyes in what appeared to be a strange prayer-like ritual. He then opened his hands out to the Guild King like offering a dish.

"Iron King, you come into the rolling plains uninvited. You march across burial grounds and burn villages that have done you no wrong. You sit in the Peace Place and ask for 'settlement,'" the orc struggled with the unfamiliar word.

"All the while you sneak out and steal that which is not yours. The Warchief, chosen by his tribe, demands you leave these lands and return his son. If you refuse, the Warchief will call all the tribes to him and they will be more numerous than the grass of the hills."

The Guild King sat quietly for a moment. He rubbed his chin and leaned forward in his seat. His eyes narrowed as he glared at the orc in front of him.

"Which chief?" he asked. "The orcs have so many I can't keep count," he said laughing and leaning causally back in his throne.

"The mighty Warchief of the Wazog," the orc replied, insulted by the question.

"Is he not just the Warchief of the Wazog and their allies, though?"

"The other tribes will hear the drums and..."

"The other tribes are desperate," the Guild King interrupted in a harsh, serious voice. "They fear the men in iron and they fear me. They know axes alone will not stop me.

They long to sing the Life Song with me. The old Warchief will beat the drums, but none will answer his call. The Wazog have raided the other tribes too long. They have made themselves strong on the blood of others. Is not, 'You eat what you kill,' an orc saying. You have killed the bond between you and the other tribes, now you must eat it. The other tribes wish to see the smoke of your burning bodies. They wish to see your life force severed.

"I will march on the Warchief and lay him and his tribes to waste. Unless..." the Guild King raised a finger to intensify the point. "Unless the Warchief sings the Life Song and delivers to me all the books of dark arts and every Shaman's tongue. Thus their corruption will be cleansed from this world and your people made whole with the Divines.

"In return for this, I will allow the tribes to live as they do now with minimal garrison. Agree and the Warchief will have peace and his son will be returned to him unharmed. I swear it. Refuse and none of your tribe will see the winter."

The orc clenched his teeth; his hands returned to fists. His eyes glanced over the crowded tent. He spat on the purple carpet. Gasps echoed through the tent.

"No Wazog would agree to this in the Peace Place. You chant for war, iron king. We hear and accept." The orc stormed out of the tent. Mumbles and whispers were quickly exchanged between members of the assembly. The Guild King stood, bringing silence to the tent.

"My war council will meet in the war tent," he ordered before promptly leaving through the way he came. Umbra sighed and shifted under the weight of his armor.

Duke Johes came up from behind him. "I hope you were not planning on sleeping tonight," he jested.

Umbra grunted and shook his head. "I am afraid sleep is a dream while on campaign."

"Yes," Johes laughed while stretching and watching the crowd leave. "So it will be war after all."

"So it seems," Umbra replied.

The Duke was a shorter man with a pointed white beard. His frame was slender compared to Umbra's, but his muscles were strong. He wore simple chainmail armor with a steel breastplate. The gold sigil around his neck seems out of place on such a common-looking person.

"How are you, Johes?" Umbra asked.

"My health is good. My guild is rich, and my wife is fat. I know many with much less." Umbra nodded his agreement. The crowd began to lessen, allowing a hole for Umbra and Johes to exit. The night air was cool, cooler than expected. Umbra breathed it in.

"The weather here is so strange," Umbra commented. "It is summer at day and winter at night."

"A strange land all around," Johes replied as he crossed his arms to defend himself from the cold. "I hear kidnapping the Warchief's son was your idea."

"It was." Umbra moved through the crowd and made his way towards the war tent. Johes followed close behind.

"I'm sure you had a different outcome in mind."

"I did," Umbra admitted.

"You cannot think of orcs as men. They have no owner-ship, as we would understand it. Any title or position is not held by the person, but by all his ancestors, too."

"Sounds like hieratical law to me," Umbra stated continuing down the row of tents.

"It's very different than that. When an orc becomes War-chief, he loses his birth name and is only known by his tribe. Thus, he is the tribe and the tribe is him. He is his ancestors in flesh and his children are him, not just from him. They share one life force."

"So why would the old Warchief refuse our offer?" Umbra asked coming to a stop and facing Johes.

"I don't know," admitted Johes. "I personally thought your plan would work. The orcs have no afterlife, only life force. The only true death to an orc is dying with no son, and then your life force ends."

"So again, why refuse us?"

"Perhaps the old Warchief does not believe we will actually hurt his son," Johes suggested with a shrug. Umbra stared at Johes for a moment.

"If it comes to it, I will kill him myself," Umbra said. He then began to walk again.

"I will pray to the Divines it does not come to that," Johes muttered.

Umbra paused. "You hold sympathy for these orcs?"

Johes smiled shyly and shook his head. "My lord Baron, I am against this war."

Umbra stood where he was, unsure how to reply, as Johes moved past him and entered the war tent. Lord Beritor and Lord Duke Herrion had already arrived and were standing around a round table covered in various papers and maps. A large arrangement of candles in the center of the table dripped wax onto the pages. Umbra came to the table and set his hands down on the rough surface. He leaned on the sturdy structure and fought against his fatigue.

Night settled back onto the camp. Guard dogs barked at the strange sounds of the strange land. Men returned to snoring in their tents and dreaming the morning will never come. The Guild King entered the war tent and immediately started to shift papers and maps about.

The Guild Masters, who had been waiting for nearly an hour, were silent. They waited patiently for the Guild King to review everything. Umbra swallowed hard seeing the annoyance in the Guild King's eyes. Apparently, he found the failing of Umbra's plan unexpected and generally inconvenient to his campaign. It seemed the Guild King had more faith in the idea than Umbra believed.

"How many hunters will the Wazog be able to muster before we corner them?" he asked. Umbra moved several maps to different places forming a more complete picture of the land.

"Sire, we can assume the orcs will try to head to the river and connect with other tribes. We have nearly half our cavalry patrolling that river. They should be able to intercept any messengers or reinforcements. If we move quickly, we can cut them off in these hills. The scouts say the hills are high enough to hide our approach."

"How many men will we be able to field?" Johes asked leaning over the maps to see them better.

"Around fifteen thousand infantry and two thousand cavalry," Umbra replied. "We will move faster if we leave the camp and luggage here with a guard and march light."

"You didn't answer my original question, Umbra," the Guild King pointed out. "How many hunters will the orcs field?" Umbra straightened his back and crossed his arms.

"Our estimates range from twenty to twenty five thousand, sire. Far less than we feared, also the orcs seem to have no cavalry or archers. Moreover, they are raiders and hunters. They are not acquainted with large scale war."

"The Divines blessed us then," the Guild King stated letting out an anxious breath.

"That is how the Prophets would see it, sire," Umbra commented.

"But not you, Baron?"

"Sire, as Duke Johes would say, we cannot treat orcs like men. Orcs are known to be brutal fighters."

"Brutal yes," Lord Beritor added, "but not very smart. We will out maneuver them, sire."

"I only advise caution," Umbra stated.

"Always good advice," the Guild King agreed. "If the old Warchief won't deal, what do we do with his son?"

"Kill him," Lord Beritor proclaimed waving a dismissive hand. "He is no good to us now. Chop his head off and send it to the other tribes as a message. Let them see what happens when you are stubborn and won't see reason." Duke Johes shook his head in disgust.

"You will gain nothing by killing him," he said.

"And you are the expert on orcs?" Lord Beritor countered.

"It doesn't take an expert to see the flaw in your plan. You would be destroying the Warchief's life force. He would lose all reason to exist. He would become emboldened, frantic even. The rage it would cause among the orcs could never be quenched. There is nothing more dangerous than a beast with nothing to lose."

"Life force? I don't even know what you are talking about," Lord Beritor laughed. "Sounds like rubbish to me. What I do know is that we must keep our word. We said to the Warchief, deal or we kill your son. He refuses to deal therefore the son must die: simple as that."

"Sire," Johes said turning towards the Guild King and ignoring Beritor entirely. "After we defeat his father, the son will be useful in forcing a peace deal beneficial to us, but only if he is alive."

"I take the word of Duke Johes seriously," Baron Umbra began, "but I cannot believe the old Warchief would have such disregard for his son. I take his defiance as a bluff. He believes we will not harm Del'Caf in fear of losing our leverage. Thus I suggest we cut off a hand and send it to the old Warchief to show the nature of our resolve."

"Do we know if the Warchief is the power or just the ass on the throne?" Lord Duke Herrion asked breaking his long silence. The other members of the council looked at each other unsure of the question.

"What do you mean?" Umbra asked.

"Well, like you Baron, I find the old Warchief's disregard troubling. Is it possible age has forced his advisors to take the reins, so to speak? It would not be the first time such a thing has happened."

"Unlikely," Johes said shaking his head.

"Why?" Herrion asked thoughtfully.

"The orcs would see such acts as offensive to the tribe. The Warchief is the tribe embodied; one cannot go against that."

"Then even more reason to kill the green skin," Lord Beritor said with a casual wave of his hand. "His death will dishearten the whole tribe."

Johes glared at Beritor with an expression of sheer shock. "Have you heard nothing I said?" he asked.

"I have heard you, Duke. However, I fail to see the negative as you do. If we kill the pup, it will hurt the Warchief's judgment. You yourself said he would become irrational. That could become our advantage, and why should we care if his tribe becomes enraged? What people love invaders? Personally, the overly cautious nature of the Duke makes me ponder his intentions. Maybe the poor state of his guild makes him fear battle."

"How dare you!" Duke Johes growled in a low voice.

"It is understandable, your guild is nearly a forth of our forces and most of them are fresh off their mother's tit."

"My boys are the finest in all the lands of Galsag!" Johes barked. Lord Beritor snickered.

"Oh please, I have seen your training methods."

"I will not be spoken down to on guild matters by some highborn who founded a guild for tax purposes!"

Lord Beritor began to laugh aloud. Duke Johes took a step forward in anger. The Guild King raised his hand and all grew quiet.

"Tell me, Lord Beritor," he began in a soft voice. "What good is a dead hostage? Will one pay ransom for a corpse? Also, why give the enemy fire to feed his blood thirst? The young orc will remain our guest, unharmed in any way. Perhaps the old Warchief is bluffing, perhaps he is not. Can we know the motives of orcs when we rarely understand the motives of men?

"All our scouts and spies say the Wazog tribe can unite the orcs. This must not happen. So, we will march with the bulk of our forces and destroy the Wazog. A garrison will be left with the camp and any supplies we cannot carry. This will serve to confuse our enemy's scouts. The army will travel light and sleep in the mud for a few weeks. We will leave at first light."

The Guild King stood back from the table. "If there is nothing else, my lords, I am exhausted." The Guild Masters chuckled politely. The Guild King smiled and left. The Guild Masters bowed as he did.

Umbra stretched and yawned. "So war it will be. See you all for the march. It will not be a pleasant one."

Lord Beritor began to walk out of the tent when Duke Johes cut in front of him, rudely pushing him aside. Lord Beritor smirked at the gesture. Lord Duke Herrion sighed.

"Why do you insult the good Duke like that?" he asked.

"He invites insult," Lord Beritor replied.

"He seems to take your remarks personally."

"How do you know it is not personal?"

"Because we are highborn," Herrion commented, "and highborn do not make anything personal. It's bad manners."

"Among the highborn you would be right, but our current masters are soldiers with titles undeserving of their families. You expect me to believe you don't suffer under these guildmen's rule? I know you better than that. They are thugs and sell swords only in power by virtue of bloody victories."

Herrion nodded, unable to dispute much of what his friend said. "If I remember right, Lord Beritor, you supported the Guild King in the North Wars: a time when many highborns felt as you do and went to the North's King Olfrie for assistance."

Beritor waved a dismissing hand. "The Prophets had already thrown their support behind the guilds. It was suicidal for the Lords to challenge the combined might of the guilds and the Prophets. One thing has always been true in Galsag- where the Prophets go, so goes the kingdom. Like you say, Herrion, it was not personal."

"So survival is your family's words?"

"Might as well be."

"And is that what you are doing here, Lord Beritor?" Herrion gestured his hands around the tent. "Surviving?"

"Yes," Beritor proudly admitted, "and when the guilds lose their ill-gotten power, I will survive that too."

"No one would dare test the Guild King's power."

"No, but they most certainly might test his successor. The Guild King has no noble blood. His power comes from the sword. Once he dies, so does his authority."

"The Prophets have already sworn to uphold the heir, as have his grandfather, Lord Drako."

"But will they?" Beritor pondered aloud. "All it takes is one man of power to say no to him and the whole scale of power in the kingdom shifts. The guilds have more weight on their scale for now but these lowborns won't keep it."

"It is a mistake to call them lowborns," Herrion corrected.

"You consider them our equal?" Beritor asked shocked at the notion.

"No, of course not," Herrion assured, "but they are not lowborn either. They were conceived in war, birthed in battle, and raised in steel. Lowborn? No – they are bloodborn."

If you war, war only evil. If you love, love only good. If you mourn, mourn only the righteous.

The First Word
Harrowed 5:19

Blowing snow blocked out the sun. The wind whistled through the roaring melee. Hundreds of men clashed over a frozen river. Arrows filled the sky while blood turned the snow red. Umbra struggled under his fur cloak. He knew the place well.

Slushing through the icy water, Umbra moved past the endless fighting. On the edge of the battle stood a beautiful woman whom Umbra felt he ought to know. Tears of blood were flowing down her cheeks.

Umbra awoke to Stephen shaking him in his bed. "The orc has escaped," Stephen said hiding his fear of Umbra's displeasure. Umbra sprung to his feet leaving his strange dream behind.

"What?"

"The orc has escaped, my lord," Stephen repeated.

"I heard you the first time." Umbra said, throwing on a tunic. "How did this happen?"

"We believe it was the orc messenger. He killed his escorts then released the hostage."

"He has to be brought back," Umbra ordered finding his belt and tightening it around his waist. "Am I clear? Without him this campaign could turn against us."

"I understand, my lord."

Umbra walked out of his tent. Riders and men were darting everywhere panicked. Umbra turned to Stephen and asked, "How many men did you send after him?"

"Erik took fifty of his knights, my lord."

"Send another hundred cavalry. And wake the Guild King and organize the Broken Lances to march. The king will want to hit the Wazog soon now. Tell the men to bring nothing they cannot carry, and bring me my horse."

"Yes, my lord," Stephen bowed low before leaving. Umbra returned to his tent and sat at his writing desk. He rubbed his temples with two rough fingers, hoping his headache would retreat. He walked over to a basin of water and splashed his face. The cool drops of water ran down his chin and fell to the ground.

The woman he saw in his dream stood out in his mind. He struggled to recognize her. The image of her tears refused to leave even as he pulled his armor from its stand.

He started to slide into his under-padding when he realized he had no aides to assist him with the ties on the back and sides. He dropped the pad to the ground and poured himself a cup of wine instead. He was lifting the glass to his lips when Raven bursted into the tent with a face red with anger.

"Did you issue the order for me to be left behind when the army moves?" she demanded. Umbra calmly sat down his cup and tapped a finger on his desk in thought.

After a moment, he pointed at Raven. "You can help me

with my armor," Umbra said picking his pad back up.

"Answer my question!"

"I don't know how it is with Mesmers," Umbra stated, "but in Galsag, people tend to speak to lords more politely." Raven's face turned from red with anger to red with embarrassment.

"I'm sorry; I can be brash at times."

"I noticed."

"My lord, please – answer my question. I wish to know."

"I will, if you help me with my armor." Raven sighed and approached Umbra. He lifted his arms as Raven tied the straps on the padded undershirt. Raven looked at all the parts of the armor and swore under her breath.

"How do you wear all this?" she asked.

"Years of practice."

"So, my lord Baron, did you ban me from traveling with the army?"

"You make it sound personal."

"Isn't it?" Raven yanked on two cords pushing the wind out of Umbra's chest.

"No," he coughed. "I banned all delegates and persons not directly needed on the field. A battle is not the theatre, little Mesmer. The army will be traveling light and has no wagons to spare for your luggage."

"I am not a simple delegate," Raven insisted.

Umbra laughed. "Oh – pray tell why not?"

"I am charged with the oversight of the cannon, how can

I assist in their use if I am a hundred miles away?"

"The cannon are staying here," Umbra stated.

"What? Why are you marching without your greatest asset?"

"Cannon are heavy. They take a lot of horses to move and slow down the whole march."

Raven finished with the pad straps and helped Umbra slide his legs into each of the greaves.

"How will you defeat the orcs with no cannon?" she asked.

"The same way we have defeated dozens of enemies before our deal with your mother; with blood and steel." Umbra lifted his chest plate onto his shoulders with a grunt. Raven stood to her feet and began to tie the metal plates together.

"I know you hate Mesmers," she said, "but that is no reason to endanger men needlessly."

"You know that, do you?"

"Yes," Raven insisted. "Stephen told me about your guild." Umbra grew somber and instantly cold.

"He had no right to tell you about that," he muttered.

"You know not all Mesmers are..."

"Are what?" Umbra interrupted harshly. "Death merchants? Impious ironmongers who would sell their hearts for gold and silver? Who spit on the Divines and the First Word with their contemptible lifestyles? The Great War could have ended at the Mesmer's whim, but the profits were just too tempting."

"What are you talking about? The Mesmers were neutral in the war."

"Yes, a status they used to great benefit. Your so-called neutrality allowed your people to sell cannon to both sides, did it not? Galsag and Northrim had fought wars before, true, but the cannons allowed the Great War's butchery to last thirty years.

"I was born to the sound of cannon and screaming men. I watched cities burn and castles crumble. I walked with the masses of serfs driven from their homes. I saw their faces drained of hope and filled with despair. You think Stephen's tale is the reason I hate Mesmers? No, my lady, my hatred of your people is far deeper than one slight."

Raven was silent as she finished the final strap on Umbra's armor.

"I'm going to be mayor after my mother," Raven whispered still holding the tied cords in her hands. "Tradition would have my brother, but everyone knows he has no heart for rule. If I am going to run the last free city in the world, I need to see what it is to rule. You say you grew up witnessing my people's works; well I have not. I need to see what the world really is, not what people tell me." Umbra shifted in his armor. He adjusted the chest plate to his comfort. Stephen walked into the tent.

"Your horse is ready, my lord."

"Thank you, Stephen." Umbra walked away towards Stephen.

"My lord, please," Raven cried chasing after him. Umbra

mounted his horse. Stephen handed him his hammer. Raven grabbed onto Umbra's saddle and looked up at him with desperate eyes. Umbra sighed.

"You cannot bring any aides or luggage," he said as she leapt in joy. "I mean it, my lady. It was no jest about the wagons having little room."

"Thank you, my lord," Raven said bowing low.

"And you are to remain near the King's guard at all times. The last thing I need on my conscience is a dead woman."

"Of course, my lord."

"I just hope you don't get saddle sores easily," Umbra chuckled. Stephen laughed as well. Raven glared at him. Stephen stopped laughing. Umbra laughed harder.

In the distance, a horn blew. Umbra and Stephen turned to listen. Stephen patted Umbra's horse to comfort it.

"That is Erik's horn," Stephen commented. "He must have found the orc."

"Must have," Umbra agreed.

Across the open plains, Erik finished blowing his horn. His brother Thomas drew his sword. They rode at full gallop over the hill. Troops of knights paralleled them on the opposite hill. The two orcs fled into a prairie with swords they stole from their murdered guards. The swords were clumsy in their large hands.

Thomas darted towards Del'Caf. Del'Caf swung at Thomas' head. Thomas leaned left, barely avoiding the sword's edge, before quickly counting with the butt of his handle to the orc's skull. Del'Caf fell with a thump.

The other orc turned to fight when Erik rammed him with his horse. The collision knocked both the orc and Erik's horse to the ground. Thomas leapt from his mount and ran to his brother's aid.

"Erik," Thomas cried. "Are you alright?"

"I didn't think that would happen," Erik stated.

Thomas laughs. The orc messenger staggered to his feet and began to run away when several knights dashed down and surrounded him. Two dismounted and forced him to his knees and bound his hands.

"If you cowards would leave your beasts," the orc yelled, "and fight as true hunters, I would drench the ground in your blood."

"And if you would stop fleeing like frightened deer, I would not need the horse to chase you, green skin!" Erik yelled back with a laugh. He grabbed Thomas' hand and rose to his feet.

"Easy," Thomas said concerned.

"Thomas, I'm fine. Tell me, green skin," Erik said approaching the caught beast. "Is it customary in your land to betray the banner of truce? Your Warchief is without honor. He sends a messenger with the façade of dealings. When, in truth, he wishes to be a thief!"

The orc began to laugh at Erik. Erik glanced to his brother, puzzled. "Why are you laughing?" he asked. "Thomas, why is he laughing?"

"I am not here on the orders of the Warchief," the orc chuckled.

"What are you talking about?"

"It is the duty of all Wazog to protect the Warchief's life force, so the spirit of our tribe may live forever."

"The Warchief did not send you?" Erik asked.

"We must inform the Guild King," one knight exclaimed.

"We will do no such thing, Sir Martin," Erik ordered.

"But, my lord, this means the Warchief may not know about his son. A settlement could still be made."

"I have no doubt the Warchief already knows about his son," Erik replied. "His lack of response is proof no settlement can be reached. We will speak no word of this."

"But, my lord, it has barely been a day. Perhaps a true messenger from the Warchief is yet to arrive."

"I said no word, Sir Martin, on pain of death. This is a sign from the Divines. They want no settlement, and I will not see us cursed over it. Now take the runt orc back to camp."

"Yes, my lord," Sir Martin obeyed, leaving with Del'Caf lying unconscious across a horse. Thomas waited for them to leave before speaking.

"I have never thought you a religious man."

"I'm not," Erik stated grabbing the orc messenger by the neck and lowering himself to the orc's face. "I am going to let you go, and you are going to sound the war drums among the tribes and tell the Warchief we are coming for him. You will not tell him his son is our hostage. If you do, there will be no war between our people. And no one wants that. But, if he believes his life force is safe, then the Warchief will give us a battle for the ages. Then we will see whose blood covers the grass."

"Untie me and I will show you," the orc hissed.

"Uh huh." Erik knocked the orc over the head with his sword handle. The orc tumbled over. Erik cut the ropes from the orc's hands and mounted his horse. Thomas followed.

"Umbra will gut you and hang your body from a tree if he finds out. You wouldn't be the first lord he has strung up," Thomas informed.

"Umbra is old, so is the Guild King. New leaders must rise to replace the dying, and one cannot prove his merit in the practice circle. This will be the last great campaign of our age: the last chance of glory and title. We would be fools to pass it up. I will not let Umbra steal the moment I have been training for my whole life just because he grew a conscience."

> *The Guild's victories over their numerous enemies can be explained in one name: Umbra. Many cite the courage of his Broken Lances, and they do deserve credit, but dogs are only as brave as their alpha.*
>
> **History of the Guilds**
> **By Elder Lighours**

The early morning air was cool, and the ground was covered in thick dew. The first colors of the sunrise were barely visible past the horizon. The rhythmic trot of tens of thousands of men turned the road to a river of mud. Stephen drank the last of his horn of wine and rode up past the marching column.

Line after line of black-cloaked fighters filled the scene. At the head of the column was Raven, covered in mud and dirt like everyone else. Stephen approached her and chuckled to himself. Her head was nearly in her lap as she rode. Stephen reached out and touched her shoulder. Her head jumped up as she awoke.

"You know it is dangerous to sleep while riding. You could fall and break something."

"I didn't even know I was sleeping," Raven yawned.

"How many hours did you rest last night?"

"The same as everyone else. four hours, or so."

"My lady, you do not need to stay up with the men to pitch camp and post guards. Once we stop, you can lay down your mat and go to bed. In fact, we would prefer you do."

"I know, but I feel terrible sleeping when no one else is. I must admit, I never knew a march was so tiring."

"This is a forced march. Not all marches are like this. We are trying to cover a lot of ground quickly, and we are not concerned about luxuries such as sleep."

"Or cooked food, or clean clothes," Raven added.

"The mud suits you, my lady," Stephen laughed.

"Mud seems to be the true uniform of a soldier."

"Yes, and soon we will add the final ingredient."

"What is that?" Raven asked.

"Blood, my lady, lots and lots of blood."

Raven shook her head in disgust. "I don't think I would be a good soldier," she sighed.

"I respectfully disagree, my lady. I believe you would make a fine soldier. Anyone who would choose to march in this horrible place for two weeks, because they felt they should, would be a great soldier. I have no doubt you will one day lead men to war with great success."

Raven laughed.

"When I was growing up in the Council Manor, I used to pride myself on not being soft like the other children. I was always willing to get dirty and bruised. Now all I want is a bath and a pillow."

"I suppose you will be asking for clean clothes and fresh bread after that."

"Don't taunt," Raven pleaded.

Stephen shifted in his saddle. "What is Mesmer city like?" he asked. "I have heard all kinds of stories about the last free city, but I don't believe them."

"Why? What have you heard?"

"I heard there is magic everywhere, like in the times before the angels left, yet you have no gods. I heard you have no lords, or knights, and that all people have equal say."

"Is that all?"

Stephen shrugs. "They also say you can have three whores for two coppers."

"Is that all?" she asked with a shy giggle. Stephen shook his head and bit his lower lip.

"They also say it is very beautiful."

"It is a beautiful city," she agreed.

"I hope to see it someday." Stephen lifted up his wine horn only to remember it is empty. Raven, amused, gave him her wine sack. He took it with a smile and drew a long drink.

"Castle Pearl is only a few days away," Raven stated. "Why have you not visited?"

"My duties don't allow me much time for leisure, and my travels are always official."

"Well, when I return home, I will send you an official summons. Then you can visit me officially."

"I'm charmed, my lady, but what would be your official reason?"

"I am the daughter of Miss Edoweyhn, Mayor of Mesmer City. I will think of something," Raven smirked.

"I would like that," Stephen admitted.

"Then it is settled. I will show you the market; oh, you must see the silk lane. There are artists there who will weave your likeness into a silk canvas. And food from all the world on every corner. It is an amazing thing to see."

"Then I look forward to it."

The sun broke the horizon and filled the plains with light. Smoke from a hundred campfires rose into the sky. Stephen peered at them with a sober look on his face.

"What is that?" Raven asked following his gaze.

"Stay here," Stephen commanded, riding ahead of the marching army.

At the top of the ridge, he saw the source of the pillars of smoke. Thousands of orc camps covered the hills. Drums began to beat in one part of the camp, soon spreading to the entire horde. Stephen's horse jerked under him, startled by the noise. Umbra rode up behind him.

"How many would you say there are?" Umbra asked.

"Well over thirty thousand, my lord Baron."

"Almost double what I feared," Umbra lamented.

"How did the scouts miss this?" Stephen asked.

"They didn't. I gave the Guild King their report three days ago."

"And the Guild King marched on anyway?"

"He seeks a decisive victory. Destroying such a horde will take the fight out of the orcs. Every orc hunter who would oppose us is here. After today there will be none to stop us."

"And what if they destroy us? Does the Guild King think his army invincible? Or has he come to believe his own legend?"

"The Guild King trusts his soldiers to do their duty and depends on the Broken Lances to earn their reputation. We are his vanguard."

"He depends too much on us," Stephen protested. "We are hard men, yes, but still just men."

"We are not just men," Umbra snapped in anger at Stephen. "We became more than mere men when we charged the ramparts at Tilton. We became more than men during the bitter winter in Longlast. We became more than men when we held the stone bridge against the Horsespear men. We are the Broken Lances, and the mood of the army is set on us. I will hear no talk of defeat from any wearing the black cloak, especially from my second in command." Stephen regretted his bluntness and bit his tongue.

Several battle horns sounded across the various guilds. The columns of men sped to a double quick. The lines began to form, and the rear elements halted.

"This will be a bloody battle," Stephen stated.

"Yes, yes it will be. And we will lead the charge, as we always have. Glory will be for the Guild King, and our souls for the Divines."

BLOODBORN
2

The orcs were always known, but none cared of the strange green beasts in the south. Galsag had traded for fur with them for centuries, but none had considered them worth conquering till the Guilds turned a greedy eye south.

Before then, few had seen an orc fight. Even fewer had lived through the experience, but war is much more than personal skill. History has shown the more orderly line tends to have the day, but even history has a surprise or two for the unprepared.

History of the Guilds
By Elder Lighours

Jt was midmorning by the time the battle-lines were drawn. The Guild King surveyed the field as the wind whipped about his royal purple cloak. The Guild Masters sat on their horses around him. A company of the King's Guard surrounded them.

The two armies stood on opposing hills with a deep valley between them. The orcs seemed to have no structure or lines, but their sheer numbers gave the Guild King pause.

The Guild King scratched his face with a cracked thumbnail. "The orcs appear to have no version of cavalry or archers, yet they place themselves out of arrow range. So, it seems they understand the concept."

"Maybe we should move my archers forward then, sire," Lord Beritor suggested.

"No, it could expose them to a charge, and from what I understand, the orcs charge rather well."

"The orcs are aggressive fighters," Herrion said. "They will not fight a defensive battle. We can draw them where we want them."

"True," the Guild King agreed looking back at the Guild Masters. "Lord Beritor, you will lead your Sword Brethren into the center of the valley. Lord Duke Herrion and Duke Johes will wait until the orcs attack. Then they will move their guilds against the orc flanks. Lord Beritor, who is your best cavalry captain?"

"Sir Conner of Tilton."

"Fine. I ask each of you to lend me your cavalry. I promise you will get them back after the battle. Sir Conner will lead the combined cavalry, ride around our troops, and attack the orcs to the rear. Baron Umbra, you will keep your cavalry and the Broken Lances in reserve."

Umbra was taken back. "Sire, I must protest," he began.

"I will not hear it, Umbra."

Umbra opened his mouth to press the issue, but then relented and simply muttered, "Yes, sire."

The Guild King looked to the other Guild Masters. "You all know your orders. I expect every man to do his duty. For Glory and Honor."

"For glory and honor," the Guild Masters repeated. They saluted their king and left for their commands. Umbra sat quietly on his horse near the Guild King. Raven glanced at Stephen from a few paces back.

"The Broken Lances aren't joining the battle?" she asked.

"It would seem not," he answered.

"You wish they were, don't you?"

"I didn't leave my family and march to the edge of the world just to watch a battle."

"You have a family waiting for you?" she asked shyly, not sure if she wanted to hear the answer.

"Yes. A mother and two sisters," Stephen answered. "I also have a dog I miss rather intensely."

Raven hid her girlish grin.

Behind them, Lord Beritor rode out before his large force and ordered the advance. Brilliant blue banners blazed the symbol of the Sword Brethren as rows of infantry marched forward.

In the front, lines of spear and pike men trudged on with little more than leather armor and dry mud for protection. After them advanced swordsmen and axe men in sturdy mail and plate coats. Following in the rear were hundreds of archers and crossbow men with nothing but their shirts and simple helmets.

"I always liked the Sword Brethren's banner," the Guild King remarked as the guild passed by. "Such a simple design, but it creates great imagery. Reminds me of the sun rising behind a sword stuck in the ground."

"I believe gaining your favor was Beritor's intent, sire," Umbra said emotionless.

"His intent is to flatter me into forgetting he is no different than the noble lords who opposed me in the North Wars. Pompous and corrupt. Willing to backstab over a wheat field. Ah – I suppose it worked."

"Yes sire," Umbra replied.

"You don't have to hide your anger, Umbra. You're not good at it anyway."

"Sire, you have never held my guild back before. Why now?"

"I need you, Umbra. And I need those boys of yours. There is a war coming unlike any we have ever seen. Galsag must be ready for it. I pray the Divines bless me with death before it comes, but my son, Umbra, my son will see it. He will need all the help he can get, and you can't help him if you are dead on some forgettable battlefield to the south."

Umbra wrinkled his brow in confusion. "What war do you see, sire? Northrim is broken, the Vycesie is our ally, and the lords are weak. Who but the orcs still stands against you?"

The Guild King sighed. He looked across the sea of fighters advancing on the enemy. "Being king is the single hardest thing I have ever done; harder than being a soldier, harder than being a Guild Master. As a soldier, you blame your captain for the orders given. As a captain, you blame the king. Who does the king blame – the Divines? That would be a hard argument to sell. My decisions affect more than even I will ever know. I am a man playing with fate by every stroke of my pen or utterance of my tongue. This will be my last war, Umbra, I swear it."

The Sword Brethren came to a halt at Beritor's order in the base of the valley. The orc horde roared and thundered in defiance. The archers in the rear loosed a volley of arrows into the enemy. Scattered clusters of orcs fell under the deadly attack. In response, the orc army charged forward.

The front row of pikes lowered their weapons, bracing for the onslaught. The orc mass collided into them like a wave hitting a shore. Blood sprayed as orcs were skewered on the spear poles, and men were crushed under orc axes.

The battle had begun.

Even from the top of the hill, the Guild King could see the orcs had the advantage in close combat. The Sword Brethren archers continued to pepper the orcs with arrows as the swordsmen rushed into the fray, but the onslaught showed no sign of slowing.

The banners of the Order of Spears and the Halbruders began to move towards the flanks. Their formations advanced as one man and one line. The Guild King squinted to see the distant figures tearing at each other. A messenger dashed up on horseback.

"The Sword Brethren are holding, sire. Lord Beritor wishes me to inform you he is confident of victory."

"Bah," the Guild King gawked. "That man's ego is only matched by his coin purse."

"The Order of Spears is charging, sire." Umbra pointed with a thick finger to the left of Beritor's formation. The Guild King looked as a mass of Duke Johes' men broke from the lines and charged into the orcs.

"What is Johes' doing?" the Guild King spat in annoyance. "Herrion is still an arrow's shot away. Johes is endangering the whole flank."

"If Herrion can move up and around, he might catch the orcs in the rear."

"No, send the cavalry around," the Guild King ordered. Umbra waved his hand, and hundreds of men on horseback darted off. "If the cavalry can get around the orc's flank quickly, they may lessen the pressure on the Order," the King explained, mostly to himself. He clenched the reins of his horse and breathed deeply.

The cavalry galloped down the hill behind the charging Order of Spears and around to the exposed rear of the orc horde. Suddenly, men began to fall from their horses. The knights looked about, confused, when a wave of spears flew out from seemingly nowhere.

"Spear throwers," the Guild King muttered. "They hid spear throwers on their sides to ambush any flanking movements. Why would they think to do that?" he asked Umbra.

"I do not know, sire."

"Is there any evidence the orcs have studied our battle tactics?"

"Sire," Umbra stated. "There is little evidence most orcs can even read."

Wounded men began to drift past the royal entourage.

"They fight like demons, sire," one shouted as he walked by holding a bandage on his arm.

"They can rip a man in two with their bare hands!" yelled another.

The Guild King ignored them and focused on the field. The right corner of the Sword Brethren began to break, and orcs poured into the ranks of archers, slaughtering as they went.

"Messenger," the Guild King barked.

"Sire?" the lad asked riding upon his pony with a royal banner proudly in his hand.

"Ride to Lord Duke Herrion and tell him to move his ass. The entire battle line will be threatened if he doesn't engage soon."

"Yes, sire!" The messenger rode off as another approached.

"Duke Johes has been killed, sire," he said. "Sir Wolfstang has assumed command."

"May the Divines receive his spirit," the Guild King muttered.

"Truly," Umbra answered lowering his head.

The Guild King looked up to the messenger. "Tell Sir

Wolfstang to break the attack and withdraw his men one hundred paces."

"Yes, sire." The rider darted away with his message.

"Messenger," the Guild King barked.

"Sire."

"Ride to the cavalry pinned on the hill, and order them to regroup behind our lines."

"Yes, sire!"

"Sire," Umbra began carefully. "Send in the Broken Lances. We could turn this battle with one well-placed charge."

"No, if I am to send in the Broken Lances, it will be at the critical moment when the Divines decide a victor."

Lord Duke Herrion's guild finally made it to the battle, and the front lines advanced into the orcs with steady precision. His archers lined up and sent in volley after volley upon the orcs. The horde shifted its might from the Sword Brethren and began to attack the Halbruders, but Herrion's men were ready. They pressed into the orc mob killing as they went.

The Guild King worked to slow his breathing. A minute in a battle felt like a day, and this battle already felt like a month. The King tried to relax his clenched jaw as he saw the lines wax and wane in the center of the valley.

"If we lose this battle," the Guild King muttered silently. "I will lose this campaign and thus my powerbase. My throne's foundation is glory on the field. A defeat could end me."

"Your throne is more legitimate than that, sire," Umbra

assured. "A single setback will not undo decades of rule."

"Pray we do not find out."

The Guild King watched as the messengers rode to their objectives. The lads found the company leaders and conveyed their messages. A single knight on horseback shouted orders at his foot soldiers. The Order of Spears broke off from the orcs, as best as the men could, and sprinted to a new line with their knight leading them.

"They will break," Umbra warned. "The Order is disorganized. They won't stand another charge."

"No, they must hold, at least until the cavalry can assist. The left flank is going to decide this battle, my friend. All cost must be paid to win it."

The cavalry pushed through the barrage of orc spears and returned to the guild's lines. They began to reform behind the Order when the orcs charged at the new defense line. The Guild King quietly clenched his horse's reigns, even as his face remained as unchanging as stone. He felt his heart beat faster as he watched the orcs plow into the battered lines.

"They are going to break," Umbra urgently warned.

The Guild King cursed under his breath and bucked his horse forward. Umbra and the royal guards rushed to follow him as he galloped down the hill towards the fleeing men. Raven tried to follow after them.

"GO BACK!" Umbra barked. "Stephen, protect her!"

"Yes, my lord," Stephen replied.

The Guild King reached the rear ranks of the Order of

Spears. Men were fleeing in scores. The Guild King rode in among them drawing his sword and holding it high above his head.

"Who are you!" he shouted at them. "Are you not the Order? Are you not the line who held when the Horsespear men charged? Have you not marched with me from one side of the world to the next? Will you run now? Will you turn your back on your honor? On your King!"

"On the King," an officer yelled. "Rally on the King!" The beaten men rallied around the King's horse and formed a line in front of him. The brutish orcs formed at a stone's throw from them and roared in bloodrage.

"You are the Order of Spears," barked the Guild King, "and you will hold!"

The orc horde rushed into the line. They hurled mighty axes, breaking wooden pikes and crushing men. The mounted knights rushed in at their back, cutting at arms and legs to disable the giants.

An orc grabbed a sword by the blade and ripped it out of the knight's hand. Three crossbow bolts struck the orc's chest before he fell.

The Guild King barked for his personal guard to enter into the fray. The stately armored men charged in without question. They pierced and cut into the orcs from atop their large steeds.

The Guild King withdrew a few dozen paces to Umbra and the rest of his personal guards.

"Sire, let me bring up my guild. Without support, this

line will falter."

"I agree. Send in the Broken Lances, but have Stephen lead them."

"Sire!" Umbra protested. The Guild King quickly raised a firm hand.

"I will not hear it. Stephen will lead them." Umbra bit his tongue and saluted his king. He turned his horse and rode back up the hill to where Stephen and Raven waited with the messengers.

"Lead the Broken Lances forward. Aid the Order of Spears, and crush the enemy," Umbra ordered his old friend.

"Yes, my lord," Stephen replied. As he left, he briefly looked at Raven. "Take care, my lady."

"You are the one who should take care, sir," she corrected. Stephen smiled and rode off.

Long is the suffering of the wicked.
Much is their dismay. They drift like wood
in a river. They know not the right way.

The First Word
Nightfall 4:23

Duke Erik Longcoast drew in a long and deep breath. He shifted in his saddle and gripped the handle of his sword tighter. The sounds of battle raged just past the hill slope, out of sight of Erik and the Broken Lances. Erik paced his horse back and forth in front of the formed up guild.

"Erik, stop. You are making my horse anxious," Francis complained.

"We should be in the battle," Erik stated.

"We are 'in' the battle," Francis corrected. "We are simply in reserve."

"Are we not vanguard?" Erik spat out. "Who has ever heard of keeping your best to the rear?"

"A king is not obligated to share his battle plans with the likes of us," Koll remarked.

"No, he wouldn't want anyone to see the obvious flaws in them."

"That is enough, Erik," Francis snapped.

"Or what?" Erik shouted. "Or what?"

"Enough from both of you," James the Red interceded. "We will engage when ordered and not a moment before. We serve our king diligently, even if that means staying in reserve."

"I guess the old man is right," Erik scoffed spinning his horse again. "I trained my whole life for this day. Ever since I could hold a practice blade. A knight lives for war. It is his only art. For a knight to sit on the very edge of battle and not draw his sword would be an offense to the Divines."

"Be weary of your wishes, young Longcoast," James said. "You may have it granted." James pointed towards the hill as Stephen rode down to them.

"We have been ordered to charge," Stephen announced.

"I will be leading the attack. Follow me with your men, and I will show where the Guild King wants us."

"Where is the Baron?" Koll asked.

"He was ordered to stay behind. Now tighten up the ranks and prepare to advance."

"Yes, sir!" Erik shouted gleefully darting to his men.

Sir Martin was standing among the swordsmen looking at the Captains rush to their units. He shifted his weight on his sore feet and adjusted his shield straps. The man next to him chuckled.

"Sir Martin, you slumming it today with us lonely foot soldiers?" the man asked.

"The damn horse hurt his leg again," Sir Martin replied. "So yes, I am a foot soldier today." The swordsman laughed a deep belly laugh.

"What breed is it?"

"It is a brown rouncey," Martin said.

The swordsman laughed again. "Fucking rouncey. A knight of your class should have a destrier." The swordsman said this as if he was an expert on horses.

"The rouncey travels better. Destriers are better in battle, but not on long campaigns."

"Well, not your rouncey it seems," the man laughed again at Martin's expense.

Erik rode close to the rank and saw Martin. "Sir Martin! Is your horse still lame?"

"It is, my lord."

"Bad for you, but great for me. Now I have a man I trust

to lead the infantry."

"Yes, my lord," Martin replied.

Stephen rode out in the center of the whole guild and drew his sword. He spun his horse about and checked if all units were ready to move.

"You know who you are?" Stephen shouted to the guild. "You are the solid rock! You are the sword in the enemy's gut. You are the lance in our King's hand. You will pierce the enemy. You will rout the enemy. And if you die, it will be with the blood of a hundred foes on your blade. You will not be forgotten. For our losses, and for our gains! We are the Broken Lances! Advance!"

"Forward!" Erik cried drawing his sword as well. The guild moved up the hill and over the slope. There, Erik gained his first glimpse of a real battle. As far as eyes would strain he saw tens of thousands of men and orcs mixed in brutal melee.

The cries of the dying thundered along with the roars of combat. The sheer size of the chaos nearly took Erik's breath away as he realized how real it all was. Waves of wounded men abandoned the field dragging sword, shields, and comrades behind them.

"I must be brave," Erik muttered to himself as the guild marched down the hill and closer to the battle.

"Steady men," Stephen shouted.

A band of men ran past Erik, fleeing the fighting.

"Cowards," Erik mumbled. Stephen turned his horse and waved his sword in the air.

"You ready, you war-dogs? Charge and send these beasts to the black!"

The ground shook as the whole of the Broken Lances rushed forward into the mobs of orcs. Erik bucked his horse and rocketed into the fray. Instantly he was surrounded by a moving mass of chaos.

An orc swung at him and missed. He countered with his sword to the orc's head. Blood sprayed up, covering his face and chest. It dripped into his eyes and off from his nose. Erik's heart rushed with fear and excitement. He felt as if fire was literally in his veins.

He swung at another orc and cleaved the beast's arm off. Erik turned, stabbed an orc, then another and another. The rush of battle overcame him. His vision became crystal clear as all fear danced away. He forgot all danger or threat. He knew only his blade and his next victim.

He was so consumed by the fire that he barely noticed the unnaturally large orc charging at him. The orc slammed into Erik with such force it sent him flying from his horse and into the mud. Erik struggled to sit up when the orc stomped down on his chest. The chest plate prevented Erik's death, but his blood coughed up from his mouth.

Erik reached for his sword. He could feel it with his fingertips. The orc raised his axe over his head and brought it down on Erik. By sheer force of will Erik shifted his head far enough to avoid the blow. The axe blade slammed into the ground, and the orc struggled momentarily to recover it.

Erik abandoned his sword and quickly fumbled at his

belt to find his dagger. In one motion, he drew the blade and stabbed the orc in the leg. The orc roared in pain and stepped off Erik. Erik scrambled to his sword, and with a fast swing, opened up the orc's guts.

Long rope-like organs poured out onto the ground as the orc tried to roar but couldn't. He fells to his knees. Erik sliced the orc's head off and watched it roll. Erik stood to his feet and took a step when an axe was swung at him.

He dodged the attack only in time for another to come. Erik blocked it, but the blow sent shockwaves down his arms. The orc roared and pressed his weight into the axe. Erik, knowing he would lose a match of strength, pushed the axe to one side and cut the orc along his forearm.

The orc, unfazed, smacked Erik across the face sending him flying several feet. He landed face down in the blood soaked mud. Erik lifted himself up and found himself face to face with the blank eyes of a dead knight.

The frozen expression of the corpse looked into Erik. The man seemed almost graceful now, like a person at peace, as if he was at rest with his unfortunate fate and the injustice of it.

Behind him, Erik heard footsteps fast approaching him. He grabbed the dead knight's sword, spun on a knee and held the sword up to block the incoming blow. The axe landed so hard it pushed Erik deep into the mud. The orc immediately swung again, and Erik was forced to grab the sword blade with his free hand to stop it. The blade cut deep into his palm as the axe struck. Erik screamed in agony.

Annoyed by Erik's defiance, the orc kicked Erik to the ground. Discontent with dying, Erik stabbed at the orc in one final effort to gain victory. The blade hit a lucky strike to the orc's throat.

Refusing to give up easily, the orc swung his axe one last time and landed it on Erik's right arm. Erik screamed as the bone snapped and the flesh tore. The orc fell over dead.

Erik stumbled and tried to move his fingers, but the whole arm proved useless. Blood flowed down his sleeve and dripped to the mud. Erik struggled to his feet and limped away from the fighting. He could see the archer's lines. He drifted towards them, dizzy with blood loss.

He was near safety when an orc stepped in front of him. Erik, knowing he couldn't fight, fell to his knees. Tears began to roll down his cheeks. The orc growled like a dog and charged at Erik. Erik squeezed his eyes closed and tried to think of home when he heard the orc grunt, followed by a loud crash. Erik opened his eyes. The orc was dead before him with a spear in its back. Erik looked about for his savior.

Stephen turned his horse and came near Erik. Stephen leaned down and extended out a hand. Erik reached up for it. A hammer fell on the back of Stephen's head. Blood and bone splattered Erik. The horse bucked and tripped in the mud. Erik last saw the shadow of the beast engulfing him before it fell.

Life is a wheel, death but a rung. What is made is undone. But when the time is complete, and the world made new, we will see what is true.
A world without the black mark on the soul. A world full of treasures for a man to behold.

The First Word
Nightfall 117:45-47

The sun hung low in the sky. The wind swept up the smell of death and misery, and spread it for all to enjoy. Murders of crows circled the endless feast of dead men and orcs. Healers darted across the field, lifting men up on stretchers as Prophets pray for their souls.

The moans of thousands of wounded and dying men echoed in the deep valley. Occasionally a scream would cry out as the surgeon's blade did its work. The dead face of a young knight stared at Umbra. Among all the dead on the field, this one held his attention. Raven approached on horseback.

"He was Sir Clinton," Umbra said without facing her. "I remember him first coming to us. He didn't have the skill of other recruits, but he had twice the heart. I've never seen a man work so hard to earn the black cloak or so proud to wear it. Now he will be buried in it."

"Is that not honorable?" she asked.

"Honor is an amusing thing. A man can live his whole life well, make a mistake, and die in dishonor. Where another man can be a liar and a thief, die in battle, and be buried a hero."

"Mesmers believe to die in battle means the man lacked the needed skill to survive."

"If skill is all it took to win a battle, then the orcs would have carried the day."

"If this is a victory I do not wish to see a defeat." Raven stated staring across the battleground. A shiver ran down her back.

"The only thing as terrible as a battle lost," Umbra said walking past her, "is a battle won."

"What happens now?" Raven called out to him as he left. Umbra paused and faced her.

"Well, we will stay here for a few days to bury the dead and let the seriously wounded pass comfortably. Then we will march back to camp and feast nonstop for a couple of weeks. In that time, the orc chieftains will gather, and peace talks will begin. After the treaty is signed, a garrison will be left to build a fort or two. And we will march back to Galsag as heroes and conquerors and all that nonsense."

"How do you know the orcs will deal?"

"I know," Umbra assured with a cocky smile.

"How?" Raven pressed.

"Because orcs love battle, but not war. Prolonged conflict is not something they understand. Change is something they fear. They are a people who have done things the same way for thousands of years. They will bargain, even with us, to keep their ways."

Raven nodded her understanding. "All of the black could not match what I have seen today."

Umbra continued up the hill alone when Francis rode up and rendered his salute. "We captured the old Warchief, my lord."

"Good, where is he?"

"Chained up past the hospital tents."

"And what were our casualties, Sir Francis?"

"I have not heard the final for the army yet."

"What about the Broken Lances, how many of our brothers are we leaving here?"

"Six hundred, my lord, and about that number wounded." Umbra sighed heavily. He rubbed his face and glanced behind him at the battlefield. "There is something else, my lord. Erik was severely wounded."

"Will he live?" Umbra asked calmly.

"The healers do not know yet. They said he may not keep his sword arm."

"I see."

"Also, my lord," Francis paused not sure how to continue.

"What is it, Francis?"

"Stephen is dead, my Baron."

Umbra drew in a long breath and nodded. "Thank you for this report, Sir Francis."

"Yes, my lord." Francis saluted and rode away.

Umbra could already smell the reek of the hospital tents as he came over the hill. He started his way down into the rows of bloody men laid out on the grass. It was a familiar sight to Umbra, but one he never grew used to.

A large tent stood independently from the other tents. The banners of the Order of Spears flew in front of the entrance. The two tent guards saw Umbra approaching and stood aside without question. In the center of the tent stood a wooden table; on the table laid the Duke. A bloody fatal wound sat squarely in his chest. Umbra neared the bed and touched the Duke's hand.

"May you rest with the Divines, my friend."

"His last words were an order," a rough voice said behind Umbra. Umbra turned to see a large man with white hair and sunken eyes. His shoulders were broad as a horse and just as powerful. A gold pendant hung around his neck.

"What were they, Sir Wolfstang?"

"He said, fill in the line, and don't let the archers run."

Umbra nodded slowly. "The battle is always easier than what comes after," he commented looking to the Duke.

"Unfortunately so, but it is how the Divines made it."

"Yes," Umbra sighed. "You did well today, Sir Wolfstang."

"I did my duty, as any man should."

"If I remember right, you said a similar thing after the battle of Snow Cap."

"I did, and I still feel the same way."

"No man had ever beaten the Horsespear men on horseback until you. Most thought you were mad to lead that cavalry charge," Umbra reminisced.

"It cost me dearly," Wolfstang admitted, exposing a deep scar on his arm. "I have never seen a weapon quite like the horsespear. I still see those long spear heads cutting through man and horse in my dreams."

"It was a bloody day, much like today," Umbra added.

"I wish it was the last bloody day," Wolfstang commented.

"I know I intend it to be my last."

"There will always be more wars to fight, Baron. You of all people should know this."

"What was the final count on the army, Sir Wolfstang?" Umbra asked changing the subject. "Do you know?"

Wolfstang thought for a moment. "I do not know the final count, but I overheard an early one."

"What was it?" Umbra asked, unsure if he really wanted to know.

"Seven thousand wounded, of which two thousand are not expected to last the night. Another five will never leave the field."

"A bloody day indeed," Umbra remarked.

He shook his head and left the tent, unwilling to stay any longer. The sun had fallen completely behind the horizon by then, allowing the moon and stars to shine. An oddly cold wind caught Umbra, making him shiver briefly.

Thundering horse hooves declared a person's approach.

Umbra glanced to the direction of the sound. Raven rounded the hilltop at full gallop. She darted between the wounded who loudly complain at her passing. Raven's horse slid to a halt before Umbra, throwing up a rain of mud in the process.

"Is it true?" she asked, eyes wide. "Is Stephen dead?" Umbra stared emotionless at her. She looked like a frighten child. Umbra found he hesitated to answer. He could not say why.

"It is true," he muttered softly.

Raven attempted to speak, but her words turned into a dry cough. Her lower lip quivered once before she regained her composure.

"Well," she forced out, "he was a good man." Raven bucked her horse and darted off into the dark without another word.

"Yes, he was," Umbra agreed.

He took a step forward when Lord Duke Herrion stumbled out of a tent laughing. A mug of ale rested in one hand and a bottle of wine in the other. Herrion noticed Umbra and walked towards him before he fell face-first in the muck. Umbra rushed over and lifted Herrion to his feet. He reeked of beer and vomit.

"Umbra," Herrion suddenly cried out in joy. He tried to take another drink, but his mug's contents now stained the ground.

"We won, Umbra!" he yelled.

"Yes, we indeed did."

"Have you seen the old Warchief yet? He is a pile of laughs. We have him chained to a couple rocks. We tried a stake, but he broke the damn thing. Anyway, chained to a rock he is, and he just sits there and growls at everyone. His hair is bright white, like snow, and long. It is in really long braids and he growls at everything. He is three hundred years old, you know. He was old before the Great War. Can you imagine living so long? Not that it matters, they die as we do. They are bloody and cleaved like my men. Oh, Umbra, my men," Herrion wailed falling to his knees, despite Umbra attempting to hold him up. "They killed so many of my men."

Umbra tried to lift the Lord Duke up, but Herrion slapped his hands away like a toddler refusing to be picked up by a stranger. Umbra, embarrassed and unsure what to do, folded his arms and looked around for help. Herrion clung undignified to Umbra's legs weeping loudly.

Three knights passed by the tents up ahead, and Umbra whistled at them. They stopped in their tracks and hurried to the Baron's call. Herrion tried to crawl away, but Umbra grabbed him by the arms.

"Do you know who this is?" Umbra asked.

"Yes, my lord," the center knight said.

"Good. Take this man to his tent and leave him with his attendants."

"Yes, my lord," the knight said reaching for Herrion. Umbra snatched the knight's hand.

"Tell no one of this, or I swear by the three Divines I will have you stripped of your knighthood and flogged."

"Yes, my lord," the lead knight said picking up Herrion and carrying him away.

"My men, Umbra," Herrion cried. "My men. Who will speak for my dead?"

"That is the worst I have seen him," Lord Beritor said startling Umbra.

"Please, don't walk up behind me," Umbra requested.

"Apologies," Beritor replied with a chuckle. "So what do you think of our victory?"

"Hard won," Umbra replied.

"That is an understatement. It will take a year just to settle all the inheritance claims."

"Some woes are greater than others, I suppose," Umbra muttered sarcastically.

"Yes, yes, you don't like me. I understand, but I am not your enemy, Baron."

"That does not make you my friend."

"True, but perhaps ally."

"What do you want, Lord Beritor?"

"Who do you suppose will stay behind to manage these new lands?"

"Peace is not certain, yet you already talk as if it is," Umbra remarked.

"All but certain."

"The Guild King has already promised governance to the Prophets."

"Yes, quite a high price for their support in the North

Wars. Yet, I never understood what the Prophets seek to gain with leagues of barren terrain."

"It was the Divines' will," Umbra answered.

"Oh please. You and I know the Prophets don't speak to the Divines; they frequent brothels and gaming houses, sure, but not the Divines."

"I don't know that. The Prophets are the Divines' messengers. Have some strayed from the righteous path? Yes- but they are still our source for the true words of the Divines."

Beritor raised an eyebrow at Umbra. "But you admit that the Head Prophets don't have the truth in them?"

"I will admit that their power opens them to corrupt thinking," Umbra phrased carefully. "I will admit that I am not a Prophet, and thus I cannot see as they see. I truly believe the Divines love us, and I truly believe they speak to the Prophets, corrupt or no."

"So what do you think these corrupt leaders really want with these lands?" Beritor asked.

"I don't know," Umbra admitted somberly.

"I don't either, but I do know Philipus is not going to rule here. I hear rumors they requested a steward. Someone to deal with the daily affairs."

"And you want to be this steward?"

"Oh heavens no," Beritor laughed. "I can barely stand being here now. One of my captains though; he could do it and a fine job of it."

"And what would you gain? I cannot imagine you doing

anything without benefit." Beritor smiled, deciding to take the remark as a positive.

"There are thousands of leagues of lands here ready to be plowed, and thousands of orc ready to plow them. When those tariffs come in, I want to be the one gathering them."

"You mean skimming off the top of them."

"Commission for my services, even your most honorable Broken Lances collects taxes."

"Lord Beritor, I have never met a man so clearly my opposite," Umbra hissed.

"From you, that is a compliment."

"Take it as you will," Umbra replied waving his hand at him.

Lord Beritor smirked and walked away. Umbra waited until he was gone to travel the short distance to the old Warchief's cage.

The orc was much as Herrion described with long white hair in two long braids. His body was covered in scars, and one of his large fang-like teeth was jaggedly broken. Umbra leaned his head against the iron bars and stared at the defeated chief.

"You come to mock me, man?" the old Warchief asked in a deep grumbling voice.

"No orc, I don't wish to mock you. I respect you in more than one way."

"Respect? Respect would be to kill me rather than chain me like a beast."

"We still need you."

"What need does the iron king have of me?"

"You can convince the other chiefs to seek peace."

"Peace?" The Warchief spat the unfamiliar word out of his mouth. "Why would we want to sing the Life Song with you?"

"To save your people, to save your son." The Warchief chuckled deep in his throat. Then the chuckle erupted into laughter.

"My son rests far from you, iron knight. Even if my whole tribe and clan bled on your blades, my life force will endure." Umbra tilted his head, puzzled.

"Your son Del'Caf is our prisoner and has been for several weeks." The old Warchief glared at Umbra.

"You lie," he spat. Now it was Umbra's chance to laugh.

"We took him from the village at the base of the rocky hill; where the two rivers meet." The orc's eyes went wide with surprise then turned red with fury. The Warchief exploded into a fit of rage, tearing and yanking at his chains while roaring with all his might. The cry was so loud it drew the guards.

"Let him scream," Umbra ordered them.

After several minutes, the Warchief finally stopped, completely out of breath. "Scream all you want, Warchief," Umbra said gazing into the orc's eyes. "But when the other chieftains arrive, you will sing the Life Song to the Guild King."

"And if I do not?"

"Then I will personally refuse you your son's life."

VICTORS

3

Northrim, though similar to Galsag, is distinct among the nations. Its cold climate has made a people so hard, not even the Prophets or the elves try to influence them. They have fiercely maintained their culture and way of government longer than any other human tribe.

They are a people ruled by one man. They have no nobility, no barons and no dukes. There is only the king, the knights and the common man

History of the Guilds
Elder Lighours

Roll pressed into the woman under him. She dragged her nails down his back, and he pulled on her long black hair. The strains of hair were soft and cool between his fingers. He felt his release and fell onto the blankets covering his tent floor. He breathed the fire out of his lungs as his new friend sat up. She brushed her hair out of her face and used a rag to wipe her inner thighs. Koll ran his fingers down her back. She quivered when he hit her spine.

"That tickles," she giggled.

"Good," Koll said siting up and wrapping his arms around her. She fell into his chest and played with her hair.

"So that is going to be two silvers," she said.

"I'll give you four if you stay for a while," Koll replied. The woman shrugged.

"I don't mind. I could use a break anyway. Most of these soldiers just want to go and go and go."

"They are happy to be alive," Koll explained letting her go and grabbing a wine skin. She snatched it from his hand playfully and filled her mouth with wine. Koll shook his head as she crawled into his lap and kissed him passionately, spilling wine between their lips. Koll coughed and wiped his mouth. She sat back down and took another drink.

"What is a battle like? Since you boys came back from the field a few weeks ago no one has spoken of it," she asked leaning forward. Koll grabbed the wine sack from her and shrugged.

"It's a battle."

"Were you afraid?"

Koll forced a half smile. "Of course, but it wasn't as bad as I thought it would be. Once it starts, it just happens."

"So you don't mind battle?"

"No, I don't," Koll said flatly. "I am at a lost why so

many are scared of it. You do your duty, and you die, or you don't."

"And your duty is murder?" she asked. Koll flinched at her bluntness.

"Violence is a tool, like a shovel, or a hoe."

"I bet farmers have more peaceful sleep than soldiers."

"Perhaps, but a farmer can't pay a camp wench four silver to insult them," Koll pointed out.

"The truth insults you?" she asked.

"No, of course not. It is just more complicated than you make it."

"How so?" she asked lying on her belly next to Koll. She rubbed her hand up and down his upper leg.

"My duty is to the king and the kingdom," he said ignoring the hand rubbing near his groin. "Just as is a farmer's duty. He, however, provides wheat, and I provide my sword. Without soldiers, who would protect the kingdom?"

"Oh, I don't disagree. Once, a knight saved me and my sister from a bandit. But I don't recall the orcs ever invading Galsag. Maybe I am wrong."

"You don't find our cause righteous?" Koll asked annoyed, pushing her hand away from him.

"What is righteous?" she asked. "The First Word condemns what we did in your tent, but does not condemn what you did on the battlefield. Which is more of a black mark on the soul?"

"The orcs worship demons," Koll rebutted. The woman laughed and rolled onto her back.

"Your innocence is cute," she said rubbing her breasts. "I sometimes wonder what it was like when I was innocent. Maybe I never was."

"You must have been a child at some point."

The woman pondered the point for a moment then shook her head.

"I grew up during the North Wars. I don't remember being allowed to be a child."

"Bloody business, the North Wars. I grew up during it too, but up in Northrim, not here in the south." The woman's eyes drifted away, lost in memory.

"Longlast never bowed to the Guild King during the war. We Southies are proud of that."

"Proud of what?" Koll scoffed. "Preventing the unison of your country?"

"No, preventing the south from becoming a puppet to some upstart."

"You are awfully political for a camp wench," Koll stated.

"All Southie girls are," she replied.

"So you don't support the Guild King?" Koll asked shocked. "He stabilized the kingdom. He brought strength back to Galsag. He made the providences rich. The people are safe from bandits and invaders, now more than ever. He is a good man."

The woman shrugged. "Well, you know him better, to be sure," she admitted. "But I feel no safer now than I did when I was child. As for wealth, maybe in the north silver lays bare in the street, but here…" she gestured with her hands to her bare body with a small smile.

"No place is perfect," Koll defended.

"True, but some places do get the better deal."

"Would you rather be ruled by noble lords again? At least under the Guild King, merit is the currency of the realm. A man can become anything; no matter his birth."

"And yet most knights and Guild Masters are still high-born," she laughed.

"It takes time to change a system," Koll stated.

"Yes, but is it really changing, or more the same?"

> *A King should be of royal blood, or married to royal blood. He should be a keeper of word and an upholder of truth. No wrong doing should be found in him, and his reign should be just. The Divines will bless such a man and curse any pretenders.*
>
> **The First Word**
> **Harrowed 8:47**

The coal burned with a glow in the fire pot. The bright light filled the tent, shining off its many luxuries. At the entrance stood two weapon racks filled with dozens of expensive and heavily decorated swords. The ground was covered in furs from around the world. The walls were lined with shelves of trophies. In the back was a large bed with red and purple sheets. A single set of armor stood in the corner.

Umbra fiddled with his silver cup. Its red wine stared back at him. He moved uncomfortably in the cushioned chair. Its ornate wooden frame rubbed his back. The songs of thousands of drunken soldiers roared across the camp. The Guild King sat across from Umbra, gazing into the fires embers. His cupbearer stood near him with a full pitcher.

"I see you are wearing a new tunic," the Guild King commented without moving his eyes from the fire pot.

"It was my treat to myself," Umbra explained. "Something to look forward to on the long march from the battlefield."

"When did you buy it?"

"Excuse me, sire?"

"Buy it," he repeated. "You didn't get it here. So when did you buy it?"

"In Doraxe, before we left."

"I have never known you to purchase new or luxurious things."

"Sire, this was hardly the most luxurious tunic they had. There was one with gold inlay and a silver border. I believe it cost a common man his full year's wage."

"Such treasures for man to behold," the Guild King muttered, quoting a famous verse from the First Word.

"Your reign has made many wealthy," Umbra stated.

"And many more poor. I remember the first time I entered Doraxe and went into one of those highborn shops. I was disgusted that men could live so well while the people starved. Now I understand it all too well. Riches are a small comfort with the burden of power. I must admit, I have come to like my pomp."

"My new tunic is enough for me," Umbra said.

"I wish more were like you, my friend. So many always want more. It is never enough for them. You know I have agreed to hand all the lands of this campaign over to the Prophets, do you not?"

Umbra glanced at the cupbearer and shifted uneasily in his chair. "I have heard it said, yes."

"Have you also heard there are some who wish a steward to be named, to handle the daily tasks of rule?"

"I have heard this also. Should we be speaking policy in front of your aide?" Umbra asked gesturing to the young cupbearer. The Guild King chuckled.

"David has been my aide for five years; I trust him to test my wine and food. I think I can trust him to keep his lips sealed."

"As you wish, sire," Umbra said.

The Guild King noticed his discomfort and turned to his cupbearer. "David, go see if the cooks have any chickens prepared. I think I want a late meal. Both legs, half a loaf of bread and another pitcher of wine."

"Yes, sire," David said bowing. He sat the pitcher down and exited the tent.

"Lord Beritor mentioned it on the road," the Guild King

said as soon as David was gone. "Usually I avoid his advice, but he states a compelling one this time. The common people are losing their trust in the Prophets. They see them as corrupt toads looking to fatten their own bellies. Giving the Prophets the orc lands will double their holdings. I could be seen as their puppet in the people's eyes."

"And a steward would stop that?" Umbra asked.

"If I pick the right one, it might lessen it. Lord Beritor thinks Sir Connor would serve well. What do you think?"

"Will Philipus agree to a steward in the first place?"

"If I press him, yes, but it has to be the right kind of man." Umbra leaned back and casually drank his wine.

"Well, Sir Connor seems to be the perfect choice. He is a true guildsman. He has some noble blood from his grandmother so the highborns won't fuss. He is an honorable knight and a wise statesman, but is it wise to allow Lord Beritor access to such gains?"

"And who would you suggest instead?"

"What of Sir Francis Drako?" Umbra asked.

The Guild King snorted.

"How is a Drako a better choice than a Beritor? I would rather take a chance on Sir Connor than risk empowering Victor Drako."

"Is that wise, sire? Lord Beritor is well known for his blind ambition."

"And Victor Drako is well known for his large armies," the Guild King exclaimed. He stood to his feet and refilled his cup from the pitcher. "The Drakos are the only noble family left that could threaten me. Peace depends on Victor's mood. Why else do you think I married his daughter? If I give his son stewardship, it could tip the power balance in the whole kingdom."

"Sire, you are not looking at this correctly," Umbra said, careful not to come off as rude. "The Prophets will be the legal owners, the Drako Family gains nothing. In fact, it will weaken Victor to have his heir so far from the kingdom's dealings."

"Do you truly trust this Francis so much?" The Guild King asked, plopping back into his seat.

"I have trained him for years now. He is a good man who does not bow to just anyone's whim – including his father's."

"You are a strange man, Umbra," the Guild King mused taking another drink. "Your guild is rich enough to field ten thousand, and yet you raise only a fraction of that. A hundred honorable men long to be your friend, and you treat a Northrim hostage and my rival's heir like your sons."

"I see more in a man than his birth or title," Umbra replied coldly, as if to remind the Guild King they too were outcasts once.

"Very well," the Guild King sighed. "I will put the Drako boy up for steward. Philipus will not reject him for fear of his father."

"Thank you, sire," Umbra said.

"Don't be so quick to thank me, this will cost you. We need to make some decisions about the orcs, and I want your support."

"I am at your service," Umbra stated.

"I want the Broken Lances to gather up all the hunters among the orc tribes and take them back with us to Galsag."

"Why, sire?"

"To train them, of course. The orcs will be a great addition to our forces and maybe even help recoup our losses here."

"Sire, I don't think the orcs will be willing soldiers for their conquerors."

"Then we must make them willing. Show them the advantage of cooperation."

"And how will I do that?" Umbra asked.

"You won't, your Steward will."

"Why would I need a Steward?"

"Because, I need you to help me to run this blasted kingdom. I'm tired of doing it all on my own."

"Is that not for the inner council to do?"

"It is, but with Duke Johes dead, we have an opening. I intend you to fill it."

"Sire, you honor me, but I have no wish to sit on the inner council. I hardly enjoy being part of the Hall of Guild Masters."

"Oh, I know you don't," the Guild King laughed. "But I am not giving you a choice in this matter. I need someone I can trust on the inner council, and you have been sitting in the shadows too long."

The Guild King's face turned somber. His eyes became cold and distant. "There were too many orcs at the battle, my friend. Thinking about it makes my mind drift to scary places. I see shadows within shadows, and all of them are crowding around me..."

"What are you implying, sire?" Umbra asked concerned. The Guild King shook his head and drank down his wine.

"Nothing," he said with a smile.

> *The dark arts are from the demons of old and should be contested against and burned whenever seen. Any tongue that utters a spell must be cut out; any hand that practices magic must be burnt.*
>
> **The First Word**
> **Harrowed 3:30**

Lord Herrion picked his teeth with his fingernail. The tent of meeting was overflowing with guild captains and delegates. The orc chieftains stood outside awaiting the talks to begin. Herrion noticed Baron Umbra, closer to the Guild King than usual, with concern poorly hidden on his face. The Guild King himself sat on his raised throne in full armor. Lord Beritor quietly approached.

"Do you think the King chose to wear armor as a show of strength," he asked.

"No doubt he did," Herrion replied in a whisper.

"And the nervous expression on Umbra's face, do you conclude he worries how this affair will end?"

"I have no doubts Umbra realizes, as do I, the impossibility of guessing the Warchief's actions."

"I think he will spit on the King's terms and try to murder us all."

"That is possible, I suppose," Herrion admitted. "It depends how he feels about us having his son. Will that be leverage enough?"

"Umbra gives these beasts too much credit," Beritor insisted. "He already proved he doesn't care about the lad. By the Divines, I don't know why we are still wasting bread on him."

"The King and Baron Umbra have unwisely placed all their eggs in one basket, I will agree with you there. Still, I do not know what the old Warchief might do with his son captured and his army defeated."

The tent grew silent as the entrance opened and five orcs entered. They all carried the marks of several battles on their skin. Upon their eyes and brows, they carried the burden of their people's future. Herrion recognized the sorrow. He had seen it before on the faces of noble families forced to surrender their lands and titles at the Guild King's command.

The orcs faced the Guild King in unison. The tent was silent, besides the low murmurs of whispering bystanders. One orc stepped forward.

"You called us here, iron king, and we have come. What

do you seek?"

"Peace," the Guild King replied opening his arms like a father to a child. "I wish for the Life Song to be sung eternally between us."

"You iron knights do nothing without price. What do you want? Why did you come here?" the orc chieftain shot back.

"I seek neither your people nor your lands, but your Shamans worship dark gods, and it is an affront to the Divines. I demand the tongue of every Shaman and every black book of magic." The orc chieftains exchanged glances.

"What are our ways to you, iron king? Why do you care what songs our Shamans chant?"

"Because the Divines demand this evil be stopped!" the Guild King barked.

"For many winters your people and mine have traded and learned each other's tongues. Why now do you wish to harm us?"

"It is not harm I bring, but salvation. I must remove the taint that is in your lands. Give me the books and the Shamans, and I swear to you, the rest of your people will be free." The chieftain turned back to the other orcs again, and they whispered amongst themselves.

"And if we refuse?" the spokesorc asked. The Guild King leaned forward and glared at them with dead cold eyes.

"Then what happened in the valley three weeks ago will only be a taste of the death I will bring your people."

"You make bold claims, iron king, but there is strength

in the tribes yet! Why should we agree to such black marks as you suggest?"

The Guild King waved his hand, and the old Warchief was dragged into the tent. The other chieftains gasped in disgust at the Warchief's undignified appearance. One chieftain growled at the Guild King in anger.

"You can break a Warchief's body," he snared, "but he is the spirit of our people, and that will never be broken."

"The Warchief is not broken," the Guild King corrected. "He has simply come to understand my reasonable offer."

"The Warchief will never sell his people to you, iron king; no matter the amount promised."

The old Warchief lifted his head. All eyes darted to him. His tired gaze drifted around the tent. It went from his fellow orcs, to the Guild King, then to the crowd around him.

He saw the royal guards in their iron suits piercing at him through darkened helmet slits. He saw a young woman staring intensely at him. He matched her stare, and she instantly looked away with a fearful shiver.

The old Warchief sighed and lowered his head. A low growl started deep in his throat. Herrion found his hand gripping his sword, not sure what to expect. The growl continued for a moment before it changed into the most haunting and beautiful song Herrion had ever heard.

The old Warchief sang passionately, yet his lovely tune was devoid of all cheer or gladness. It, instead, was filled with sorrow and loss. The other chieftains stood stunned, daring not to move during the song.

"Have I just heard the much-talked-about Life Song?" Herrion asked himself.

When the old Warchief was finished, he set his eyes firmly on the Guild King.

"I once saw a young group of hunters chase a mighty beast. The beast fought and clawed at them for many hours, injuring several. But finally, the hunters conquered the beast and slayed him. That beast had no herd. He had no cubs and no mate to look after. He was a lone beast with nothing but his own flesh. Such beasts can fight until the end. His life force held no other vessel than himself."

The old Warchief turned to his fellow orcs.

"My brothers, our life force has more vessels than our old bones. We are not like the mighty beast, free to fight as we wish. We are not free to die as we wish."

The Warchief then returned to the Guild King.

"I agree to your terms, iron king, if you agree to mine. There will be no more burning of our villages, no more murder of our people. We will live as we did before – as much as we can. I have sung the Life Song, will you continue it?"

The Guild King rose to his feet and surveyed the whole assembly.

"I find your terms agreeable, orc. I promise all who obey our laws can live in peace. Be warned, though, I will not sing the Life Song with any orc who worships the dark gods, hides black books, or gives shelter to criminals. Do you agree?"

"I agree," the old Warchief announced.

Head Prophet Philipus rolled out a large desk with a

massive scroll on it.

"This is the peace agreement," he explained, "all you must do is come, touch the pen, and peace will be made between us."

Philipus held out a long black wooden pen. The orc chieftains looked to the Warchief. The Warchief stepped forward and raised his hand. He paused, drawing in a long breath. He extended his finger and touched the pen.

Philipus smiled as the Warchief walked away. All the orc chieftains, one by one, came and touched the pen as well. After the last one, Philipus dipped the pen's nib in ink and signed the bottom of the scroll.

"Now let it be known that in the eight month of the seven hundredth and ninetieth year since the First Prophet, peace was made between the orc and man. May the King forever reign."

"May the King forever reign," the crowd repeated as one.

"Iron King," the old Warchief spoke. "What of my son?"

"He will be my guest at my capital and serve as my advisor on all orc matter."

"Will he be safe?" the old Warchief pressed.

"Of course, I give my word. No harm will find him. You are all free to return to your people and inform them of your wise decision."

The old Warchief turned and left the tent, knowing there was no more he could do. The other chieftains slowly followed.

The Guild King grabbed a cup and toasted, "To peace."

"To peace," the crowd echoed as they downed their own cups and looked for more to fill them. The Guild King drank down his wine and fell back into his throne with a grin on his face.

> *There were only five survivors of the assassination of the Black Spear Guild, later called the Broken Lances. Most notably were the Guild King and Umbra, but there also were Stephen of Ashcord, James the Brown, and Caz of Dalecrow.*
>
> *All but one died in battles over the next thirty years.*
>
> ### *History of the Guilds*
> ### *By Elder Lighours*

Baron Umbra stood before the slab upon which his friend Stephen now laid. The healers gently cleaned the body for its travel home. Umbra rubbed two small coins between his fingers. He approached the body and laid them on Stephen's chest.

A healer sewed the torn flesh of Stephen's head around a wooden bowl to replace the shattered skull. The act would give Stephen a much more presentable appearance at his official funeral in Ashcord; and for that, Umbra was grateful.

Sir Francis entered the tent quietly and cleared his throat to announce his presence. Umbra waved the healers away.

They collected the tools of their craft and scurried off.

"You wished to see me, my lord?" he asked properly.

"Yes, I need to talk to you."

"I'm at your service," Francis responded.

"Have you heard the Guild King is keeping me in Doraxe?"

"I have heard. I assume you will make James steward with Stephen gone."

"Yes, that is my plan."

"I will do all I can to serve him, my lord," Francis pronounced.

"You are not coming back with us, Francis," Umbra stated bluntly. Francis narrowed his eyes, looking over Umbra to see if he was serious.

"Why would I not be returning to Black Shield?"

"Because you are staying here," Umbra said, crossing his arms.

"I don't understand."

"They have made you the new Steward of the orc lands. You will need to build forts and check points to keep the peace. I suggest you build a castle by the river to protect the supply lanes, and towers along the roads."

"My lord, why was I chosen for this honorable exile?"

"It is not an exile, it is an opportunity."

"It seems more like an exile, my lord."

"The Guild King has already decided," Umbra informed Francis, stepping forward and patting him on the shoulder. Francis shook his head as he digested the heavy news.

"Who would I be answerable to?" he muttered still unsure how he felt.

"Officially, the Prophets," Umbra answered. "You will be required to uphold their laws as well as the law of the land."

"Will I have problems with the Prophets?"

"Not if you do your job. They will have a Prophet come to advise you, and to inform on you, I'm sure."

"When would I be able to visit my home?"

Umbra shook his head slowly. Francis nodded.

A trembling hand reached into his belt pouch and drew a folded note. "Can you have a letter delivered to my sister?"

"Of course," Umbra replied. "Don't be disheartened by this. You have my full faith. I cannot think of one I would rather trust with this task."

"Yes, my lord," Francis said.

"Good, now find James and tell him to come in here."

"He is right outside, my lord," Francis said blankly.

"Then your task is an easy one, is it not?" Francis smiled awkwardly and walked out of the tent.

James soon entered after him. "Yes, my lord?"

"The Prophets will gain all the orc lands," Umbra opened.

"I'm not surprised; no guild wants the burden anyhow." James looked past Umbra and glanced at Stephen's body. He felt a twinge of discomfort talking politics in the presence of the honored dead.

"There are conditions though," Umbra continued. "The

Guild King will press Philipus to name a steward. I put Francis' name forward, and it has been accepted."

"He is a bit young, my lord," James confided. "A good knight, to be sure, but steward of new lands is not an easy position, even for the most elite of statesmen."

"He will do fine," Umbra asserted.

James nodded his head and smirked. "I am surprised you didn't consider me," he laughed.

"I didn't realize you were so eager to leave the Broken Lances," Umbra said, almost as if he was hurt by James' comment.

"It is not a matter of leaving, my lord. But I have served for many years and have only honor to show for it. I am grateful, but I do long to leave my children with something more substantial."

"I see," said Umbra shifting his weight as he thought. "I suppose I never saw you as ambitious."

"I am ambitious in my own way. It is right for a journeyman to expect elevation to master once his tutorship is done. I am ready for a position. You trained me well, my lord."

"Well, as the Divines would have it, you were promoted this very night. I will not be returning to Castle Pearl. I will be taking Duke Johes' place on the council until, Divines' willing, a better man can be found. Thus, I am declaring you Steward of Black Shield and Master of Castle Pearl. Your first task will be to replenish our numbers and take on the unsavory task of training the Guild King's new recruits."

"My lord, I am honored beyond words, I will not disappoint you," James said bowing low. "What new recruits?" he asked standing back up.

"Well the orcs, of course," Umbra stated.

"The orcs?" James burst out laughing. He stopped when Umbra's expression remained somber.

James shook his head. "My lord, the orcs are our enemies and little more than beasts. You can't be serious about trying to train them."

"I am not trying; you are," Umbra clarified.

James searched for words. "My lord, one cannot train a bull for war. The orcs are animals."

"Then make them into men who are our friends, rather than animals that are our foes. I have full faith in you, master trainer."

"My lord Baron, this cannot be done."

Umbra grabbed James by the shoulder and replied, "For your sake, I hope it can."

SWALLOWED PRIDE
4

There are three great cities in Galsag: Anchor, Tilton, and Doraxe. I leave out Mesmer City for the Mesmers would take offense to being included in Galsag.

But of those three, Doraxe is the greatest and the oldest. It has endured nine sieges and has not once been breached.

History of the Guilds
  Elder Lighours

The city was alive with a thousand eager citizens, desperate to gain a view of their returning heroes. Every alley, every street side, and every roof stood packed from the crowd. Flower petals rained from the sky on the passing precession as the temple bells tolled.

The Guild King held his hand up, receiving the praise freely. The three Guild Masters of the campaign rode close behind him. Umbra stared up at the downpour of red petals.

"It's like snow," he muttered to himself, "a blizzard not of ice, but of blood."

"Bless you Baron Umbra!" an old woman cried out from the crowd. Umbra glanced at her as she tossed flowers towards him. "The Divines bless the Broken Lances," she yelled.

"Long live the Guild King and his Black Baron," someone cheered. The Baron was unmoved by the praise. Praise had never been a joy to him.

"My guild," Lord Beritor mumbled while staring at the somber Baron, "has fought in as many battles, and is as deserving of honor as the famous Broken Lances."

Herrion hid his amusement at Beritor's sour expression. "Umbra is a common man," he explained, "and the people love the success of one of their own."

"His popularity rivals the King's. That makes him dangerous," Beritor hissed, "to the king and the kingdom."

"Your concern is touching, but I doubt Umbra is any political threat to anyone. I hear he would become a hermit if the King would allow it."

"If he has no political ambition, then he should hand his popularity over to one who can do some good with it," Beritor commented as if popularity was a basket one could pass to another. "His refusal to use his influence is selfish. Give me the ear of the King, and the heart of the people, and I would change the world."

"Yes, but for better or for worse?" Herrion wondered

aloud. Beritor glared at him, offended. Herrion laughed it off and proceeded down the street.

The stairwell leading to the royal citadel was filled with Guild Masters wishing to greet their king. At the top of the stairs, near the gate, were the Queen and her little prince. They moved down towards the street with their guards creating a path before them.

The Guild King dismounted, and the Guild Masters bowed in honor. The stoic Queen waited for her husband to draw nearer.

She was middle-aged, but well-formed and pretty despite her years. She wore an elegant dress with a gold cord wrapping her dark brown hair. The boy next to her was nine or ten, with bright yellow hair, and had the features of his father.

She nudged the young boy as the King approached. He ran to his father and was swept up into his large arms. The prince laughed as he fought the prickle of his father's coarse beard on his soft cheek. The King sat him gently back to his feet. The Queen stepped closer. They exchanged a smile and a formal kiss.

"My queen," the Guild King said.

"My king," she replied. "It is good to see you well."

"As it is to see you," he replied.

"I missed you, father," the little prince stated grabbing his hand.

"I missed you as well, my son."

"Was the war hard?"

"No war is easy," the King laughed, "but yes – this one was hard."

"Then we will praise the Divines in their mercy for making it short," the Queen said taking hold of the princes' hand and leading him away from his father. The royal guard escorted the royal family up into the citadel with the Guild Masters trailing behind them.

The Guild King's citadel sat atop a sharp cliff in the center of the city. A broad river flowed at the rock's edge, reflecting the white washed stone of the castle towers. The inner courtyard was lined with statues of past heroes and tended trees to honor them.

Sir Snaca and Guild Master Frederick watched as the royal couple walked the paved path.

"How does one give a king ill news?" Frederick asked aloud.

"Carefully, I would suppose," Snaca responded.

"I was opposed to this war from the very beginning. I pray it will prove worth it to the King."

"The minds of kings are complex things. I would not worry. Your loyalty is not in question. If the King did not see you as fit, he would not have made you steward in his absence."

"I am the Master of the Hall," Frederick reminded. "It is my sworn duty to protect the Guilds. I was the logical choice to be steward. My abilities, or the King's trust in them, had little to do with it."

"Then if you wish to maintain your high position, you

should support me in my solution."

"You need not worry about me, Snaca. I know what must be done," Frederick said walking towards the King with a forced cheery expression.

"Ah – my loyal stewards come to me with their report," the Guild King said with a grin. "Leave me, my love. Matters of state beckon me."

The Queen somberly bowed. "As my king desires. For all know a woman has not a thought in her head worth hearing." The Guild King's grin lessened, but he did not acknowledge the comment. The Queen turned and left with her prince by her side. Silence lingered between the three men for a moment.

"Congratulations on your victory, sire," Frederick finally said.

"Thank you, Master Frederick. I am glad to be home. May it be my last campaign."

"We all pray for that, sire."

"I hope the yoke of steward was not too burdensome."

"Of course not, sire, though an old guildsman such as myself would hardly wish for the honor his whole life."

"Honestly, I wonder if I want the honor my whole life as well," the Guild King jested with a smile. "I hope you will continue in your role as Master of the Hall."

"However the king needs me, I will serve."

"Good. Now, walk with me good friends, and give me your report. I wish to know if my kingdom is better or worse without me steering her."

"Sire," Frederick began walking a few steps behind the King. "Sir Snaca has been a great help in my duties. His knowledge of accounts and laws are second to none."

"Yes, why else would I have made him my Treasurer General?"

"Yes sire. In your absence, we have waged a war of our own against crime in the city. We have lessened poverty and started several work programs to improve the roads nation-wide."

"We have also increased revenue to the crown and ne-gotiated several deals with various guilds to increase trade," Snaca added.

The King nodded approvingly. He entered into the pal-ace in silence. He waited until they were away from even his guard's ears.

"So what is the thing you fear to tell me?" the King asked his advisors. "Has a plague broken out? Has diplomatic re-lations with an ally strained? Is there a true threat to my life? Your faces reveal your worry no matter how many lay-ers of deceit you add."

Frederick and Snaca lowered their heads in shame.

"Sire," Frederick began. "I take full responsibility, Snaca only obeyed my orders."

"I advised the action, sire," Snaca interjected. "It was what was needed."

"What is it?" the King asked, growing short.

"The treasury is drained, sire."

"What?" the King nearly shouted, his face turning red.

"In one breath you tell me taxes are up and the coffers draw empty? This does not fit, my friends."

Snaca and Frederick hid their faces. "Sire," Snaca dared to speak. "Three wars in twenty years is a costly thing to any king. The cost is amplified when the war is waged so far away from his base of supply. The price of feeding your armies in the orc lands was astronomical."

"I only marched with a handful of the larger guilds. Pray tell, what made their bellies astronomical?"

"Every guild, according to law, has the right to set taxes in their own land. This includes tariffs," Frederick explained. "Many guilds saw it fitting to demand taxes from your wagons."

"And you allowed this blackmail?" the King ranted.

"It is the law, sire," Frederick defended himself. "It was not in my power to deny them."

"I should have their heads for treason," the King barked. "Is it not treason to steal from the crown?"

"Not according to the law, sire," Snaca stated.

"Then this law must change," the King decided.

"Not an easy task, sire."

"Is not the Hall assembling in a few days? Draft a bill, man. I cannot think of a better time to change it. No Guild Master would dare oppose me with the glory of my recent triumph."

"You are most right, sire," Snaca said bowing. "I will draft a new bill at your word."

The Guild King saw a young man in Mesmer clothing

walking past as Snaca spoke. "Draft it," he said pushing his way past them. "Charles!" he cried, cheerfully opening his arms as if to embrace a lost son. The young man looked to the King and bowed with a grin.

"My King."

"Oh stand up straight; you need not protocol with me,"

"It is a matter of habit; I will work to break my manners for your sake. It is good to see you unharmed by the green beasts."

"Oh please," laughed the Guild King. "Do you honestly think I would allow a horde of savages to defeat me? Now, on to something important, how is my patronage treating you?"

"Sire, I'm not sure I can stand it much longer. Your love and generosity spoils an artist. I play the lute all morning, paint all afternoon, and fuck till bed."

The Guild King let out a deep belly laugh. "And this is a bad thing?"

"An artist's muse comes from pain, and trouble. These soft sheets will be the death of me," Charles sighed.

"I can always move you to the street and solve the problem."

"No, sire. I prefer the slow death of comfort."

"Very well then," the King laughed again. "Ah Charles," the King laid an arm over the young man's shoulders. "You are the desire of women and the terror of men."

"Married men most of all, I suppose," Charles jested.

"Yes, yes. Now Charles, the people need to know about

my victories in the south," he whispered. "What good is all that blood on the field if it gains us no glory back home? I expect paintings, songs and some plays about it."

"Well sire, the Hall of Guilds does have a rather large wall in need of flattery."

"Oh, I like that. Let them walk past a mural of me leading the charge into the orc's lines. My sword draw, my face strong, my beast unflinching before death."

"Did you?" Charles asked.

"Did I what?"

"Lead the charge?"

"Of course not, I'm the king; but that is not the point."

"I will work without rest, sire," Charles declared.

"No need for all that," the King dismissed. "I only need the best work of your life. This was my final war, the art dedicated to it should be worthy of it." Charles nodded in understanding.

Snaca and Frederick watched the King and the Mesmer drift away from them. Snaca slowly leaned towards Frederick.

Frederick sighed heavily. "The bill will never pass through the Hall," he said. "I have truly betrayed my king now."

"The only way to save the kingdom is to rock its foundations a bit," Snaca said coldly. "Of course the bill will not pass, but in it being presented, other issues will come to light. The King must be made to see the situation more clearly. Sadly, the kingdom's change has gone largely unnoticed by our loved sire. When he walks into the Hall of Guilds, he still sees the hard, selfless men he bled with twenty years ago instead of the fat, lazy men who sit there now. It is time for the King to see the hard truth."

> *From a young age, loyalty is taught to the Northern peoples. Loyalty and honor is the cornerstone of their culture – where advancement and gain is the cornerstone of many of their neighbors.*
>
> *To a Northrim knight, disobeying an order is the same as falling on his sword. And many would prefer it.*

History of the Guilds
Elder Lighours

Umbra breathed in the cool morning air. The citadel guards were changing their watch as the servants scurried to prepare the morning meal. Umbra walked the courtyard and enjoyed the calm of the artificial forest. The trees around him were all carefully pruned and trimmed even as their leaves changed color for the season.

Koll paced anxiously down the path. He saw Umbra approach but did not say anything. He forced a smile and a nod.

"Lovely morning, is it not?" Umbra asked.

"Yes, my lord. Very lovely."

"Colder than I expected," Umbra continued, "but we are high on a cliff."

"Yes, my lord."

"You sleep well? Was the room to your liking?"

"It was very comfortable," Koll answered.

"The meals will be good, too. Last assembly I attended ended in a three-day feast. A large bull was roasted as well as several hogs and chickens."

"I look forward to it," Koll stated. Umbra chuckled.

"You wish I had let you return to Castle Pearl with James."

"I do."

"I need you here," Umbra explained.

"I know."

"But you still wish you were released."

"I grew up in a palace," Koll said, "in plush beds with servants roasting my meals. Being here draws up memories."

Umbra understood his pain. "How is your father?" he asked in an attempt to be comforting.

"Old," Koll replied. "My nephew will be king soon. He turned fifteen this year. By the Divines, I remember him as a lump in my sister's belly. I have never met him. Not even once."

"Do you regret being taken out of the succession?"

"No, no I don't. I would have made a poor king. Kings have to compromise and hide what they think. I have never been good at that."

"Northrim is not like here. There, the king's word is absolute; his will, unquestioned."

"That also is too much for one man," Koll muttered. "It

is a wonder my father lived as long as he has. Such weight on one man. I don't remember much of him before the war. I remember he had a desk high up in the tower, where he could gaze over the whole kingdom. The children were rarely allowed up there. Once he beckoned me, sat me on his knee, and pointed out to the land. He told me a good king exists to serve, not be served. That he is but a steward of the land. A gardener, I suppose, and his duty is to protect it even at the cost of his life."

"King Olfrie is an honorable man and a good king," Umbra said. "It was unfortunate he backed the nobles in the North Wars. I would have preferred to have been his ally than his foe."

"What was it like fighting your own countrymen?" Koll asked. "Did you feel like a traitor?"

"I had lived in Galsag for decades when the North Wars broke out. My duty was to the Guild King. Any duty I owed Northrim was paid in the Great War."

"My lord Umbra," Sir Snaca cried out as he hustled across the courtyard.

"Yes?" Umbra asked turning to the panting man.

"My lord, I am Sir Snaca. We meet several years ago when the second prince was born."

"Yes, I remember," Umbra replied. "What do you need, sir?"

"The King saw fit to place me in your service, my lord. So I can acquaint you with your new duties within the inner counsel."

"Very well," Umbra stated. "When will the counsel gather?"

"Before the opening of the Hall, my lord. The King will wish to gain advice on his new bills before going before the Guild Masters for approval."

"What sort of bills?" Umbra asked with a raised brow.

"I do not know," Snaca insisted, "but I would suspect a new bill will be drafted to levy laws and taxes on the newly conquered lands."

"The Prophets control the orc lands, what are they to us?"

"The King would be foolish to allow such riches to slip through his fingers without so much as a tariff," Snaca explained.

Umbra began to speak when a trumpet sounded from the gates. The three men looked to who had arrived at court. A large company entered through the gate on horses surrounding a single lord. The knights wore the finest armor in Galsag. In their hands were large banners with a white dragon on black silk.

"Lord Victor Drako," Umbra muttered. "Tell me, Snaca, when was I going to be informed of the Lord's coming?"

"I apologize, my lord. He was invited by the King himself as the honored guest of the Hall."

"What is the Guild King playing at?" Koll wondered aloud. "Why would he invite his rival to court?"

"I do not know," Umbra admitted walking closer.

The troop of knights fanned out to make a square. A

kingly man with long white hair and an intense gaze dismounted his horse. He wore clothes made of black silk with a coat of fur over his shoulders. The assortment of rings and jewels on his hands and neck would lift the lowest peasant into the highest nobility.

The Queen carefully exited the castle to greet her father. He kissed her on the cheek and embraced her. She returned his affection coldly.

"How was your journey?" she asked politely.

"Long, thank you for your concern." Victor stated. "Have the Mesmers arrived yet?"

"No, we expect them this evening."

"Then tonight's feast will be an interesting one. All the King needs is the Vycesie and King Olfrie and all the world will be at his table."

"It is good to see you as well, father. I have been well, and so have the children," the Queen said as if he had asked a question.

"Ah yes, how is the young prince? Is he strong? Is he brave? Or smart? Tell me he is at least smart."

"He is very smart," the Queen assured. "He speaks Elf well now and is learning the ancient tongue."

"Good, good. He will make a good king."

"Yes, father."

"I'm very happy with what I hear about him. You have raised him well."

"I live by your example," the Queen flattered.

Maxwell approached his father and sister. "And where is

Francis? Is he here as well?" he asked.

"The King saw fit to place him as Steward of the orc lands, brother" the Queen explained. "I thought he sent word."

"No," Maxwell complained, "he has sent no word."

"Well, we have word of it now," Victor stated flatly. "I would have liked to have seen my eldest son and rightful heir, but since he decided our name was best honored gallivanting around with butchers, I will continue to suffer his absence."

"Many would call his promotion honorable, father," the Queen reminded.

"Would they?" Victor asked. "Praise the Divines my other children were not so disobedient, or our house would be in ruins by now. But instead we are again royalty, and our line will rule this land forever."

"Yes, father," Maxwell and the Queen both muttered.

"Now, let us see if we can find something worth eating in this stable your husband calls a palace."

> *To rule is to serve. A man who serves but himself is not a man but a fool. Your authority is granted by the Divines to cover those under you. As they have given it, so can they take it away. The rod should be used firmly but always fairly.*
>
> **The First Word**
> **Treasures 2:8**

Francis' eyes opened. His breath formed a fog over his face. He sat up in his straw bed and stretched with a yawn. The sun hid behind the horizon. Francis slid to his bed's edge and rubbed the back of his neck.

Standing to his feet, he leaned down and touched his toes. After popping his back with a few quick jerks, he moved to his washing basin. He splashed some oil on a sharpening stone and glided his dagger across the stone to cut a razor edge.

After whipping a bowl of soapy cream, he prepared his face and sides of his head for shaving. Then with artistic precision, he dragged the blade over his skin leaving a smooth surface. With the excess cream washed off, Francis held out a small mirror and trimmed the remaining hair on the top of his head with scissors.

Contented with his work, Francis donned a single cotton tunic and tied a cord belt around his waist. A pair of beaten sandals awaited him outside his tent. He slipped them on and began to jog around the camp.

Rows of tents covered the yard. The beginnings of a castle surrounded them. Guards patrolled the wood walkways and huddled near the fire pots.

Francis embraced the cold wind and chill of his accruing sweat. Francis finished his laps and dropped to his hands and toes. He lowered his body then pushed back up again. He repeated the action until his chest and arms burned.

Leaping from the ground with a pounding heart, Francis sprinted to a log and hurled it over itself. He continued to flip the man size log all the way to the well where he stopped for a drink.

Several men in chain mail approached him wearing the tunics of the prophet's. A young man in prophet robes was among them. Francis finished his drink and faced his guests.

"My lord," one of the knights said with a bow of respect. "I am Sir Gregory, sworn to the Divines. May I present Prophet Minor Jayden from Doraxe."

"I am to be the Divines' voice and counsel in these dark lands, so that the light of the First Word may spread through the region like a flame in a dark room."

Francis nodded his head. "You mean be Philipus' spy." Jayden uncomfortably chuckled and looked at Sir Gregory with a confused glance.

"I am at your service, my lord," said Jayden, "as is every knight in the Divines' service. But these lands are under Prophet control; as ordered by your King of the Guilds."

"Is he not also your king?" Francis asked.

"I am the Divines' humble servant."

"Of course, and tell me, how did a Prophet Minor gain such a high responsibility as aid to the Steward of the Orc lands?"

"I would assume the same way a humble knight gained the position of Steward even though he is not yet thirty," Jayden answered. Francis grinned.

A soldier ran up to the group and bowed. "My lord, the orcs have arrived with the Shamans."

"Thank you," Francis replied.

"So soon?" Jayden asked.

"I am under orders to withhold aid until all Shamans and dark books are accounted for. It had the effect of encouraging the clans to obey quickly before winter comes."

"I see," Jayden commented.

"Excuse me," Francis said walking through the group. "I need to change into more dignified attire before greeting my orc guests."

"Of course," Jayden said.

Jayden waited until Francis was back in his tent to speak to Gregory. "What do you know of him?" he asked.

"Only what is well known," Gregory replied. "He is a Drako, Victor's heir. He joined the Broken Lances against his father's will and made Captain quickly."

"I heard he left the Battle of Two Hills without a scratch. Impressive, considering two of his fellow captains did not."

"Impressive indeed, if you assume he was engaged in the battle as his other captains."

"Are you saying he wasn't?" Jayden asked shocked and amused.

"I'm saying I believe what I see, not what I hear."

Jayden laughed to himself and pondered. "So he is either a coward who held to the edge of the fray while his comrades died, or a hero with skill enough to save himself."

"My experience teaches me men often sit in the middle somewhere," replied Sir Gregory.

"And where would we be without your experience?"

Jayden mocked. Sir Francis exited his tent cladded in armor. Around his neck was the gold sigil of his new office.

"Shall we?" he asked the Prophet Minor and his escorts.

They walked together out of the courtyard and into the open plains. Several dozen orcs and their families had gathered outside. None of them were large or impressive like the hunters Francis had faced in the battle.

A cart filled with books and scrolls sat to Francis' left; to his right was a line of chained orcs. Francis walked up and down the line of orcs, looking over each Shaman. They stared him down, proud to the end. Jayden kept his distance and covered his nose and mouth with a cloth.

"Those are the Shamans, I presume," Jayden said.

"Yes," Francis replied. He paused in front of one of them and opened up the orc's robes exposing the heavily tattooed chest. "Only Shamans have these kinds of marks. That is how you know them."

Jayden picked up one of the orc books and fumbled through its pages. "Most fascinating," he said.

"Can you read any of it?" Francis asked pointing at the book in Jayden's hand.

"No, and even if I could, it is forbidden."

"You are right," Francis said grabbing a torch and tossing it into the cart. The fire grabbed at the pages quickly. Soon the whole cart roared in flames.

"Our word with the iron prince is kept," an orc chieftain said, approaching with one of his chiefs. "Now, send us the wagon you promised. Winter draws near, and the herds have all left for better grounds."

Francis turned to the chief and chieftain. "You are missing a Shaman," he stated.

"No, this is all of them," the orc chief asserted. Francis smacked the chief across the face.

"Do not lie to me, and you will address me as 'my lord.'" The orc spat out some blood but said nothing. Francis grew impatient and raised his hand again. The chieftain casually stepped in.

"Yes, my lord," he said. "We understand. We, the Torguk tribe, will submit as our Warchief has ordered."

"Better," Francis replied lowering his hand. "Now every clan has a Shaman, do they not?"

"They do," the chieftain said.

"And the Torguk tribe has seven clans, do they not?"

"It does."

"Then why do I have six Shamans chained before me and not seven?" Francis barked.

"Dor'thor Shaman cut off his life force rather than be silenced," the chief interjected. Francis instantly struck the orc again.

"I warned you about lying, orc!"

"My name is not orc," the chief spat. "I am Chief Urk'gral of the Torguk tribe." The orc growled as he glared at Francis. Francis stood stoic, not even looking at the orc.

Then, in one fluid movement, Francis drew his sword and sliced the orc chief open. The other orcs began to move, but the human guards quickly drew their own swords. The chieftain raised his hand at the crowd. They immediately backed down.

Francis leveled the blood-soaked blade to the chieftain's throat. The orc did not flinch. The two glared at each other for many moments.

"You seem calm," Francis said, "for a chieftain who just lost one of his chiefs."

"The Warchief ordered us submit, so until he speaks, I will submit."

Francis smiled at the strangeness of the words. "You are interesting people," he commented. "Where is the missing Shaman?"

"My chief spoke truth."

"Then why did you fail to bring me a body or some sort of proof?"

"An orc must be burnt before the sun falls on his death," the chieftain explained. "Else his life force will never find its new place."

"And how am I to determine if you speak the truth?" Francis yelled in the orc's face.

"You know the truth," the orc said, "for I spoke it." Francis pressed the blade harder against the orc's green skin. Blood danced down the blade and dripped to the ground, but the chieftain stood unmoved.

Francis laughed. "What is your name, orc?"

"Mur'kog."

"When I think of orc nobility, I will think of you," Francis said, drawing his sword away. He motioned to his men.

The knights grabbed the Shamans and pressed them to their knees. Mur'kog did not turn from Sir Francis, even as the cries of the Shaman's rung out and their severed tongues were tossed into the mud.

"The food wagons will be sent out tomorrow," Francis promised. The chieftain said nothing. Francis turned back to the camp and motioned his men to follow. The smoke from the books was rising like a black cloud over the fort.

Jayden caught up with Francis inside the half-built walls. "Was that necessary?" he asked as Francis cleaned the orc blood from his blade.

"Completely."

"I fail to see how."

"When the Guild King won his throne, he had problems with the southern lords. They raided his roads and disobeyed his decrees. There was fear of revolt in the court. That ended when the Guild King sent the Broken Lances south. Baron Umbra found every scrap of rebellion, rounded them up, and hung them off the towers of Longlast Castle. Since then, there have been no raids on the king's roads."

> *Galsag has always been a proving ground for the ruthless and the clever. The only place in the world that rivals its political wonder is the Vycesie's lands with its immortal elven court.*
>
> **History of the Guilds**
>   **By Elder Lighours**

The feast's fire roared under the slaughtered hog. Servants cut meat from its charred flesh and served it to many guests. A long table sat on a raised platform looking over the filled hall. The Guild King tore into his meal and gulped down his wine. His modest wife gently cut her food and chewed it slowly. The young prince sat on his father's armrest leaning on his shoulder. Victor Drako sat past the Queen next to Baron Umbra and the other Guild Masters being honored at the feast.

"I hear my lord Baron Umbra will be joining us tomorrow at council," Beritor said to Herrion.

Herrion shook his head. "Don't get too used to him. My lord Baron has no stomach for the court and is only here out of love for the King."

Master Frederick leaned over the table to look both lords in the eyes. "I cannot think of a better replacement for the empty spot. It is about time we have more true guildsman at court. I fear the King may be surrounded by highborns pretending to have his best at heart – as is their way."

"Master Frederick, aren't you dead yet?" Beritor asked with a smirk.

"No my lord, I endure. My many years in the army and in guilds have made my bones like steel and my heart iron. I will outlive you all, I suspect."

"You are not that old, my friend," Umbra stated. "I am your senior by five years, if I am not mistaken."

The Queen finished her plate and gently cleaned her face with a cloth. "What bills do you plan to put before the Hall this year?"

The King grunted.

"Can a man not even eat a meal without talk of state? What makes you think I have any bills ready?"

"I certainly hope you have some, my dear husband, considering the kingdom is near bankrupt."

The King sat down his wine somberly and drew much closer to his wife. "And where, pray tell, did you hear that?" he whispered.

"My love, while you were slaughtering green men in the south, I was here; listening to the walls. A palace wall has a lot to say if you take the time to listen to it, and I have much time."

"You are a difficult woman to love, my queen," he said with snide.

"And you are a hard man to help," she countered. "Do you plan to present your bill openly in the Hall?"

"It is how things are done."

"It may be how things are done, but it is not how you will pass this bill, my love."

"And you know matters of state better than I?"

The Queen giggled under her breath. "I know no Guild Master will vote for a bill that increases his taxes or strips his rights away."

"You know that?"

"I do," the Queen asserted. "Dear husband, if you wish to see your bill passed, bury it in an appealing bill. Maybe something to do with the orc, harsher laws maybe. No guildsman would oppose that."

The King pulled away from the Queen uninterested, but even as he tried to put her words out of his mind, the truth of them lingered.

The young prince grabbed his father's arm and pointed to a rough-looking man with a great beard. "Who is that, father?"

"That is Simon von Ox," the Guild King replied, "of the Order of Spears."

"What has he done?"

The King laughed. "Recently, very little. He is a brave man, though. Fought in the North Wars well enough."

"And who is that?" the prince asked pointing to another man. He was a younger man with fine features.

"That is Sir Edward Brighouse, of the Halbruders. He led the Lord Duke's infantry in the Battle of Two Hills."

"And her?" the prince asked pointing to a young and well-endowed servant girl.

"I don't know her," the King said with a touch of lament in his voice. "Yet," he added with a wink at his son.

"Were the orcs scary?" the prince asked.

"Oh – no more than any other foe."

"When will my uncle come home?" the prince asked. The Queen raised her head and glanced at her husband before returning to her meal.

The King patted the lad on the knee. "When his duty is done."

"When will that be?"

"I don't know," the Guild King admitted.

"Do you miss your uncle, young prince?" Victor asked. The prince looked at his grandfather then to his father for guidance.

"Answer your grandfather, son."

"I do, my lord."

"I feel your pain," Victor stated lifting his glass. "A toast – a toast to my son, who sits in honorable exile from this court by decree of our most wise and loving king."

The Guild King raised his cup. "To Sir Francis Drako," he called out, echoing down the stone hall. "Steward and trusted friend of this court. His absence, although necessary and painful to us all, is a loss."

"You are most gracious, my king," Victor replied, "to call him a friend of your court when he has, in fact, never – to my knowledge – been a part of your court."

"Any member of the Broken Lances is a friend of my court, whether his duties allow a visit or not."

"You cannot know how much that warms my heart, sire, to hear such things from your own mouth. For a less keen man would look at your actions and think the king was against him. He would think the king meant to steal his heir though promotion. Of course, being a much wiser man, it is obvious to me my king would never do that to his loving father-in-law."

"Then I will thank the Divines for your wisdom," said the King, "for a lesser man would have insulted the king in his anger and thus risked losing the king's blessings and love."

"Yes," Victor agreed. "A lesser man could have. It is fortunate then that not only am I a man of great wisdom, so I know your love when I see it, but I am also a rich and powerful man, so the loss of a king's blessings would not be so painful. Though I sleep securely, knowing I will never lose them."

The Guild King raised his cup again. "To your slumber," he toasted. "May it be long."

Victor smiled and raised his own cup. "And to the crown prince, may his reign begin early in life." Both men drank down their wine.

"Not too early I hope," the Queen muttered touching the King's arm.

The door to the great hall opened wide and a Mesmer herald, dressed in fabulous pomp, entered. The crowds at the tables grew silent as the Mesmer waited. The King sat down his glass, moved his son to his own chair, and sat upright in his own.

"I present," the herald yelled out, "Our Most Loved Mistress, Mayor of Mesmer City, Baroness of Eden, Rightful Ruler of the Mesmer, and Defender of the Common, Lady Edoweyhn." A row of dancers dressed as fairies jumped and sprang down the cobblestone floor, amazing the guildsmen at their tables. Next was a line of musicians with small children throwing flower petals along the way. Then a large carriage, covered in gold and finely crafted wood, came into the hall. Every side had decorative paintings and brilliant trim.

A servant with a fluffy shirt and tights for pants stepped

to the front of the carriage and opened the door. A woman with a long, flowing dress and many exotic furs for a coat stepped out into the hall. Her hair was encased in gold wire to form wing-like structures. Diamonds the size of apples hung around her neck. Her face was painted nearly white with red spots on the cheeks.

The whole hall stood to their feet and lowered their heads in respect. She walked forward to the King's table and bowed in the Mesmer style. The Guild King rose and bowed in return.

"Lady Edoweyhn, I welcome you to my court."

"And I am glad to be received," the Mesmer Mayor replied. "And I pledge continued love and support of my people as we are the most natural of friends."

"I trust your journey was safe," the Guild King said.

"It was safe enough. Your diligent work to make your kingdom well has paid off, at long last."

"You have my Lord Drako to thank for the safety of the roads," the King said gesturing a hand to Victor. "For it was his lands you passed through most."

Lady Edoweyhn bowed. "I thank you, Lord Drako."

"It is my pleasure, my lady."

"My lady, if your travel has not made you too weary, please come and sit with us," the King offered. "We are celebrating a war won and peace made."

"I am honored to dine with you. It brings me much joy to know the horrid beasts of the south now know their place."

"Much like the brutes to the north?" Umbra muttered

under his breath.

"Now," said Edoweyhn, "I trust my daughter is not too weary from her campaigning to come see me." Edoweyhn looked over the crowd for her Raven. She did not find her. The King cleared his throat.

"My lady, your daughter did not accept my request to dine with us tonight."

Even under the white paint, all saw Edoweyhn's face turn red with anger. "And where is she?" she asked.

WAR SPOILS

5

Just as Northrim is defined by loyalty and Galsag by its diversity, the Mesmers are defined by abundance. Every Mesmer home is decorated with fine items of gold and silver. Every Mesmer gentleman or lady sees it as their duty to dress in the latest fashions.

The balls and parties of even the lowest merchant would bankrupt most lords, and the debauchery in their bedrooms would shame most whores.

History of the Guilds
By Elder Lighours

aven wandered through the filled tavern. Drunken men grabbed at the bar wenches as they passed by with filled mugs of ale. The fiddle and the drum sung between the shouts of brawlers and the splash of vomit. A crowd congregating in the corner caught Raven's eye. She carefully squeezed through the spectators to see the source of their interest.

Three men sat around a small table. A pile of coins and jewels sat in the middle next to a stack of playing cards. One man was obviously the wealthiest with his fine clothes, large belly, and gold chain. The man next to him was of more humble origins, with the look of a man in over his head.

The gentleman across from them, by whom the crowd seems most intrigued, was another matter. He was boyishly handsome with well-kept black hair. He had blue eyes and a gentle smile. His coat was in the Mesmer fashion, as was his shirt and his shoes.

He peeked at his cards then at his opponents. "So, good men, what will it be?" he asked. "Mr. Moor, do you believe our dear Guild Master Duncan has the ace?"

"No, Mr. Charles, I do not," Moor replied. Duncan laughed. His big belly jiggled as he did.

"Is the good Mr. Moor actually going to fall for this trick? I know my cards; this Mesmer the King keeps, does not."

"I disagree, Master Duncan," Charles said. "I know your cards. You have them written all over your face. You might as well have a mirror instead of a nose. In fact, I wager two more golds that you have nothing more than a pair of fools."

Charles casually sat his bet in the center of the table. The Guild Master's lips pursed in displeasure. He tossed in a matching wager. "Brave man," Charles commented.

"It is easy to be brave when victory is assured," Duncan replied. "I never realized music composition and painting paid so well, Mr. Charles."

"What should I say? The King is a generous man. Bet is to you, Mr. Moor."

Moor looked over his cards, then to the three coins he had left, then to the treasure sitting in the middle of the table. "I am all in, Divines have mercy," Moor said dropping his final coins.

"My, my," Charles chuckled. "Have some iron in your blood after all. I suppose it is time to lift our skirts and show what we got, aye?"

The Guild Master flipped over his cards, three nines. The mob clapped, certain he had won. Duncan sat upright, feeling confident. Mr. Moor smiled and tossed his card into the open, four fives. Silence fell on the crowd. Duncan's face grew red with anger. He smacked his fist on the table and stormed out. The crowd was stunned.

"Well played, my friend," Charles said clapping. "Was that not well played?" he asked the crowd, urging them to clap as well. Mr. Moor grinned and reached for the pot. Charles caught his wrist. "But you forgot about me, sir." Charles laid out his cards, two kings and three fours.

The color drained out of Moor's face. His head fell to the table and he began to weep. Charles sighed and began to collect his winnings. The crowd, having seen the end to the drama, dispersed. Raven, however, stayed in the shadows.

Charles was counting his bounty when Mr. Moor fell to the floor. "Please sir," he begged on his knees. "That was all I had. Please, for the sake of my children." Charles tried to ignore him, but he persisted.

Charles rubbed his forehead in thought.

"If you can't afford to lose, you can't afford to play," he explained.

"Kind sir, have a heart for the sake of my little ones. I am a fool, I know. I only wished to gain an advantage in this cruel world."

Charles sighed and shook his head. He grabbed a handful of coins and tossed them at Moor's feet.

"Thank you, sir. Thank you. You are a gift from the Divines."

"Yes, yes," Charles muttered. "Now, don't play anymore, my friend. You have no gift for it."

"No sir, thank you." Moor grabbed his coins and left quickly.

Raven smiled and approached Charles.

"Awful kind of you," she said, gesturing to the fleeing Moor. "Not often does a gambler give away some of his winnings." Charles shrugged causally.

"It is a flaw of mine. I am a sap for saps."

"Must make being a gambler difficult. As I would understand, saps make the best playmates."

"It is true my conscience hurts my profits, but taking a poor man's coin purse hurts my peace. And I enjoy my sleep."

"Do you know who I am, good sir?" Raven asked.

"Yes, you are Lady Raven; daughter to our most honorable and fair Mayor. The best we ever had, I say. Or at least

I say it around those who could have me beheaded. How is the Free City, by the way? I so rarely visit anymore."

"It is fair," Raven replied. "Why did you leave? It is rare to see a Mesmer, who is not a merchant, outside of Eden."

"Ah, my lady. It is rude to ask a stranger his secrets, but if you were to... perhaps, play a hand or two of cards; we could get to know one another. Then we would not be strangers."

Raven smiled and looked away.

"I believe I was once told to never play a Mesmer at cards."

"Good advice," Charles mused. "But seeing I am a Mesmer and you are a Mesmer, what could be the harm?"

Raven bit her lower lip as she pondered. She slid into Moor's old chair and drew a few silvers from her coin pouch.

"You must forgive me, I travel light," Raven said holding up her coin purse.

"And without guards, it seems. Not wise in this city, my lady."

"Are you offering me protection, Mr. Charles?"

"Only for a small price," Charles asked with a smile. "Are you in danger, my lady?"

"No," Raven said drawing close. "But misbehave and you will be." She pointed past him to three men sitting on the other side of the tavern with no drinks or food. Charles nodded.

"Five card fancy?" he asked shuffling the playing card deck.

Raven tossed a coin into the pot. "That sounds fine."

Charles passed out five cards to her and five to himself. They both carefully looked at their hands. Raven sat down one and took one from the deck. Charles took two.

"So how do you find Doraxe, my lady?"

"I find it unclean and dull to the eyes."

"Well, then you have obviously not seen the palace. I provided much of the art."

"I just came from there," Raven stated tossing in another coin.

"And how did you find it?"

"Much like the city," she smirked. Charles made a hurt face and dropped a coin to match her bet. Raven laughed at his pain and showed her cards, two pair. Charles glanced at his three queens. He laid the cards face down on the table.

"Seems you have me," he said.

Raven smiled and collected her winnings. "Good game, Mr. Charles."

"Good game, my lady. Perhaps we can play again, sometime."

"Perhaps," Raven muttered standing. She paused for a moment. "Perhaps you are right about me not knowing the full beauty of Doraxe. Perhaps you can show me."

"It would be my privilege," Charles replied.

Raven smiled a last time and took her leave. Her hidden bodyguards followed after her. Charles played with the cards in his hand. Mr. Moor plopped into the seat next to him. Charles shook his head at his friend.

"I believe the plan was for you to win this evening, Moor."

"Well, plans change, my good fellow. I saw that lily eyeing you and jumped at the chance. Did you enjoy my performance?"

"Not as much as she did," Charles chuckled.

"You take her for a coin or two?" Moor asked. "Her silk blouse was worth more than that fool Duncan whole."

"No, I allowed her her coin," Charles stated.

Moor was shocked. "The great Charles lost?"

"No, my good man, I do not see it as a loss. For with a few coins and some kind words, we have purchased something much better."

> *A man should have one wife, for she is his soul, and so the Divines will smile on him. He should love her as his own flesh for she is his flesh. Do not be like those submitted to the black mark. Do not treat your wife with contempt.*
>
> **The First Word**
> **Treasures 17:41**

David touched the Guild King's arm, trying to wake him. The King snored all the louder and ignored his servant. David gently shook the King who awakened abruptly.

"Your morning meal is ready, sire."

"Tell the servants to bring it later," the Guild King scowled, rolling over and snuggling next to the nude barmaid in his bed.

"The Baron Umbra is wishing to see you before the inner council meeting," David explained. The Guild King glared at his servant and with a roll of his eyes sat up. David brought him a washing basin. The King splashed his face with water and shook off the excess.

Drying himself with a towel, he barked for the girl to leave and slipped into his clothes. The barmaid quickly covered herself with her clothes and fled the room. The King shook his head.

"David, make certain she does not run down the hall past the Queen's quarters like the last one did."

"Of course, sire," David said springing to his feet and going after her.

The Guild King tied his own belt and shook the remaining bit of sleep off. He opened a small wooden door and entered into the room where Umbra was waiting patiently.

Umbra bowed low upon seeing the King. "Sire, forgive me for waking you."

"What is it, Umbra?" the Guild King asked falling into the nearest chair and resting his head against his hand.

"I read the bill you have prepared for the Hall of Guilds."

"The whole thing?" the King asked shocked.

"With the help of the young Northrim prince, yes."

"My friend, only you would stay up all night reading a routine bill on new laws on conquered lands."

"It is my duty as a member of the inner council to review all bills before they are taken to the Hall so I can better advise you, sire."

"What is it, Umbra? Why are you here so early and why are you speaking so formally?"

Umbra slid into a seat near the King. "Sire, I have issue with this bill. I wanted to talk to you before the inner council meeting."

"Issue, what issue?"

"Sire, these laws you are passing on the orcs, they break our peace agreement," Umbra said carefully.

The King glared at him insulted. "They do not! Part of the agreement was they would submit to our laws."

"Sire, this bill would make it illegal to hunt, illegal to wear animal hide, and illegal to travel in groups of more than five. I am no lover of the orcs, but this bill clearly attacks their way of life. They will revolt, sire."

"I highly doubt that. They are bled dry and these laws will bleed them further."

"I protest this bill in the name of your honor," Umbra stated.

"In the name of my honor?" the Guild King chuckled. "Oh – I see; it is the young prince Koll that stirred you up. He always was soft skinned and tender hearted."

"Sire, I feel this way," Umbra contented. "It is not right to go back on your word."

"How dare you!" the Guild King snapped, leaping to his feet. "I am keeping my word to the letter. Our agreement with the orcs stated they must obey our laws. If I wish to pass a law that says every orc must walk on his hands, the green bastards shall or die for it. Be careful, my friend, you are on the wrong side of this argument. The Hall will pass this bill without debate. You wish to know why? Because they hate green skins, almost as much as they hate the Southies."

Umbra lowered his head. "Sire, no doubt you are right, but when we made terms with an enemy before, we kept to the spirit and not just the letter of the peace agreement. Does that change simply because the foe is a different people than ours, because their ways are strange to us? I am not wise enough to see the difference, sire."

The Guild King slipped back into his chair and rested a hand on Umbra's shoulder. "I appreciate your desire to uphold my honor, but you must trust me on this. All that I do is for the good of the kingdom. Can I count on your support?"

Umbra looked up to his King. "You can count on my silence, sire."

"Thank you, my friend. You will see. I am not as mad as I sometimes seem."

"You are the sanest person I know, sire."

The King laughed. "I will have to work on that then." Umbra smiled, rose and left the King.

Koll, who was pacing to and from, met him in the hall. "What did the King say? Did you bring up our concern to him?"

"I did, and now I will drop it," Umbra said walking on.

Koll followed after him confused. "What do you mean, drop it? He is going against his own word."

Umbra shot a glance at him. He grabbed him by the arm and walked him into the shadows out of others' ears.

"You shut your mouth, boy. He is king, and it is treason to call him a liar or bring his honor into question."

"My lord, he is..."

"He is doing nothing illegal. He will present the bill to the Hall, as is right, and if the Guild Masters vote against it, it will not become law. This is how we live here. You should understand that by now. The King drafts the bills, and the Hall approves them. There is no law saying what bill the King can or cannot present. He could draft a bill tomorrow saying everyone must walk on their hands and, if the Hall passed it, it would be law."

"So would you walk on your hands, my lord?"

"If it was passed?" Umbra asked. "I would buy shoes for my hands that day."

"That is not right, why should the innocent suffer

for the foolishness of their leaders?"

"It is the way of the world."

"Then the world should change," Koll bursted out.

"And will you change it?" Umbra asked. "You have never seen a world in chaos, Koll. You have seen war, true enough, but you never lived in a world without rules. I was a boy during the Great War, the son of a common shoemaker. One day, a band of knights passed our home while my father was away looking for food. They were Northrim soldiers, men from my own country.

"My mother tried to fight them off, so they killed her. They locked me in a shed and dragged my sister into the barn. She was such a lovely girl, Koll. You would have liked her.

"They ravaged her so violently her breast was torn off. After she bled to death, they grew bored and left. When I finally got free and saw her..." Umbra shook his head slowly, lost in his own memory.

"Umbra, I..." Koll began.

"My heart aches for the orcs. It truly does, but I will not see such things as I saw in the Great War happen here, even if that means being silent when I wish to speak. If I had authority to stop this, I would. But our system, though not perfect, is what we have. We must trust in our King, for I know he is a good man. And if the King stumbles then we must trust the Hall to correct him; that is our way."

Umbra left Koll there. Koll leaned against the wall and watched his Guild Master go. "You taught me the Guild King stands for truth and justice," he muttered to himself. "If he compromises, what right does he have to be king?"

Umbra entered into the council chamber and took his seat. Lord Beritor and Herrion were already present. Beritor thumbed through the lengthy bill on the table.

"Interesting approach the King is taking with the orc lands," Beritor stated. "It almost seems he wishes for revolt."

Umbra shivered at the thought that he agreed with Beritor on something.

Herrion grabbed a few pages and glanced over them. "It does seem to attack the orc directly. To what ends, I wonder."

"The harshness is to guarantee its passing," Umbra stated. "He is playing to the Guild Masters' prejudices towards orcs, just as his tax clause plays to the prejudices against the southern lords still in power."

Beritor and Herrion's ears perked up.

"Tax clause?" Beritor asked. "What tax clause?"

Umbra flipped through some pages and pointed to a small paragraph in the middle of the page. Beritor snatched the page and read it aloud.

"'The King does reserve for himself, for the safety and benefit of the kingdom whole, the right and privilege to decide all taxes, tariffs, and dues within lands held by Guild, Prophet, or Lord sworn to the Guild King.' By the Divines, the old man has gotten clever all of a sudden."

"Watch your tone, my lord," Umbra snapped.

"You don't see what this means, do you my dear Baron."

"It is a knock back at the Southie Lords who taxed our supply wagons during the campaign," Umbra explained.

"No, my friend," Beritor said almost gleefully. "This is direct move against the rights of the guilds. Settings its own taxes have been the right of guilds since the beginning. And now the King is trying to steal it under their noses with their own vote with a blotted bill about orcs. Clever, clever."

"You're a fool," Umbra argued. "I..."

The door opened and the King entered. The lords rose to their feet and bowed. Head Prophet Philipus followed behind the King.

"Sit, my lords, sit," the King ordered calmly. "We have some things to discuss before the Hall meets this afternoon. I have prepared a bill of new laws to present to the Hall on how to deal with the orc lands. I know my lord Baron has read them. Have you any thoughts, my lords?"

"No, sire," Herrion stated. "I do not doubt they will pass in the Hall."

"Neither do I, sire," Beritor stated.

"Good, now until we grow tired of him, Baron Umbra will sit in Duke Johes' chair. We thank him for this sacrifice; for we know it is much."

"Welcome to Doraxe, Baron," Philipus greeted.

"Thank you, your worthiness," Umbra replied.

"Now, what is the condition of the Prophet's new lands, Philipus?"

"The Steward is currently building a castle to serve as a headquarters and has been successful in rounding up all Shamans and black books."

"Any sign of revolt?" the Guild King asked.

"No, the Steward is doing well in managing the tribes' needs and complaints." Umbra hid a prideful smile.

"Good, anything else, your worthiness?"

"Yes sire, with your permission."

"Of course," the Guild King sighed.

"There is a heretic cult growing in the city. They speak against the authority of the Prophets and are spreading lies about the First Word among the people."

"What kind of lies?"

"They preach the Prophets are unnecessary and every man can find the Divines on his own."

The Guild King laughed. "Does not the First Word clearly establish the Prophets as the Divines' messengers?"

"Indeed it does, sire."

"So why would they believe otherwise?" the Guild King chuckled.

"They are misguided, sire. Simple people often are," Philipus explained.

"So what do you want me to do about it? Heresy falls under Prophetic law."

"It does, sire, but the city falls under royal jurisdiction. A loop-hole these heretics take full advantage of."

"I do not like unrest," the King stated. "Do you know their leaders?"

"Yes sire. They are led by a young woman named Natalia."

"You speak of the Divinities?" Umbra asked leaning in.

"Yes," Philipus answered.

"Sire, I must protest," Umbra stated. "The Divinities are a fringe group to be sure, but they are hardly heretics. They do not wish to see the Prophets destroyed; only reformed."

Philipus sneered, "Their leader claims to be an angel sent from the Divines, sire."

The Guild King laughed. "Why can't these cults follow human lunatics? Do we not have enough of them wondering about?"

"The First Word teaches," Umbra persisted, "that angels did live among humans, sometimes for years, in order to guide them."

"That was before the Prophets," Philipus scoffed. "There is no need for such things now."

"Did the Divines ever say such a thing?" Umbra challenged.

Philipus glared at the Baron. "If I didn't know better, I would say you support the Divinities."

"Enough," the Guild King ordered. "Lord Duke Herrion, are you not the Head of the City Watch?"

"You blessed me with that title, sire."

"Then you will take your best men into the city, find these Divinities and see if heresy is present."

"Yes sire."

"Sire," Philipus spoke up. "I ask a Prophet be sent with him, to act as an expert on Prophetic law."

"Very well," the King said with dismissing wave of his hand. "Now, if we are done, I..."

David entered the chamber and hurried to the King's side. He handed him a scroll, which the King opened and read. He sighed heavily.

"Send one hundred of the castle guard, with dogs, and bring him back," the King said tossing the scroll back at David. The rest of the inner chamber looked at each other curious. The King shook his head. "Our orc hostage, the Warchief's son, has escaped."

The landscape of Galsag is as different as its people. The north has rolling hills with a warm sun, green fields, and large forests. The south has cold, scattered mountains with fog covering dry, flat lands broken only by forests of dead wood. The east is the most pleasant. It has all the prairies with forest made of short brush and inviting trees.

History of the Guilds
Elder Lighours

Tree branches smacked Del'Caf across the face as he ran deeper into the forest. He had never seen so many trees before.

His foot caught on a root, driving him into the bed of wet and rotting leaves. He spat dirt from his mouth. The familiar sound of galloping horses mixed with barking hounds echoed through the forest.

Leaping to his feet, Del'Caf rushed onward. He knew he could not outrun the troop after him. His only hope was to hide and let them pass.

He found a large tree with most of its leaves still on its branches. He climbed up the trunk and rested on a high and massive limb. A touch of security washed over him.

The sound of his pursuers grew as they approached his hiding place. The knights and their dogs passed the tree without pause or hesitation. Del'Caf smiled, confident he had made good his escape.

Then one dog returned to the base of the tree and began to sniff the base. Del'Caf held his breath, hoping against hope something else will gain the dog's attention. The dog began to bark frantically.

A lone knight returned to the tree to investigate what the hound had found. Del'Caf knew it was only a matter of moments before he was discovered. He hastily climbed to his feet, balancing on the branch. He waited until the knight rode under him before he leapt from the tree towards the knight. The knight barely had time to peer up before he was crushed under Del'Caf's feet.

The dog attacked in a flash, biting into Del'Caf's forearm. Del'Caf grabbed the dog by the top of the head and squeezed until he heard the animal's skull crack. He pried the hound's jaws from his flesh.

Stumbling over to the dead man, he looked for a bandage, or rag to be used as one. He heard the others approaching. He fled the scene with blood running like water from his wounds. He shook off the lightheaded feeling and kept on.

In front of him emerged a farmhouse with a small barn to its side. Del'Caf ran to it without a thought of who may be home. He opened a back door to the barn and locked it behind him.

The barn was simple but neat and well maintained. Hay covered most of the ground, and any wall space not devoted to a stable or pen stall was covered in rusty tools. The animals in the stalls seemed to pay little attention to their guest as Del'Caf ducked his head in the filled water trough. He drank his fill of the murky water and washed off his arm. The bite marks gushed even more blood as he cleaned them.

The barn's main door opened. Del'Caf spun about, ready to fight. A young girl, almost a woman, stood still at the barn entrance. In one hand she had a milk bucket and in the other a long, thin stick. She did not seem afraid, but she moved no closer either.

"Who are you?" she asked.

"Del'Caf."

"Why are you in my father's barn?"

Del'Caf was unsure what to say. He wished her no ill, but one scream could bring his kidnappers. He considered if it would be safer to kill her before she had the chance, yet her odd calm stopped him.

"Are you not afraid of me?" he asked.

She shrugged. "Should I be?"

Del'Caf took a step forward. She turned her ear towards him.

"You have no sight," Del'Caf stated, amazed.

"No, not since I was a babe."

Del'Caf took another step. She stepped back slowly.

"You have no need to fear me," he explained, "but I am fleeing men you must fear. They kill at will and will end you without thought. I have seen it."

"I understand," the girl said, setting down her bucket and using her stick to find a way to him. "I smell blood."

"A hound bit me," Del'Caf said cuddling his wounded arm against his chest.

"I see." She reached into her apron and pulled out a white bag. She slowly walked to the barn door and sprinkled some powder on the ground. "We have wolves here. They don't like how the powder smells. They won't come near it. It should work on dogs as well."

"Why help? I am a strange one to you."

"There is kindness in your voice," she said sitting down on a nearby stool. She beckoned her guest closer. Del'Caf reluctantly obeyed. She reached out her hand and touched his wounds. She gently felt around the gashes. Del'Caf flinched in pain from her touch.

"Sorry," she said with an embarrassed smile. With one hand, she held his arm, and with the other, she pulled some bandages from her apron. Carefully, she sprinkled salt on the bandage then wrapped the arm.

"Men from the iron king chase me," Del'Caf admitted to her.

"Why are they after you?" she asked as she worked.

"The iron king set low my father, and took me as a war prize."

"So you are a prince?" she giggled.

"That word is strange to me."

She pondered for a moment on how to explain the meaning. "It is a leader's son," she finally explained.

"Yes, I am that."

"Then I will not regret helping you," she stated. "Are you from the south?"

"Yes, that is your word for it."

"What is it like there?" She finished wrapping the arm with a small knot.

"Simpler. Less trees. Not as wet."

"All the men are returning from the war," she stated. "Were you in the war?"

"Yes," Del'Caf said. "Many of my kin died in the fight."

"I am sorry. My father said the orcs are like wolves and had to be beaten back before they consumed us."

"Where is your father?"

"He traveled into town to sell a calf. He will be back later tonight. This wound will need to be stitched. I am afraid I do not know how to do it."

"I will be fine," Del'Caf stated.

"I am sorry, I wish I could do more."

"Do you and your father live all alone?" Del'Caf asked looking about.

"Yes," the girl said, tying off the bandage. "For many years now."

Del'Caf inspected her work and shook his head in approval. "You have the healer's touch."

"That is what my father always told me."

"Where is your father's mate?"

"My mother? She passed to the Divines giving me life."

"I am sorry."

"Don't be, she is in a better place now."

There was a rustling sound from deep in the woods. Both persons looked towards the noise.

"I must go," Del'Caf stated standing.

"Yes, I am afraid so."

Del'Caf sighed. "Thank you for your kindness, but I will not endanger you by straying longer."

"I understand," she said with a smile.

She reached into her apron and brought out the bag of powder. She felt for his hand, but could not find it. Del'Caf gently touched her hand with his fingertip. She laid it in his hand.

"Their dogs won't find you anymore."

"What is your name?" he asked.

"Samantha," she answered.

"Live well, Samantha."

"Goodbye, southern prince."

Del'Caf quietly left the barn and returned to the endless forest. Samantha picked up her bucket, walked to her cow and began to milk.

RIGHTEOUS HATE

6

In the beginning, before man reached grace, angels lived on the earth and flourished. But when they grew jealous of their counterparts, they rebelled. The war between the angels and demons ravaged the sky for many a century. But the angels prevailed and locked the demons away. Now only a few are known to still walk openly in the world.

The First Word
Summerset 2:34

Sir Snaca dipped his pen in the ink well and wrote another line on his paper. Hall Master Frederick entered the room with a book wrapped in leather under his arm. He sat it down in front of Snaca. Snaca sat down his pen and uncovered the work. Symbols of dark arts decorated the cover. He tossed the leather protection back over it.

"Is this the only one?" Snaca asked.

"It cost me a fortunate to acquire this one. The Prophet's campaign against the orc Shamans has been ruthless. One copy of each text is taken to the Prophetic Library and the rest are burned. What does Philipus, and for that matter you, want with these anyway?"

"Power," Snaca answered. "Philipus wants a monopoly on power. The fool." Snaca turned to Frederick and pointed to the book. "This is not enough, I need more."

"There are no more," Frederick informed annoyed. "Feel lucky to have that one."

"Luck is not quite what I am feeling right now," Snaca sneered. "My master requires more, find them. He and Philipus are in race. A race to find whom will get the power first. And believe me, you don't want that moron Philipus to win. We still have time. It will take him years to translate the runes and even more to understand what they mean."

Frederick shook his head. "What kind of master do you serve who duels the Head Prophet and can read ancient orc runes."

"The texts are not written in orc," Snaca replied. "They are written in something much older. My master is the last one who remembers how to read it."

"Then why do the orcs have them?"

Snaca chuckled. "Because my master gave it to them for safe keeping."

Before Frederick could ask another question, Lord Beritor burst into the room.

"We have him," he declared.

"Have who?" Snaca asked without even turning to him.

"The Guild King, we have him."

"What do you mean?" Frederick asked with a raised eyebrow.

Beritor handed them the page with the tax clause and pointed to the proper lines. "He is trying to strip the guilds of their right to tax."

"By the Divines, you are right," Frederick stated handing the page over to Snaca to read.

"Surprising move," Snaca stated. "I did not give him that much credit for brains."

"Don't you see," Beritor exclaimed. "We can expose this trickery in the Hall. It will embarrass the King, not to mention make me the defender of the guild rights."

"Interesting," Sir Snaca said. "Yes, this may be our opportunity. When the Hall meets tomorrow, you will point out this underhanded deal. The Guild Masters will be outraged. You will defend them, rally support. How many Guild Masters could we count on to oppose this bill, Frederick?"

"All of them, I'm sure," Beritor interjected.

"Don't be so certain," Frederick stated. "The King is still very popular among the Guild Masters. He will have supporters."

"Then we must do all we can to find them and convince them to stand against this bill," Snaca said. "We must make sure the bill does not pass. Then when it is defeated, we will make our move."

"And what move is that?" Frederick asked.

Snaca looked at him blankly. "Kill the King, of course."

"What?" Frederick snapped. "Are you mad?"

"No, I am very much at peace."

"You can't kill the King," Frederick continued. "I will have no part in this!"

"No part?" Snaca asked.

"No part!" Frederick yelled. "I agreed to help you, but assassination was never part of the deal. We were to help strengthen the kingdom, not behead it."

"What did you think would happen?" Snaca asked. "We would just wait for him to die?"

"YES! The King is old." He turned to Beritor. "What good does it do you to kill the King and throw unwanted suspicion on your reign? Let him die in peace."

"The King is a man of the sword; a peaceful death was never his destiny."

"This is treason!" Frederick exclaimed.

"Oh come, come," Snaca laughed. "You have long passed the line of treason. And you will help us, Frederick. You will help us or the King will learn how you took a small fortune and grew it into a considerable estate at the crown's expense near the end of the North Wars."

"I don't care," Frederick said defiantly.

"You don't care? You do not care?" Snaca asked, nodding his head and walking towards the old Hall Master. "You don't care that the King will not only kill you but seize all your property. Then your wife and children will be left in the streets to starve while your head rots on a spike, or worse. You don't care about them? And here I thought you a loving father. I can see it now, your little girl crying to mommy how hungry she is and mommy not able to help. How pleasant."

Frederick lowered his head. "I curse my cowardice. If I was a braver man, I would kill myself and leave a letter to the King about you."

"Fortunately for me, you are not a braver man," Snaca sighed. "Now go and stir up support for our future king."

Frederick rose slowly and left the room somberly.

"We should kill him before he becomes a danger," Beritor stated as the door locked.

"He will never be a danger to us. Like he said, he is too cowardly." Snaca returned to his writing desk and began to look over the book Frederick brought him.

"How do you plan on killing the king?" Beritor asked. "Frederick has a point about avoiding suspension."

"Are you afraid, my lord?"

"There is a difference between fear and stupidity," Beritor spat.

Snaca nodded. "Yes there is. You should not worry about the weapon of use. I have my ways."

"What ways?"

"Ways that will find its target without rising suspicion." Snaca explained.

"Your secrecy does not endear you to me," Beritor stated. "I am risking my life by trusting you."

"And you will gain the throne."

"At what cost? Your master seems to gain nothing. What price am I paying for my crown?"

"A fair one, I assure you."

"Show me your plan," Beritor said leaning in. "My patience is running thin."

Snaca sighed and rose from his chair. He opened his closet door. Hanging on the wall was a large mirror with swirling smoke trapped into it. Beritor reached out a hand to touch the glass. Snaca snatched his wrist.

"Do not touch," he warned.

"What is it?" Beritor asked amazed.

"It is a forgotten thing," Snaca explained lighting several candles around the mirror. He then kneeled before it and began to chant strange words. The cloud in the mirror moved and grew increasingly violent. Beritor stepped back.

Snaca continued to chant as a single hand appeared from the surface of the mirror. In the deformed and boney fingers sat a jar holding a slimy snake-like being within it.

Snaca stood to his feet, bowed graciously and took the jar from the demonic hand. He turned to the frightened and intrigued Beritor.

"This is the instrument of the Guild King's doom."

A kingdom's tales do more to form its people than its laws. There is a tale in Northrim of a beautiful princess. Her father, a good man, wished her to marry a brave knight. She did not love him. He had terrible scars, and his hair had all but fallen out from wear of his helmet.

So fervent was her wish to stay unwed, she ran away from the castle and her father. The King died of a broken heart, and civil war broke out in the kingdom.

Northerns use the story to teach about the importance of selfless duty. Some prefer to see it as a tale about consequences. Either she would marry a man she did not love, or tens of thousands would send their loves to war on her behalf. In reality, life is a series of hard choices, and every choice affects others' lives whether you wish ill or not.

History of the Guilds
Elder Lighours

Raven ran a brush through her golden hair. The candle light glowed on her fair skin. Her mother, Lady Edoweyhn, stood to the side watching.

"You have grown into a stunningly beautiful woman," she commented. Raven smiled and looked on her desk for a hairpin. Edoweyhn picked up a decorative one and handed it to her. Raven set it back on her desk before discovering the pin she wanted.

Edoweyhn touched one of Raven's golden locks and felt it between her fingers. "Why were you not here to greet me when I arrived?"

"You had arrived late, mother. I had already gone to bed."

"I see – such a pity. I had hoped to speak with you then."

"Why?"

"It is not important now," Edoweyhn stated. "What was it like traveling on campaign? Was it an adventure? Did you meet a handsome man?"

Raven blushed and looked away.

"You did meet a man; is he brave? Did he dash into battle, saving his soldiers as he went?"

"No," Raven muttered. "He dashed into battle and had his head bashed in by an orc."

Edoweyhn shook her head a bit offended. "I don't understand why people are so appalled by battle. Soldiers die. It is their nature. That is what I cannot stand about the First Word and these cursed Prophets: they wish me to defy my nature."

"Mother, is there a reason for your late visit?"

"Cannot a mother tuck her only daughter into bed?"

"Is that what you want to do?" Raven asked walking to her bedside. "Very well, mother, but don't forget the bedtime story."

Edoweyhn somberly stayed were she was. Raven fell onto her blankets.

"Why are you really here, mother?"

"The Guild King and I have begun formal negotiations on a permanent alliance between our two kingdoms."

Raven's head perked up. "Permanent alliance? The Mesmers have never formally joined with another nation."

"Yes, well…" Edoweyhn sighed. "The world has changed. The Guild King has the Vycesie as an ally, Northrim as a subject, and the orcs as a conquered people. There is no one left but us. The Guild King's legitimacy came from victory in war. How long into the young prince's reign will it be until he looks for the same legitimacy? How long can he hold the strong-willed guilds together without an enemy to unite them? The young prince will betray an ally when he comes to power. I aim for it not to be us."

"You mean to marry me to the prince," Raven muttered.

"Yes, and as soon as possible."

"I'm twice his age; he is only a boy!"

"My love, if I could make him older I would, but he will grow into a fine young man. I have no doubt of that."

"Mother, I…"

"What did you expect, Raven? You are the daughter of the Mayor of Mesmer City. Your marriage was always going to be for political gain."

"Yes, but not a boy from Galsag!" Raven snapped. "I imagined a noble man, or a silk merchant, or maybe an officer in the army. Handsome, wealthy, charming and most of all: Mesmer."

"I understand your distress, I truly do. But we must do what we must do. Not for ourselves, but the betterment of our people, that is what being a leader is."

Edoweyhn approached her daughter and tried to touch her hair again, but Raven pulled back. Edoweyhn withdrew her hand. She blew out the candles and said, "Think on it," before she left her daughter in the dark.

The night wind blew through her open balcony waving the curtains with it. Raven crawled deep under her covers to escape the chill. She found herself lost in staring contest with the ceiling.

A noise came from outside. Raven shot upright. She grabbed a small dagger for opening the seal on letters and approached her balcony. A hand clenched to the stone railing. She heard the grunting of a man trying to pull himself up. She raised her weapon and dashed towards the rail, ready to strike the intruder.

Charles nearly lost his grip when he saw her. Raven quickly dropped the knife and grabbed his arm. Working together, Charles managed to climb safety up.

"Are you mad?" Raven exclaimed clenching her night-gown closed to her body to cover any peeking skin.

"It has been suggested," Charles answered with a smile.

"What are you doing here?"

"Calling on you, of course. Is it a bad time?"

"It is the middle of the night!"

"Good, then there should be no line seeking an audience."

"This is not how things should be done, sir."

"Perhaps not, but the heart knows no protocol."

"Sir, I really must..." Raven began. Charles kissed her before she could finish. Raven pushed him back then drew him in for a kiss of her own.

"Come with me," Charles said. "I want to show you something."

"I can't," Raven explained sorrowfully. "There are guards outside my room." Charles began to untie his belt much to Raven's disgust. Then she saw he had hidden a rather long rope around his waist.

He tied an end to the railing and tossed the rest out into the night. Raven peered over the edge and grew dizzy at the seemly endless drop. Charles, however, was confident.

"Come with me," he said.

"You are insane," Raven complained.

"Of course I am; I am an artist." Charles extended his hand. Raven found herself taking it. He quickly spun her around and wrapped the rope around her.

He lowered them both down the rope slowly and carefully. "Where are we going?" Raven asked feeling uncomfortable to be wearing nothing but a nightgown.

"I promised you a tour of the finer parts of the city," he whispered in her ear.

"Alright," she whispered back. "But I will hold you to the promise of only the finer parts."

"I already have finer parts in mind," Charles said as they reached the ground. A small boat sat on the riverbank.

"Your boat?" Raven asked.

"Greatest ship in the fleet," Charles said hopping in. Charles lifted Raven into the ship and gently sat her down. He picked up the oars and began to journey down the river and through the city. Lifeless clay buildings soon flanked them. Only scattered candles in the window and the moon provided light. Charles rowed the boat down a little side stream and through a sewage hole leading out to the wall.

"Where are we going?" Raven asked.

"A finer place," Charles answered.

The boat drifted along the stream until the city was a distant light. Large orchards crowded the riversides. The moon hovered high above. Charles pulled the small boat into a sand bar and rested his arms. Raven sat nervously, shivering in the cold.

"You know, if my escorts found out I left the citadel grounds, let alone the city, without them..."

Charles laughed. "My lady, I assure you. I mean you no harm."

"Then what are we doing so far from comfort?"

"Shh." Charles pointed to the trees. Raven looked just as the wind grabbed handfuls of loose leaves and tossed them into the air. The white leaves danced on the wind and caught the moonlight as they drifted down to the water like snowfall.

"It's beautiful," Raven whispered, mostly to herself. Charles moved near her.

"Life and light have no cause. No start, no pause. They exist for a moment then fade away. But beauty, beauty will always stay."

Raven leaned and laid her head on his shoulder. Her fingers entangled his own.

"Are you a poet as well?" she asked.

"I am all things," he said kissing her gently again. She grinned brightly at him.

"You are a very peculiar man, Mr. Charles," she said.

"Most interesting men are."

> *Do not consume your enemies.*
> *Convert them. If you can make your*
> *foes see through your eyes, you not*
> *only defeat an enemy, you gain an*
> *ally.*

> **The Seven Dances of War**
> **Kymmonata, General of the**
> **Vycesie**

The morning air was thick with fog. Del'Caf could tell it would be a hot day. He pushed through the brush and trees, careful to lessen his trail. He had not seen any sign of his pursers in several days, but overconfidence was the mistake of caught prey.

Del'Caf froze in place. The sounds of men and the smells of roasting food came from just beyond the tree line. Del'Caf crouched down and crawled closer. The familiar sound of the orc language was mingled with the human's. Confused, Del'Caf drew closer to see.

Dozens of orcs were sitting on the side of a sunken road eating a morning meal. Men wearing black capes stood guard around them. Del'Caf carefully slid away when the cold steel of a blade touched his neck.

"So," the knight standing over him said, "you come out here to piss and have a thought of running instead?"

"I..." Del'Caf began.

"Did we not warn you what would happen if there is a runaway? Stand up."

Del'Caf obeyed. The knight casually looked him over.

"Get back to the others, and don't let me catch you thinking again."

The knight gave Del'Caf a good push into the clearing. He stumbled into a group of orcs and sat down with them.

"Who are you?" one orc asked in their tongue.

"Mor'tag," Del'Caf lied, "of the Wazog tribe."

"Another Wazog," the orc sneered, tearing into his meal. "The stars themselves are Wazog."

"The Wazog paid the blood price," an orc next to Del'Caf growled. "I wish my tribe so brave. I am Kir'git of Urrah."

"Well met," Del'Caf said grabbing Kir'git's arm in greeting.

"I do not know you, did they add you at the crossroads with the others?" Kir'git asked.

"Yes," Del'Caf played along. "I have hid my face in shame for leaving my tribe this way."

"Feel no shame, Mor'tag. We are obeying the Warchief. It may be painful, but we have our honor still."

"You are not supposed to be here," a little orc to Del'Caf's left whispered.

"Quiet, sneak," Kir'git barked.

"Sneak I might be, but sneak you need, I think. For our

guest's name be trickery and humans dislike tricks."

"I told you to hold your slimy tongue," Kir'git snapped, reaching out to grab the sneak.

Del'Caf caught his hand.

"Hold," he said. "His words are true. I am a stranger."

Kir'git pulled back.

"What wind blew you here?"

"I ran from the iron king."

"Matters not concerning to me," the sneak said. "The count, the count. Now that matters to me. To men, orcs all one face, yet numbers they know. Soon they tally and count fifty three where once was fifty two. Then swords be drawn and blood be spilled. Trickery a treat they will not eat."

"If you wish me gone, I will go," Del'Caf assured. The sneak caught his arm.

"No... no. Run you cannot. See you flee and dead we be. Yet, stay you cannot."

Del'Caf growled. "What do you say then?"

The skinny orc handed Del'Caf a piece of bread.

"A large orc with a scarred cheek is who you seek. Soon the woods will he sneak. While he pees, take a peek."

Del'Caf tore open the loaf of bread and discovered a knife hidden inside.

"Who is he?"

"Don't listen to this viper," Kir'git exclaimed.

"Someone must die," the sneak snapped. "Care, instead, to try?"

Kir'git stood to his feet. "I will have no hand here."

"Who is he?" Del'Caf asked again.

"To you, a fool. But in your way he stands to join this merry band."

Out of the corner of his eye, Del'Caf saw the large orc finish his meal and head to the woods. Del'Caf hid the knife under his arm and followed. The large orc found a tree and squatted by it.

Del'Caf stayed out of sight and moved up behind the orc quietly. He clenched the knife in his hand. Everything in him said this is wrong. He knew his father would not approve. But he was not under his father. He was lost in a strange land that was not kind to those like him. He knew the sneak was right. Survival was the only honor now.

Del'Caf closed to only a few paces away. He leapt into a sprint and raised the knife as he closed on the orc's back. At the moment before the blade touched the flesh, the large orc spun and caught Del'Caf by the arm.

Overcome by surprise, Del'Caf was easily thrown to the side. He leapt back to his feet and tried to stab the orc again. They struggled eye to eye for several moments before Del'Caf kneed the orc in the groin. The orc stumbled over but managed to steal away the knife.

Del'Caf franticly grabbed for a rock among the rotting leaves and jumped at his foe before he could recover from the blow. Del'Caf bashed the stone against the kneeling orc's skull. The bone made a loud crack as the orc fell over.

Del'Caf stood over him looking at his limp body. He smashed the head with the rock again and again until all that remained was a puddle of blood and bone.

Del'Caf stumbled back a few steps. The bloodied stone fell from his trembling hand. He forced his breath to slow. He waited for his heart to calm itself. He hastily covered the body as best he could with leaves and returned to the group.

The humans had already begun to count them when Del'Caf fell back next to the sneak.

"Tell me," the sneak said, "will there be fifty three or fifty two?"

"Fifty two," Del'Caf muttered.

"Then safe we be and on we go."

"Who was he?"

"Matters not."

"It matters to me!" Del'Caf growled.

"Why?" the sneak laughed. "What's done cannot be un-done. He is no more; you go to do more."

"Who was he?" Del'Caf persisted.

"He Torgunk, brother of Sil'grok."

"Who is Sil'grok?"

The sneak bowed his head in introduction.

"He was your brother?" Del'Caf gasped. "You are a kin-slayer."

"No, no," Sil'grok corrected. "My hands clean. You slayer of my kin. No shame, no shame."

"You are a viper and a sneak," Del'Caf cursed.

"And you are a Warchief, or son of one at least."

Del'Caf grabbed the slim orc by the throat.

"How do you know this?"

Sil'grok struggled under Del'Caf's strong hands. "I see, I see many... things. I know... mysteries. Friend... I can be. Secret safe... with me."

Del'Caf let Sil'grok go.

"What is your game?" he hissed.

"Game? No game. To the human castle we go. Others don't know what I know."

"What do you know?"

"Life for orcs has changed. Gone the days of simple praise. Honor made by clever blood. You could be Warchief of new tribe. Your blood right, your mind clear. I will show you, but you must trust."

"I don't trust any in this place," Del'Caf asserted.

"Then on right path you have begun," Sil'grok chuckled.

The King of the Guilds shall present all bills to the Hall of Guilds for approval by majority vote. Vote will be cast by the use of black and white stones before the whole assembly or by a showing of hand.

No law shall be right or legal without the Hall of Guild's approving majority vote.

**Guild Compact
773 S.P.**

The Hall of Guilds was filled with eager Guild Masters and their patient aides. The large stone structure was second only to the great citadel it neighbored. Steps with rows and benches lined the inner chamber, while statues and murals decorated the entranceway. Huge banners flew from the ceiling, representing all three hundred and fifty six recognized guilds.

The Guild Masters talked amongst themselves about various issues. On one side of the Hall sat the highborn. They wore fine clothing and sat on the cushions their aides brought them. On the other side sat the guildsmen. They had self-given surnames like Sword and Cross. They wore rusty and beaten armor as statement of pride. They cussed and laughed at each other as they barked orders at their manservants for amusement.

Near the two massive doors, leading into the main chamber, sat several cushioned chairs on a platform. Victor fiddled with the sigil around his neck and took a drink of wine from his glass. He was uncomfortable in large crowds. All the people talking distracted him, making it hard hear his own thoughts.

A woman's voice broke into his pondering. "May I bother you for this seat, my lord Victor?"

Victor looked up at Lady Edoweyhn. "I believe it is reserved for you," he replied.

Edoweyhn lifted the edges of her dress and carefully sat in the chair. Victor snapped at his servant and had some wine and fruit brought to her.

"You are most kind, my lord," Edoweyhn said.

"It is nothing," Victor assured. "It is good to see you, my lady, How is ruling Mesmer city treating you?"

"It treats me just fine, and how is your retirement?"

"If only I could enjoy it," Victor lamented. "With my heir in the orc lands and my daughter as Queen, I barely find a rest at night."

"And what about is your darling son, Maxwell?"

"He is my comfort," Victor stated. "He has grown into a fine young man. I wish at times, he was my eldest. I would sleep better at least."

"You are too hard on poor Francis. He only wishes to find his own way."

"Yes, let us hope 'his own way' does not lead to the ground."

Edoweyhn shook her head giggling. "Are you happy to be called to the Hall?" she asked changing the subject. "I believe we are honored guests."

"What an honor! We nobles sit in silence while thugs play at state." Edoweyhn laughed touching Victor's arm lovingly. Victor pretended not to notice.

"My lord Victor, I do enjoy your company. You are a rock in an ever changing storm."

Victor raised an eyebrow to her. "How so, my lady?"

"Your opinions never change."

"That is because my 'opinions' are the truth, and I see no reason to be afraid of them."

"Of course not, you are head of the house of Drako."

Victor shook his head. "Even if I was a peasant with no land or title, I still would not be afraid."

"Well lucky for me, you were born near royalty. Otherwise, they would have cut off your handsome head many years ago."

"My blood is royal," Victor corrected, "and when the King goes to the Divines, my family will rule Galsag for a thousand years."

"I look forward to the day," Edoweyhn stated. "Have you heard the rumor?"

"Which one?"

"The most interesting one."

"Ah yes," said Victor. "You are planning on marrying your daughter to my grandson."

"It has been discussed."

Victor leaned in and whispered in Edoweyhn's ear. "You should have married me."

"I would have, but I was already married. And even the Mesmers only have one husband at a time, despite what you may hear."

The mighty doors to the Hall opened and royal guards entered. The members of the assembly grew silent. The Guild King entered in fine dress and a thick fur coat with a long trail. He walked out into the center of the great Hall and looked about.

"Guild Masters of noble guilds, both great and small, distinguished guests and all else, I welcome you to the Hall of Guilds. Where, every two years, I keep my promise to bring all changes in law and policy to you for your wisdom, council, and approval.

"My friends, you all know I have just returned from a barbaric campaign against green skin heretics. I am happy to announce a great triumph!"

The Hall leapt to their feet in thundering applause.

"I have the peace accord signed by the leaders of the major tribes and, as promised, dedicated the lands to the Divines."

The applause continued. The Guild King let it last for a time then quieted the Hall down.

"Now is the time for us to levy laws on the orcs: laws that will crush any rebellious spirit and deprive the tribes of power."

"Here, here," a Guild Master yelled out.

"Therefore I propose this bill for the Hall's approval. Hall Master Frederick," the Guild King handed it over. Frederick stood from his chair.

"The bill the king proposed was delivered to each guild the required three days before any vote. Seeing the obvious honor in this bill, I move to have it voted on immediately."

"Hall Master," a single voice spoke out of the rows of well-dressed highborns. Lord Beritor stood to his feet.

"The Hall recognizes Lord Beritor, Guild Master of the Sword Brethren," Frederick stated.

"Hall Master, this bill is simply laws for the orcs, and to apply only to the orcs, correct?"

"That is what the King said."

"Then I need to have explained provision four hundred and sixty two."

Guild Masters ruffled through their copy's pages. Beritor gave them time to find it.

Beritor read aloud from his copy. "'The King does reserve for himself, for the safety and benefit of the kingdom whole, the right and privilege to decide all taxes, tariffs, and dues within lands held by Guild, Prophet, or Lord sworn to the Guild King.' Is this only for the orcs? It seems to apply to all guilds."

"Would the King answer the Lord's question?" Frederick asked turning to the King.

The Guild King leaned back in his throne; tiredness cast down his face. He shook his head no.

"If the King cannot answer, what am I to think?" Beritor asked. "I am not wise enough to know the mystery of his intent, but it seems he wished to pass a provision which has nothing to do with the bill. I move this provision be stripped from this bill. If the King, in his wisdom, wishes to present it as a separate bill, he can do so."

"I second this," a Guild Master called out.

"Aye," another shouted.

"All in favor of removing the provision in question?" Frederick asked. Most hands rose. "The provision is removed. All in favor of the passing of this rest of the bill unaltered?" Most hands rose again. "The bill is passed." Frederick looked to the Guild King. "Does the King wish to represent the provision as a separate bill?"

The Guild King sighed and nodded his head.

"The provision is presented as a new bill before the Hall. All in favor..."

"Hall Master," the Guild King interrupted. "I wish to address the Hall in the bill's defense."

"The Hall recognizes the King of the Guilds."

The Guild King stood to his feet and walked to the center of the Hall.

"My brothers, we have fought many wars together. Many wars. And everyone knows that in war, each must make sacrifices. Men must leave their families, abandon their crops, and travel far with little to sustain them. They must sleep in fields and trudge through mud. They often go months with little or no pay, all for the good of the kingdom.

"My friends, we are in a new war. Not one against green skins or tribesmen, but against debt. The coffers of the kingdom are in chaos. We must, for the good of the kingdom, reform our tax laws so all may prosper."

"Then why did you hide it?" a Guild Master barked.

"My intent was not treachery."

"Sire, it smells of a power grab!" Beritor shouted.

"I am the King," he snapped back. "I have enough power."

"Then why do you ask for more?" another master yelled to echoing laughter.

"This would strip the guilds of effect self-rule," Beritor countered. "By removing the right to set taxes in their own lands, you would reserve for yourself who prospers and who starves. For how do we know you would not use your new tax powers to destroy guilds who oppose you? Could you not, under this new law, set trade tariffs so high no wheat merchant would bother with the affected region? Siege warfare via decree?"

"I oppose such allegations!" Baron Umbra shouted, leaping to his feet. "Our King has never dealt dishonorably with any man."

"At least not to you, my lord Baron," Beritor stated. "It is a perk of being the King's favorite."

"You speak out of turn, sir," Frederick stepped in.

"I apologize, Hall Master. I grow passionate about my brothers' rights being stripped from them through underhanded deals and blind ambition. The power of the kingdom has always, and will always, rest with the guilds – not the king!"

"Here, here!" many cried.

Beritor continued. "If the King had been more upfront with us on the needs of the kingdom, perhaps I would believe the King has honorable intent and this would be a different debate. I call this bill be put to a vote and struck down this instant!"

Several stood in applause. Master Duncan stood silently.

"Hall Master," he called out. Frederick recognized him. Duncan waited till the Hall fell quiet again.

"Tell me, Lord Beritor, are you not on the King's inner counsel?"

"I am."

"Then why did you wait till the Hall to raise your concerns about this provision? Could you have not done so earlier in private? Is it not your job to advise our king?"

"It was so well hidden, I did not find it till this morning," Beritor explained. Duncan nodded his head.

"Yes, I also find reading long bills difficult. I can see how it would be even harder for you with your company of aides who do your work for you, you highborn fraud."

Several guildsmen chuckled.

Duncan's voice grew louder and bolder as he spoke. "You spend so much time brushing your hair, it is amazing you could bless us with your presence today. But since, it seems, you had plans to disgrace our beloved king and call his honor into question, you made time. This whole affair smells of pig shit and highborn trickery."

More guildsmen stomped their feet in agreement.

"I, myself, am the King's man. If he tells me to march to the ends of the earth – I will. If he asks for all my land and treasury, I would give it. I love my king, and so should all of you. He raised us out of darkness. He gave us a country. He made us what we are. I trust him with my life. Hall Master, I move for the vote to be delayed till this issue can be discussed."

"Seconded," Umbra spoke up.

"I don't think it needs to be," Frederick nervously said. "We all see the issue plain."

"Hall Master," Duncan repeated annoyed. "A move has

been called and seconded. Law states a vote must be cast."

"Cast the vote, Hall Master," the Guild King ordered.

"All for the delay of a vote?"

Many hands rose. The Hall Master's aides carefully counted them.

"All opposed?"

Far fewer were raised.

"The vote is delayed by three weeks as stated by law. The Hall is now in recess," Frederick announced.

Guild Masters stood and moved towards the doors. Crowds of them came to greet Lord Beritor and shake his hand, thanking him for the defense of their rights. Frederick carefully approached.

"Why did you allow that to happen?" Beritor muttered through a smile. "If the vote was today, we would have carried the day for certain."

"How could I stop it?" Frederick complained. "I have my duties as well."

"If you wish to keep your pitiful duties, you best lean on Duncan. If he begins to turn people against the righteousness of our cause, I will hold you responsible."

"I will talk to him," Frederick promised. He pushed his way back through the crowd where Duncan was already speaking to many Guild Masters.

"Master Duncan," Frederick stated. "A word?"

"Of course, Hall Master." Frederick pulled Duncan away from all listeners.

"Why would you support a bill that damages your own

rights?" he asked.

Duncan snorted. "What business is it of the Hall Master where I stand on issues? This whole affair does not sit well with me, sir. Not only do I intend to stand against it in the Hall, I also plan to dive to the bottom of this treachery. I advise you, sir, to not be there when I arrive."

Duncan pushed away from Frederick and reentered the crowd. Frederick slowly rubbed the sides of his forehead as a headache came on.

> *And in that day, angels from the Divines came down and lived with man. They looked as man but were not man. They ate as man but were not hungry like man. They carried in them things none believed, and the Divines worked through them to show man the way.*
>
> **The First Word**
> **Summerset 41:16**

"Lord Duke Herrion, one of the wealthiest, most powerful men in the kingdom, has been lowered to the job of a common guard."

Herrion looked about for the source of the familiar voice. He found it when Sir Edward walked from behind a stack of hay. He was a shorter man with red side burns and a pop-marked face. A long wooden pipe hung from his lips. Dark blue smoke danced through his ruined teeth.

"Good to see you, Sir Edward. I see you still have no respect for your betters."

"Not true, my lord. I have a healthy respect for your sister."

Herrion glared at Edward. Edward drew on his pipe. Herrion began to laugh. Edward joined in.

"How have you been?" Herrion asked.

"Can't complain," Edward replied. "Ready to end my time in the city watch."

"I thought you lived for the watch."

"I did, many years ago."

The two men left the City Watch courtyard and entered the busy streets of Doraxe. Vendors and customers filled the roads with carts and stalls.

"So what is this about arresting Divinities?" Edward asked as they walked.

"Where did you hear that?"

"I'm not a fool," Edward scoffed. "I hear things."

"We are not arresting anyone for now, only investigating complaints."

"And they have to send the symbolic head of the watch to do it?"

"The King wished me to see personally if heresy is present. What are you smoking?" Herrion asked, pointing to Edward's pipe.

Edward grinned. "Only the best thing to come from the orc wars. It's called peace grass. My cousin's husband brought it back with him. Care to try a puff?"

Edward offered him the pipe.

"I most assuredly do not," answered Herrion, pushing the pipe away. "I cannot imagine breathing smoke to be good for you. Now tell me what you know about these Divinities. What do they believe? What do they do that would have the Prophets so agitated?"

"As to their beliefs, I don't know much," Edward admitted pushing through a group of passing women with baskets. "But I do know they do a lot of good for the people in cheap side. They feed them, they clothe them, and crime has actually dropped. My lord, it is hard for you to understand the impossibility of that up in the castle."

"How did they manage that; Divine intervention?" Herrion laughed. Edward grabbed Herrion's arm and stopped him in the street.

"Don't arrest them, my lord. They are good people and I don't give two dumps about Prophetic law. Don't arrest them."

Herrion slowly removed Edward's hand.

"I don't mean to arrest anyone just yet."

"My lords," a voice yelled from the crowd. The two men glanced behind them. A young man in the blue robes of a Prophet was rushing to meet them.

"My lords, I am happy I found you. I waited where you told me, but we must have missed each other."

Sir Edward chuckled.

"Yes, we must not have seen you," Herrion stated. "You are the expert on Prophetic law?"

"Yes, my lord. I am Prophet Minor Thompson. I studied here in Doraxe and in Tilton."

"Good," Herrion replied. "Then you can answer me something."

"Anything, my lord."

"What constitutes heresy? The definition seems to be an enigma of sorts."

"Prophetic law defines heresy as any teaching contrary to the First Word."

"What of other interruptions of the First Word?" Edward asks. "Is that heresy?"

"There is only one correct interruption, and that is what the Prophet's teach."

"But has not the Prophet's teaching changed over the centuries?" Herrion challenged.

"Yes, but..."

"So, at least at times, new interpretations were not heresy."

"I suppose," Thompson admitted, "but those advances were brought about by learned Prophets; not some mad woman claiming to be an angel."

"She is angelic enough for me," Edward sneered.

Thompson was aghast. "You cannot be serious, sir."

"We are wasting time," Herrion declared. "Edward, where does this Natalia preach?"

"In cheap side."

"Send an extra patrol down there and find where she is. Then tell them to wait for orders."

"You sound as if you expect trouble."

"I am a cautious man by nature," Herrion stated.

Cheap side was a ruin. Crumbling buildings were held up with makeshift material. Children, dressed in little more than sacks, ran through the alleys and gutters. The sounds of prostitutes applying their trade rang from open windows.

In the clearing, near the public well, stood a young woman in a simple dress. Crowds of people closed in on her. Herrion drew a cloth from his pocket, pressed it to his mouth and nose and approached.

A man, barely able to walk, limped up to her while she preached. She paused her sermon, leaned down, prayed over him, and touched his head. Herrion nearly dropped his handkerchief as he saw the man straighten up and walk away without his crutch.

"What kind of trickery is this?" Herrion asked the Prophet.

Edward shook his head laughing. "It's no trick, my lord. Men born blind see when she touches them."

"Then it is dark arts," the Prophet Minor stated. "It must be."

Natalia stepped up onto the well again. She waited for the crowd to grow silent before continuing. "When the Divines gave us the First Word, they meant it to be the key to understanding their will and character. But man has twisted it to his own purpose. The First Word says, 'a man will bed only his wife for she is his soul.' But the Prophets now teach a man can bed many women so long as he also beds his wife.

"If a wife is a man's soul, she is the inner most part of him. How can a man have two souls? When he beds another woman, he cuts into himself. Did the Divines, creators of all life, make it? Did they not mean what they say?

"The Prophets say only those wearing the blue robes are teachers recognized by the Divines. But I tell you, there were no robes on the First Prophet and no schools for him to study. The will of the Divines was written in the soul long before it was written on paper."

"That is blasphemy," Thompson whispered in Herrion's ear.

"Was not the First Word written after the First Prophet?"

"Yes, but..."

"Then it is not blasphemy."

"People," Natalia continued, "the First Word says, 'any who seeks the favor of the Divines will have their pains healed.' Yet the Prophets do no such healings, saying it was only for ancient times and passed after the Prophets were established. But I tell you the truth, the Divines do not change. Their promise was for now just as it was for then."

"Then why are some not healed?" Herrion cried out. The crowd turned to look at the strange guest. Natalia stared at him and bowed low.

"My lord, you honor us with your visit."

"Answer my question," Herrion demanded. "When my niece was dying of the hot cough, I begged the Divines to heal her. Why did they not?"

"Do you want the truth or do you wish to be comforted for your loss?"

Without thinking, Herrion answered. "The truth."

"Very well," she replied. "Because, Lord Duke Herrion, when your father died, and you discovered much of his estate was left to your brother, you exiled him and stole his wife. You killed your enemies and betrayed friends purely out of greed and malice. Then you stand here and ask why you did not receive the Divine's favor?"

Herrion's face grew red with fury. "Arrest her," he hissed to Edward.

"My lord, she spoke out of turn," Edward tried to consul.

"Arrest her I say!"

Edward sighed. He drew his sword and moved towards her. The crowd shoved in to guard Natalia, but she pushed through them, comforting them: it would be OK. She came to Edward. He gently placed her in cuffs. A man took a step forward in anger, but a sharp look from her stopped him. Edward took her by the arm, and they walked away from the crowd slowly and back towards the City Watch.

*And the Prophet came to a town where
a man was mad with a demon. He would
seem plain then attack those around him.
Fire would light at his voice and animals
die at his will.*

The First Word
Longlast 17:56

avid folded the blankets back from the head of the
bed and fluffed the pillows. He lighted several candles and took a tray of fruit into the massive washing room. The royal bath could hold a horse with its marble walls.

The Guild King grabbed a grape off the tray as David passed and sensually placed it into his young female guest's mouth. She bit on it and rubbed up close to the King in the steaming waters with a giggle. David sat down the fruit tray and added another coal to the stove.

"Thank you, David," the Guild King said cuddling with the woman. "Are these grapes the last of the season, you think?"

"Probably, sire," David answered. "The rest is to the wine press by now."

"Shame, there is nothing like the favor of fresh grapes. Not to say I don't also enjoy my wine," the Guild King chuckled.

"Sadly if they don't go into the press they will go into the waste pit, sire."

"I know, I know."

The girl, not liking the loss of the king's attention, bit on his hairy chest.

The King flinched. "Enough of that," he scolded. " Can't you see I am talking to my friend. How is your mother?" he asked turning his head back to David.

"She is well, sire."

"She has enough for winter? If not I could make arrangements."

"You are too kind, sire, but she lives in a Prophet commune now."

The King wrinkled his forehead. "Is she a chastened sister?"

"Oh by the Divines, no," David laughed. "She is a cook."

"A cook? I remember when she traveled with the army. She did many things but never cooked."

"So I have heard," David stated, stirring the stove.

The Guild King pushed his female companion away. "David, I didn't mean it like that."

"It is fine, sire. I know she was a camp wench. You were kind to take us in."

"I was honor bond, after what happened," the Guild King reminisced.

"Ah – if only honor was all it took," the Queen said walking into the room. The Guild King's woman guest hid herself quickly behind the broad man.

"You don't need to hide, dear," the Queen said. "I have known about my husband's whoring for many years."

"I don't remember summoning you, my love," the King

stated.

The Queen laughed. "You never summon me, thus I must summon myself if I wish to see my dear husband. I heard you had a trying day in the hall."

The Guild King turned to the naked woman in his bath. "Get out," he ordered. She complied with haste, grabbing her simple dress and dashing from the chamber. David stood in the corner by the stove keeping the fire going.

The Queen sat down next to the great spa and rolled up a sleeve. She tested the temperature then began to brush the water with her fingertips.

"I was ambushed by Lord Beritor," complained the King. "Made a fool of."

"I am sorry, my sweet."

"Are you?" the King asked. "I must wonder aloud how he found that provision so carefully hidden. Unless, of course, the one who advised me in the first place informed him."

The Queen sniffed. "Why would I wish to hurt my loving husband?"

"Spite seems to be a popular motivation among cold, unfeeling wives."

The Queen's expression became incredibly somber. "You truly think me cold?"

"Madam, I have worn armor in the snows of Northrim and found them warmer than your affections."

The Queen sighed. "I suppose I deserve that. I know I have been cold to you since..." She glanced at David. "Since the birth of our first son, but my heart is yours, forever and always. It is my only desire to benefit you."

The King lowered his head in shame. "I know the Divines have not been kind to you. It was harsh of me to call you cold."

The Queen leaned her head on the edge of the tub. The King approached and kissed her on the cheek.

"What will you do about the hall?" she asked.

"Appeal to honor," the King stated. "If there is any left."

"Among the old guard guildsmen there is, but the highborn and the younger guildsmen... They want money and you are trying to take it."

"What do you suggest?"

"A compromise. The Guilds give you the right to set tariffs and road tolls, but they maintain general tax rights."

"But without full control of the taxes, I don't believe I can refill the coffers."

"And with no control you most certainly won't," the Queen reminded.

"True."

"A compromise will easily pass in the Hall. The Guild Masters are not unreasonable."

"I fear Beritor makes them so. He is out for blood, regardless of the issue."

"But why?"

"I'm old," the King laughed. "The crows will be circling the crown before my skin is pale. He wants to set himself up as some sort of hero of the guilds. Push and bully his way to more power in the prince's reign."

"Then you have to stop him."

"I can't bloody well just kill him. He has not done anything illegal."

"So you will just let him bury you in the Hall?" the Queen gasped.

The King shook his head. "You underestimate many Guild Master's mistrust of Beritor. I had Frederick give me a tally of how the votes would go in his opinion. I win comfortably. Guild Masters may not like the new laws, but they certainly don't like the idea of Lord Beritor having influence over them."

The Queen yawned and rose to her feet. "Then I trust your wisdom on this issue, sire."

The Guild King smiled. "Do not worry, my love. I will have my tax rights."

The Queen left them with a bow.

"Bring me a towel," the King ordered David after she had left. David wrapped his sire in the large piece of linen. The King stepped out onto the marble floor and drank some of the wine set for him.

"Do you wish me to find the girl again, sire?" David asked.

"No, no. I want to rest now."

"Yes, sire."

"Perhaps the Queen is right," the King pondered aloud while walking to his prepared bed. "Perhaps a compromise would be best. But would that not make me seem weak?"

"A king must do what is best," David said. "For all people, not just those who can hurt him politically."

The Guild King nodded his agreement. "You are right, new tax laws would better the lives of many commoners. Too many Guild Masters like to press their people under heavy tax loads so they can have finer meals. You are wise beyond your years; maybe you should lead the debate in my favor."

"You honor me, sire, but debate is more than clever words."

"What is debate but words?"

"Presence, sire," David said fetching the King his nightgown. "Men follow you not because of your crown but because they know you will lead them in the right direction."

The Guild King slid into bed and laid his head comfortably on his pillow.

"Twenty years ago you would have been right," the King stated as David blew out the candles. "But now? Now I am just the man they have to bury before they can start manipulating the royal prince."

"Then show them you are still king," David stated picking up the fruit tray.

"Yes, you are right. I am the king, and I know what is best for my people. Thank you, David. Now leave me to my sleep."

"Of course, sire," David said leaving the chamber.

The kitchen was empty due to the late hour. David sat the fruit tray down and picked a few off for himself. He dumped the remaining fruit into a bucket to be given to the hogs in the morning and cut open a loaf of bread for his dinner.

"Late night snack?" Lord Beritor asked from behind him. David flinched, startled. He turned to the lord and caught his breath.

"Lord Beritor, you scared me."

"Remind me," Beritor said walking closer. "How did you come into the King's service again?"

"My father was a soldier," David replied. "He volunteered for a dangerous raid and never returned. The King took pity on me and my mother on account of my father's bravery."

"I see. So he felt guilty for murdering your father."

"My father was a soldier in a time of war," David protested. "My lord, these questions are highly irregular."

"Am I making you nervous?"

"Yes, my lord," David said trying to take a step back.

Beritor lifted David's bread from his hand and took a large bite out of it. He smiled while he chewed.

"Forgive me," Beritor said setting the rest of the bread back in David's hand. He stepped back out of the kitchen and disappeared down the hall.

David looked at the half-eaten loaf and angrily threw it into the hog bucket with the leftover fruit. He turned around to clean the tray when two arms grabbed him from behind. David struggled, but his attacker forced him to his knees. He cried out, but his voice only echoed down the empty halls.

"Unhand me!" David demanded. "Unhand me this instant, or the King will have your head!"

"I doubt it," Lord Beritor whispered in his ear.

"Beritor? What is this?"

"He is assisting me," Sir Snaca said leaving the shadows like a wolf emerging from the forest.

Beritor twisted and turned David to face him without lessening his hold. In Snaca's hand was a glass jar with a disgusting snake-like creature wriggling in it. Lord Beritor hit David in the kidney and placed one arm around his head and throat.

"What is the meaning of this, Snaca?" David struggled out.

"Regime change," Snaca replied with a smile.

"You're mad! I will tell you nothing, nor help you in any way. Even if you threaten to cut off my head, I would not help you!"

Snaca nodded. "I believe you, and I am humbled by your loyalty. Luckily, it is not your will but your body I need."

Snaca opened the glass jar and approached David. He fought frantically but couldn't get free. Snaca forced open David's mouth and tipped the jar over carefully. David tried and failed to scream as the creature fell from the jar and into his mouth. Its slimy body squirmed down his throat.

A man without the Divines is a man without a guide. He wanders the earth with no direction or wind. His heart becomes his rudder, his appetites his pilot.

The First Word
> **Harrowing 3:34**

Francis signed his name on the bottom of a piece of parchment. His aide replaced it with another. France glared up at his aide then looked the document over. His eyes ached from the hours of strain. The dying crackle of campfires outside declared the late time of night.

"What is this?" Francis asked, pointing to the scroll.

"It is an open arrest warrant, my lord steward, for any orc found stealing rations or processing more than allotted."

"So they cannot trade or hunt on their own now? What is in the Guild King's head? I have half the Nor'tog tribe imprisoned as it is. I don't have the manpower to enforce such dribble."

"Political gesturing," Jayden said entering the tent. "A way of showing the Prophets he is still in charge in reality, if not in name."

"His 'political gesturing' could cause a revolt," Francis complained, signing the paper then waving his aide away.

"The Prophets will send more men then."

"Why do the Prophets care about this place? Don't tell me it is to rid the world of dark arts. They didn't seem to mind the dark arts fifty years ago. So why?"

Jayden smiled and took a seat. "As to all of Philipus' intentions, I do not know, but I suspect it has to do with this." He drew from his robes a small bag. Francis opened it and was hit with a powerful smell coming off the dry grass leaves.

"What is it?" Francis asked turning his head away.

"They call it peace grass," Jayden explained. He pulled out a pipe and pressed some leaves into the bowl. Then he held the bowl up to a candle flame until the leaves began to burn.

Jayden drew deeply on the pipe and exhaled a deep blue smoke. He handed it to Francis.

"You breathe in the smoke?" Francis asked uncomfortably.

Jayden nodded. "It is a tradition of the orc chiefs. They smoke it when they meet in the Peace Place." Jayden's face became lazy and his eyes glazed. Francis sat unsure, fumbling the strange bone pipe in his hands.

"This cannot be good for you," Francis commented.

"Only try it," Jayden insisted. "It makes you feel light, like air."

"And the Prophet's feel closer to the Divines when they smoke it?"

"All feel closer to the Divines. Philipus is setting up smoke shops in Doraxe already. He will pay a good price for every bushel. If you send him a cart or two, you could buy a palace."

"A palace, ehh," Francis muttered lifting the pipe to his lips.

The embers glowed red as he inhaled. Francis coughed out a plume of blue smoke. Jayden chuckled at his discomfort. Francis leaned back in his chair to catch his breath.

"You feel it?" Jayden asked.

"Yes," Francis whispered, his eyes slowly become drowsy. "I feel as if I am riding, even though I know I am not."

"Men in Galsag are paying bags of gold for what you are experiencing."

"Then the Prophets have found a good source of income," Francis laughed. "My father would not be pleased with me smoking some strange grass from a pipe."

"Why?"

"Why? He is against anything that dulls the mind, in his

opinion. He believes a proper lord must always be watchful, never excessive in wine or women. My grandfather taught him that. I suppose there is wisdom in it, since my grandfather was one of the few lord to grow stronger from the Great War and not weaker.

"My father is also the only man the King fears. He stubbornly refused to create a guild even while the other lords rushed to have their carters drafted. He wanted the Drako family in all aspects of state by my nephew's maturity.

"To that end, he had me appointed minister of... something. I did not go, though. As soon as I was on the road, I made good my escape from his plotting and joined the Broken Lances. My father was furious."

Francis rubbed his face and stared off into memory. "I guess the Baron convinced him I was still an asset so I was allowed to stay. I had to earn my place, though; nothing is given in the Broken Lances.

"The day I earned my black cloak was the best day of all my days. I remember looking at Umbra when he presented the robe to me. I saw..."

"What did you see?"

"Pride," Francis stated. "I saw pride."

Francis took in another breath of pipe smoke. The blue fog filled the top of his tent.

"How much do you want for that bag you have with you?" he asked.

"Take it as a gift, my lord steward."

"You are too kind."

"It is a small act, I assure you."

Francis nodded then laughed. "How does one like you become a Prophet, Jayden?"

"One like me?"

"Yes, highborn, educated." Francis replied. "You should be running a county, not aiding me. Come now, I told you my story, tell me yours. Are we not friends?"

"Of course we are friends, steward."

"Good, then spin me your sad tell."

"I am highborn, as you said. Unlike you, I did not have the good blessing of being first born. When my father passed, my brother held no desire to share our considerable inheritance – most of which was willed to me. I had the law on my side, but my brother had swords on his. The law offers little protection against swords. My brother gave me a choice, renounce my family and become a Prophet, or die. I chose the Prophet's life."

"Seems to have worked out for you," Francis said carelessly.

Jayden's gaze hardened into an iron stare. Francis sunk into his chair. "I was forced to abandon my wife and daughter." Jayden said. "I had to receive word by letter of my brother taking my wife. When my daughter took ill from fever, I was studying in the tower. When she died, I was not allowed to see her. So no, my lord, it did not work out."

"Apologies," Francis muttered feeling ashamed. He drew in on his pipe and felt better instantly.

"It was years ago," Jayden shrugged off.

"How old was your daughter?"

"She would have been ten this year. Losing a child is the worst thing imaginable. I would not wish it on my enemies. It is like losing a part of your soul. Like your soul is a block of stone and a hammer has knocked off a chuck."

A silence hung over the two men for a moment. Francis began to speak to break it when Gregory entered the tent.

"Sorry for the intrusion, my lord, but an orc chieftain is here to speak with you."

"And you assumed I would wish to speak to him?" Francis asked.

"Apologies, I will send him away."

"No, bring him in," Francis sighed taking another draw from his pipe then hiding it.

"Should I leave, my lord?" Jayden asked.

"No, stay. I don't trust what orcs say."

Gregory walked in behind the orc chieftain. Francis struggled to remember his name.

"Who are you again?" he asked rudely. "I remember you."

"We met before when the Shamans from my clans were silenced forever. I am Mur'kog of the Torguk tribe."

"Yes, yes. What do you need?" Francis asked. Gregory stood close behind the orc with his hand on his sword handle.

"We have not the food you promised."

"I sent those rations myself," Jayden protested. "My lord, they have the food."

"All we received was bags of grass seed. It is no good for eating."

Francis laughed. "It's called wheat grain. You mill it then make bread from it."

"My people eat meat. Our stomachs know not this grain seed."

"Well grain is what I have to give. It lasts all winter if you treat it right and can feed a village on a single bag."

"We need meat."

"You can't have it," Francis explained. "I don't have any to give you."

"You have the beasts you ride," Mur'kog said.

"You mean our horses," Francis laughed. "They are not for eating."

"Meat is meat," the orc stated blankly.

Francis and Jayden chuckled at each other.

"Very well," Francis said. "I will make you a trade, you know what a trade is, orc?"

"I do."

"Good, I will give you a horse for every cart of peace grass you bring me. You know peace grass?"

"I know it."

"You know where it grows?"

"I do."

"Good, bring as much of it as you can to me, and I will get you meat. Do we have a deal?"

"We have deal," the orc said.

Francis stood and offered his hand. The orc stared at it

blankly. Francis came from behind his desk, took the orc's hand, and shook it.

"There, now we have a deal," Francis explained. The orc nodded and Gregory walked him out. Francis turned to Jayden. "Write to the Head Prophet to start construction on my palace."

"Of course, my lord steward. Should it be made of red or white marble?"

"I think I prefer white," Francis chuckled looking at the bag of peace grass in his hand. "Yes, white."

> *The Broken Lances were renowned for their fighting spirit and discipline. This was not formed out of accident but out of the radical, and often controversial, training methods Baron Umbra employed.*
>
> **History of the Guilds**
> **Elder Lighours**

Del'Caf marched with the band of orcs through the dark forest. Their human masters began to act merrier than before. Del'Caf knew they were close to the human's home. The group emerged from the woods and entered the shadow of Castle Pearl.

It sat atop a high cliff with a single road leading up a grassy plain. The waves of the sea poured up the side of the rock face and danced back down. The gates alone were larger than the whole of the Peace Place back in his homeland.

The guards moved the awestruck orcs up the road and into the massive courtyard of the castle. Men in black cloaks gazed down from the walls with disgust. A short man in leather armor towered over the courtyard atop a set of white steps. The orcs all looked up towards him as their guards stopped them.

"I am James the Red," he shouted so all can hear. "Not Sir James, not Guild Master James or Lord James. I am your master of drill, and you all now belong to the Broken Lances. These men around you with black cloaks are your betters. They have earned their right to be here. You have not.

"I don't care about your past. I don't care that you are orcs. Do well here and you will prosper in this new world you live in. Forget your old ways. They are not needed here.

"This is Castle Pearl. This is your new home. Here, you will be trained and put to profitable use. The King wishes for a division of orc shock troops. I will give it to him. Those who pass our tests and complete our training will find his life much better off. Those who don't will die.

"If this deal does not sound appealing to you, then you may leave. You may walk out those gates at any time. Of course, it is a thousand leagues to your homeland, and you will most likely be killed on sight by anyone you meet. But just so you know I am not a heartless man, I offer you a choice."

A skinny, scared, ugly little man stepped into a dirt ring

with a single knife in his hand and no shirt on his back. He smiled a grin of rotten teeth at the orcs.

"This is Mouse," James explained. "If you kill him, I will give you letters of leave and a guard with supplies for your journey home. So kill Mouse and go with the Divines."

"Alright green skins, who is first?" a guard yelled out.

"Come on, gain your freedom," another shouted. "You cowards or what?"

"Kill Mouse now is a knee unbowed," they chanted.

A huge orc stepped forward. The humans hooted and clapped their hands pleased with the challenger. A knight dropped a sword at the orc's feet. Mouse licked his lips.

"That's Bor'tak of Urrag," Kir'git whispered to Del'Caf. "He will crush the small human." Del'Caf nodded his agreement.

Bor'tak stared Mouse down. He kept his eyes on Mouse even as he reached down and picked up the sword. The weapon sat uncomfortably in his large hand. Mouse did nothing. Bor'tak charged. He swung the sword at Mouse's head. Mouse side stepped the blow and jabbed his small blade into the orc's neck as he stumbled past.

The orc tripped in shock leaning on the sword for help. Blood gushed between his fingers as he pressed his free hand on the wound. He took a step towards Mouse, and then fell over dead.

The orcs were stunned. Mouse turned to them and smiled. He wiped his blade on his pants. "Who's next?" he whispered.

The orc's lowered their heads and looked away from their defeat. Sil'grok leaned in to Del'Caf.

"See Warchief, see. This human way be. Unsure what is or is not. You fear what is not and not what is there."

"Anyone else?" James called out.

None stepped forward. James waved to the guards and disappeared back into the castle. The guards barked and yelled at the orcs and herded them into a large wooden building.

Bunks lined the walls three high. There were no windows, and the air smelled of sweat and blood. The door shut behind them. Several orcs came out of the shadows to greet the newcomers. Kir'git walked forward to them.

"I am Kir'git of the..."

"You have no tribe here, new meat." One orc proclaimed. "Your tribe is dead and the dirt is now your only mother. The humans rule out there, but in here, Stit rule." The orc pointed to a built orc with scar covered skin. Stit stood to his feet and looked the group of newcomers over. He picked up his waste bucket and tossed it at Kir'git. Kir'git caught it. Some of the bucket's content splashed up onto his face and chest.

"Go, new meat, empty it."

The other orcs laughed. Kir'git growled in anger. He dropped the bucket to the ground. The waste dumped out onto the floor boards and drained past Stit's feet.

"There, it is empty," Kir'git stated staring Stit in the eye.

Stit struck Kir'git in the face. Kir'git tackled him. The orcs formed a circle around them as they wrestled on the ground. They cheered and pointed as the two orcs mauled each other with blows and throws.

Kir'git got in a head-butt. His foe smashed Kir'git into a bedpost. They continued this exchange for several minutes. Then Kir'git was pushed into the crowd and an orc loyal to Stit hit Kir'git in the back of the head. Kir'git stumbled to the ground and Stit bounced. He jumped on top of him and began to bash on his face until Kir'git ceased to move.

The victor stood to his feet. "I am Stit, and I rule. You do nothing without my word! I am Warchief, Shaman, chieftain, and chief."

Stit spat on his beaten foe and walked away. Del'Caf picked the broken Kir'git up and laid him on an empty mat.

"I'm well," he said through the blood in his mouth.

"No, you are not."

"I win next time."

"Yes, next time you will win," Del'Caf assured.

> *All person accused of heresy shall be given a trial, not to be shorter than two days, so all evidence can be laid to the judge. The judge in all capital cases must be the ruling Lord of the region in which the accused was arrested.*
>
> **Prophetic Law**

The Guild King stomped through the hallway with his royal robes flowing behind him. David ran to keep up. The murmur of the crowd gathered in the courtroom echoed down the corridor. The King turned to David suddenly.

"Why am I judging this case again?"

"I believe it was a favor to Baron Umbra, sire."

"Yes, yes. But why did I agree? It's one girl. I have countless affairs of state I am neglecting for this shame of a trail. The Hall votes in two days. I could be talking to Guild Masters, wooing them to my side, but instead I am here, playing judge."

"Perhaps it is a matter better left to a lower lord, sire," David suggested.

"No," the King dismissed fixing his attire before entering. "I gave my word."

"Sire," Frederick called out approaching them. "They are ready for you."

"You!" the Guild spat with a harsh finger pointed at his face. "You said my bill would pass without fail."

Frederick stepped back defensively. "Sire, I swear to you, I am your loyal servant. I spoke true."

"You miscalculated. Now I am in a pitch battle with a snake. I have not had a major bill voted down in the Hall in ten years, and you risk that spirit of corporation."

"I can talk to Charles if you wish."

"No! How would that look? No, you will take a new poll of the Guild Masters. I want to know by tonight were the votes stand. Get Sir Snaca to assist. I need the numbers. The real numbers."

"Yes, sire."

The King looked to David as Frederick left. The King had a question but forgot it when he noticed how pale, even sickly David appeared.

"Are you alright, David?"

"Certainly sire, I am the picture of health."

"Yes, well…" the King mumbled walking into the court.

The courtroom rose when the Guild King entered. The prisoner stood in an open floor flanked by teams of seated Prophets. The common folk filled the balcony. Nobles and the wealthy occupied floor level seating ready to see the spectacle.

"Sire," Head Prophet Philipus began in a proud voice. "We the Prophets bring before your most honorable court a vile criminal for justice."

The commoners immediately hissed and booed at the Prophets. The court officer called for order but with no effect. The crowd continued to cat call and make rude gestures. The court officer slammed his staff's end on the marble floor, but still they would not be silent. The Guild King shook his head.

"This is not a good beginning," he called out to Philipus.

Philipus blushed in embarrassment. He turned to the people and tried to call them to silence but they did not listen. The crowd grew louder and louder in their insults.

"Let the innocent go!" one cried.

"They kill the pure, but release the wicked," shouted another.

"Good people, this is justice," the Prophet said in desperation.

The accused Natalia then turned to the crowd and raised her hands. To the court's amazement, the commoners grew silent. The King sat up in his chair and looked more intently at the young girl.

"How does it honor the Divines," Natalia called out, "to dishonor the King? For is it not written, 'obey thy master?' If you have love for me, you will show that love to these men here and respect them as you would respect me."

Natalia turned back to the court. Philipus collected himself.

"The woman before you, sire," Philipus continued in a softer tone, "stands accused of blasphemy, fraud, and intent to stir revolt."

"How does the accused plea?" the King asked.

"Sire," the young girl said. "I have never said anything against the Divines or the First Word. So how can I be guilty of blasphemy? Nor have I ever lied to any man about any subject, so where is the fraud? And I have nothing but loyalty to the King, so where is the revolt?"

"So noted," the King replied. He leaned in his chair towards the court officer. "I believe the accused is pleading not guilty." A few Prophets chuckled. "Head Prophet, you may question."

"Thank you, sire." Philipus stared at Natalia. "It has been said you claim to be an angel. Is this true?"

"No, your worthiness. I made no claims, for a claim implies something is not yet proven. I am an angel."

The Head Prophet threw up his arms.

"Blasphemy, from her own lips, sire."

"How is telling the truth blasphemy?" Natalia challenged.

"There is no evidence to back your claim," Philipus countered.

"My works prove themselves," she replied. "For does not the First Word speak of angels coming as men to show the people the way?"

"That was for the time before the Prophets," Philipus answered.

"No it is not," Natalia stated flatly. "For the First Word was written long before the Prophets existed."

"That does not prove it is for today. Besides, there is no case in the First Word of an angel being a woman."

"So nothing is Divine unless it is specifically mentioned in the First Word?"

"Of course. Something is held true when it is from the First Word."

"Then show me the verse that speaks of the office of Head Prophet?"

Many of the Prophets gasped and talked among each other. Philipus, red with anger, glared at the girl.

"We are here to discuss your heresy, not the organization of the Prophets."

"Aren't we?" Natalia asked. "If I am to be charged with blasphemy, should we not first define the term?"

"Blasphemy is speaking against Prophetic law."

"So Prophetic law trumps the First Word?"

"Prophetic law shows us what the First Word says and means."

"So the Divines are not powerful enough to make their message clear? They have to rely on old men to 'interpret?' No, your worthiness, the Divines mean what they say and say what they mean. The First Word is plain; you only do not like what it says so you have twisted it around."

Rage flared in Philipus' face. "You will show this court respect!"

"You sound like a man beating a dog," Natalia replied. "You are unable to teach it tricks so you yell and expect it to cower."

"I will see you burned!" Philipus screamed.

"And the true face of Prophetic justice becomes clear," Natalia replied calmly.

"That is enough," The Guild King interrupted. "Let us have a new questioner."

Philipus stormed to his seat while Prophet Minor Thompson calmly stood.

"You were there when I was arrested," Natalia commented to the young Prophet.

"Yes, I was."

"What did you think of the healing you saw?"

"I am the one asking the questions, my lady," Thompson stated.

"Wait," the King stepped in. "You witnessed a healing?"

"It is a common trick fraudsters use, sire. They hire a man to fane illness so the conman, or woman, can pretend to heal them and be blessed with donations."

"It was no trick, sire!" a man in the balcony yelled out. "The man healed is my brother, sire."

"Sir, sit down and be silent," the court official ordered.

"No," the Guild King interceded. "Bring him down as a witness. I wish to hear what he has to say."

The guards escorted the man to the witness stand.

Philipus stepped out onto the main floor. "Sire, I must protest. We have no evidence of who this man is or any way to validate his testimony."

"A King must be a judge of character," the Guild King replied. "I will hear him." The Guild King stared intensely at the commoner. "Sir, tell me the truth in this matter, under pain of death."

"Yes, sire. As I said, the miracle came from the Divines true enough. It was no trick, I swear on my mother's grave it wasn't. The man healed is my brother, sire. Ten years ago, he had a cart crush his legs. His bones healed deformed, and he has not walked without a crutch since. But then this angel healed him, and his legs are made straight as an arrow."

"Sire," Philipus protested. "I object to the witness calling the accused an angel. It skews the facts. It has not yet been proven either way."

"And yet you call me a heretic openly," Natalia chimed in. "Has that been proven already? If so, why this trial."

"You will speak when spoken to," Philipus cursed. "Sire, this testimony proves nothing. The Divines work in mysterious ways. Even if the healing is real, it does not prove she is an angel."

The Guild King rubbed his chin in thought. "True, but then again, why would the Divines show such favor to a fraud?"

The Mesmers have a saying about love. It is wholesomely wicked.

History of the Guilds
Elder Lighours

Raven fiddled with the page in her hand. She had read it many times but was still uneasy with what it said. She laid the paper on her desk and rubbed her finger across the signature. The dry ink was rough on her fingertip. Her breath seemed less the longer she stared at it.

She looked to her door and the unseen guards standing watch outside. She drummed her fingers on the wooden surface of her desk. The rhythmic noise bounced around the silent room. She stopped. She rose to her feet and changed out of her nightgown into street clothes. She slid on a pair of leather boots and a coat to protect her from the cold.

Her balcony was several stories above the ground with a

great view of the city below. The view, however, was lost on Raven as she fearfully climbed a rope down from her room. The wind blew her making her sway as she slowly descended.

Light from a candle poured out of one window. Raven tried to climb around it, but a gust of wind pushed her right in front of it. A large male servant and a small boy were undressing each other, luckily too distracted to notice the woman hanging outside the window.

Raven finally found the ground and sighed a breath of relief. She didn't even want to think of how she would get back up.

Raven curled her hair up and stuffed it into a hat. She sneaked to the stables and found her horse. Jumping on, she rode quickly through the gate, but not so fast as to draw attention. The gate guards did nothing, assuming someone leaving the citadel had freedom to do so.

Raven carefully made her way through the dark city streets to the house the note mentioned. She tied her horse on a post and crept silently closer. She could see two men talking near a fireplace. She hid under the window and listened carefully.

"She isn't coming," Moor said. "You know that Charles. She isn't that reckless."

"I think you underestimate her courage."

"Or her stupidity," Moor replied. "She is a princess in all but name. What are you? Gentleman of leisure?"

"Master artist?" Charles countered.

"Professional fool."

"Private confidant."

"Expert play thing."

"Successful businessman."

"Gilded trophy."

"Unique attendant."

"You can put sugar on dung all you want; you still will be full of shit," Moor finished.

"Oh, Moor. You don't understand. I care for this girl."

"You care for yourself."

"And that allows me to love her. For how can one love someone else if they do not first love themselves?"

"Love her, do you?" Moor asked.

"Yes," Charles stated. "I think I do love her, in my own way. I don't know how else to love. Does that make my love any less lovely?"

"Spoken like a true artist. Beautiful and full of nonsense."

"It is not nonsense."

"Yes, it is," Moor assured.

"If this is nonsense, then I hope to never make sense again."

Raven blushed and thought her game had gone on long enough. She walked quietly to the door and tapped the knock three times. She heard the men turn on their boot heels.

"Sounds like she did come."

"I told you she would."

"Can't wait to meet her."

"No! Get out of here."

"What, I'm your…"

"Leave!" Charles whispered harshly. Raven shook her head as she listened to Moor stammer out the back door.

There was a pause then the door opened to Charles in a relaxed pose.

"You came," he said trying to not sound too surprised.

"Of course, I am a sucker for scandal. And a daughter of the Mayor visiting the court artist at all hours of the night is simply scandalous."

"Well, I don't want you to think I have unworthy desires."

"Oh, like what?" Raven asked dropping her coat on his couch. She glanced about the home.

"The King must be gracious to you to have such a fine home."

"He has a healthy appreciation for the arts," Charles explained.

"I never thought of the Guild King as an art lover."

Charles chuckled. "I believe he is a simple pragmatist. The people love art, big and verbose. Art decides how things are remembered. So the King is smart enough to know if you control art, you control history in the eyes of the people."

"So you make the King look good in the eyes of history?"

"Gold pays for the correct message."

"And for a nice house," Raven commented.

"Many nice things, actually."

"Clothes?"

"Yes."

"Drink?"

Charles smiled. "Yes."

"Women?" Raven asked with a raised eyebrow.

Charles thought for a moment. "Sometimes," he replied.

"You are a terrible person."

"If I believed in the Divines, I would surely be risking my soul."

"You don't believe in the Divines?" Raven asked.

"It is unbecoming of a Mesmer to worry about simple people's beliefs. I believe in beauty."

"And what is that? Beauty, I mean."

Charles gestured towards a painting still on its easel. Raven approached it. Charles lit the lamps near it so she could see.

A red velvet couch and a purple drape sat next to a bundle of flowers.

"You have impressive technic. I am surprised you were not recruited into the academy in the Free City."

Charles laughed. "I was recruited into a different school."

"I have never seen such use of color and texture. I can almost see the linen of the fabric. But honestly, Charles, is not the composition a little dull?"

"How so?"

"It's a couch next to some flowers."

Charles looked at the painting intensely. "You know, you are right," he said walking in front of the painting and pulling back a curtain to reveal the couch on the canvas.

"I think it is missing its center piece," he stated holding out his hand, beckoning her closer.

Raven stepped towards him. Charles slid her outer shirt down to show her shoulders and cleavage. He positioned her on the couch and returned to his easel.

He mixed some paints and began to touch his brush to the canvas. Raven lied down on the couch and slowly undid the rest of her blouse. The pieces of clothing dropped to the floor exposing her nude skin. Charles bit his lower lip and continued to paint.

Charles approached her. "Move your arm up here," he said resetting her body position. As he did, their lips drew closer and closer till Raven finally met his. He leaned in, engulfing her in his arms. She embraced him back. She pulled at his shirt and he helped her remove it. He was turning to his belt buckle when there was a second knock on the door.

Raven looked at Charles frightened. He gestured her to be silent and carefully drew the curtain again to hide her.

Sliding his shirt back on, he opened the door. Hall Master Frederick was waiting outside.

"Hall Master?" Charles said, shocked. "What can I do for you in this late hour?"

"You can invite me in, for a start," the Hall Master grumbled.

"Of course, do come in. Would you care for some wine?"

Charles asked pouring himself a glass.

"No, I won't stay long. I need a portrait done. A special portrait and it must be done before the vote in two days."

"You are playing with the Hall? Does the King know about this?" Charles asked.

"Yes, of course. I do nothing outside his will," Frederick asserted.

Charles fell into his chair. "Who is the portrait of?"

"Guild Master Duncan."

"Duncan? I thought he was voting for the King."

"Well, votes change in this volatile time. Duncan has influence over much of the southern guilds, more so with Duke Johes dead."

"This is rather short notice. Special portraits take time and planning. I don't like to work this way."

"I'll double your rate," Frederick said without hesitation.

Charles chuckled. "You must be desperate."

"It is not I," Frederick stated with some anger in his voice. "The King orders this done."

"When did the king use artists to deal with Hall issues? He has never asked me to paint a Guild Master before, why now?"

"I told you the commission," Frederick redirected. "Get the job done."

"As you wish," Charles stated drinking his wine.

Frederick wiped his nose and left the house. Charles allowed him to find his own way out. Raven slipped out from behind the curtain with her blouse covering her chest.

"What do you actually do for the King?" she asked Charles.

Charles took a longer drink of wine. "Don't ask questions you don't want the answers to."

> *When the wind blows black and the herds run long, then the time be. When the blood turns red and all is gone, then the time be. When the sky is lost and the grass burned up, then the time be.*
>
> **Orc Prophecy**

The old Warchief stared blankly into the roaring fire. A large pillar of smoke rose up and out of the Peace Place. The chiefs and chieftains of the Wazog tribe encircled the bonfire.

Sog'rim passed the long bone pipe to his brother the Warchief. The old Warchief breathed the blue smoke in and held it. A cloud danced out between his lips. He passed the pipe on.

"Warchief," Sog'rim's son Ugra called out. "The iron prince has crafted words against us. He has told our tribes they cannot hunt or wear the flesh of their kills. Will we touch the pen with him as we did his father?"

The Warchief grunted. "The iron prince would steal our life force with paper," he replies. "But he cannot steal it. I will send three hunters to the iron king to remind him of our dealings. He will keep his word and we will keep our ways."

"So," Sog'rim's oldest Oggrat began. "You will wear the bear and not the cloth?"

The old Warchief stood to his feet before the whole tent. "No Wazog will wear cloth. No Wazog will give up his hunt, or his hunter pride. A hunter must keep what he kills."

Oggrat sprung to his feet as well. "And if the iron prince demands it? Will the drums beat against the iron men once more?"

"I made no deal with the iron prince," the Warchief stated.

"Then let the hunters hunt!" Oggrat demanded.

"No!" the Warchief snapped with a growl. "The iron king will hear our cry. His prince steps in land not his own."

Oggrat spat in the fire.

"They all step in land not their own. The iron king came without cause and left his prince to torment us."

"The iron king is in his own land. His prince has gone against his father's word," Sog'rim answered.

"Does not a chieftain know his own chiefs? No, the iron king betrays us."

"Can even the hawk see to the ends of the world?" Sog'rim asked. "The iron king lives farther than even the birds go. No, the iron king does not know what his son does to us."

"If the iron king comes from such a distant land, why did he come here?" Oggrat barked.

"Hold your words!" Sog'rim warned.

Defiant, Oggrat growled at his father. His father growled

back. The Warchief snorted like a bull ready to charge. All fell silent.

"The iron men came just as snow falls. Just as harsh winds blow. They came just as one hunter falls on the hunt and another lives. They came; it is as it is."

"Warchief, are not our ways worth defending? What is a life force without a vessel? What is a people without their ways? Does a hunter abandon the hunt when his prey proves fierce?"

The Warchief let out a tired sigh.

"We will fight the iron men," he stated. "But some beasts die by the spear and some by the club. We hunted the iron men with our axes and their skin proved too strong. Now we must hunt with the knife. We will lie in wait and slit the throat when it draws too close."

"If we wait to defend our tents," Oggrat hissed, "they will have burned down before we draw our blades."

The young orc stepped away from the circle and towards the tent opening. The chieftains gasped at him seeming to leave without proper farewells and respect to the Warchief.

"Oggrat," Sog'rim barked enraged. "You insult your Warchief."

"A Warchief who refuses to beat the war drum is no Warchief," Oggrat muttered.

"I have killed for less!" Sog'rim screamed.

The old Warchief grabbed his brother's arm.

"Oggrat," he said, "if you leave this tent, you leave my protection."

"Your protection?" Oggrat choked on the words. "Were my kin slayed in the valley under your protection?"

Oggrat stormed out of the tent to the shock of all. Ugra rushed to catch up with his brother.

"Oggrat," he called out, running after him. "Oggrat, are you lost in the heat, brother? You insult the Warchief? He is Warchief, the spirit of his people made flesh. His drums begin hunts and his songs end them. Go back before he has forgotten you."

"He has forgotten us all!" Oggrat yelled. "He sang to the iron king too soon. The tribes still had fight. They would have fought till the rivers ran red with our blood."

"It is not ours to question."

"If we do not question, we will have no ways left. Are you made blind by fear, brother? If the iron prince is not stopped we will become as dust and just as worthless."

"Stop this! What would you have of me? There are no hunters left. The iron king took them all. The pen was touched. The deal was made. The song was sung. There is nothing left for us to do."

"No, there are still things we can do," Oggrat said grabbing Ugra's face and bringing it close to his. "Not all the hunters are dead. The drums still beat, my brother. They beat in the blood of all who would defy the iron men."

"What hunters?' Ugra asked pulling away.

"Orcs not willing to bow to the iron prince. Ones who left their tribes after the song was sung. Ones who refuse to lose life force."

"How many hunters?"

"Three packs."

"Three packs?" Ugra laughed. "You mean to slay the iron prince with fifty axes? When fifty thousand were not enough for his father?"

"I have a plan."

"Plan? What plan? Stand before the iron prince and hope his men laugh to death?"

"No, I will draw the iron prince away from his swords and walls. Then when he is alone, I will cut off his head. Without its head, his tribe will fall."

"You have no honor," Ugra scoffed. "Only dogs fight in such ways."

"Did they show honor when they murdered a village to steal our kin?"

Ugra grumbled. "No, they did not."

"Honor comes from the kill, not the tool used to kill. Is there not honor in success?"

Ugra stood uneasy before his brother. "Explain your plan," he said.

And the Divines showed favor to the old man and brought his daughter from the grave and handed her back into his arms.

The First Word
Harrowing 7:42

Herrion rode into the stable adjacent to his Doraxe home. He dismounted from his horse as the young stable boy ran up and grabbed the reins. The stable boy's eyes went wide when he saw the majestic animal.

"Is that a black destrier?" the boy asked with his jaw dropped.

Herrion chuckled. "Yes it is. Are you new here, boy? I don't know you."

"Yes, my lord. My father is one of your leather workers."

"And he taught you about horses?" Herrion asked grabbing a brush and stroking the worn-out steed.

"Yes, my lord."

"Well, what did he teach you about black destriers?"

"They are the greatest warhorses on the field," the boy said excitedly. "They are fast and strong and charge like an arrow flung from a bow."

"They are also insanely costly and quick to tire, but you are right. There are none faster. You have to be careful with them though. They will run till their hearts explode."

Herrion led the horse to the water trough. The beast buried its face in the cool drink.

"What is his name, my lord?"

"Thunder," Herrion replied.

"A good name for a warhorse, my lord. I wish I had a horse like that. I would ride him into battle and stomp them all down."

Herrion chuckled. "No doubt you would. Let me ask you,

how long does one wait to give him a drink?"

"Not long. Just long enough for him to cool down and his heart to slow down, my lord."

Herrion nodded in approval. He pointed to a different horse in the stable. "What breed is that horse, lad?"

"That is a courser," the stable boy replied. "But he has some pony in him."

Herrion nodded, impressed. "How do you figure that?"

"Well, his hooves, my lord. They are broader than a purebred courser."

"You know your horses well. Give your father my compliments. I failed to realize I had an expert in my service. I wish I had known that when I bought the damn horse. It was not till I got him home I realized he was a mix. Serves me right, I suppose."

A servant ran into the stable. "My lord, the king..."

Herrion interrupted him with a raised hand. "Take the reins, boy. Don't let Thunder drink too much."

Herrion walked out of the stable with the servant. "I ran Thunder near dead this morning," Herrion continued. "But it is good for him. He should do me proud in the joust next year."

"Yes, my lord," the servant replied politely. "My lord, the King has requested you."

"Of course, the Guild King cannot bring himself to give me a day to myself. Boy!" Herrion called.

The lad rushed out to his master's order. "Yes, my lord?"

"Saddle me a fresh horse."

"Yes, my lord." The boy ran off to fetch a saddle.

"Do you know the King's need?" Herrion asked the servant.

"No, my lord. The messenger did not say."

"They rarely do," Herrion sighed.

He saw in the corner of his eye the stable boy lifting up a saddle and struggling towards the mixed courser horse.

"Boy, not that one," Herrion called out. "He is not yet broken."

The stable boy did not hear his master's warning and came closer to the horse. As soon as the horse noticed the approaching lad, he panicked and kicked franticly. One hoof hit the boy squarely in the chest, sending him flying several feet in a flash.

Herrion rushed over to the screaming boy. He touched the pit where his rips should be. He could feel the crushed bone floating behind the bloodied skin.

"Fetch the healer!" he barked at his servant.

The aide dashed off while Herrion lifted the boy into his arms, trying to calm his agony. Blood ran out of the boy's mouth and he soon passed out.

The healer rushed into the stable. Herrion prayed as the healer took the boy from Herrion and examined him. After a moment, the healer shook his head and stood.

"What are you doing?" Herrion yelled. "Help him."

"There is nothing to do," the healer explained. "His chest is completely crushed. I will fetch him a potion to ease his passing."

Herrion grabbed the healer by the coat and slammed him into the stable door. "Why do I pay you if you can't heal? Save him or it will be your death!"

"My lord, it is not possible! His bones are not armor; you cannot take them off and pound them back into shape. I am not a miracle worker."

Herrion let him go and stepped back. "Forgive me," he muttered.

"It is tragic," the healer comforted. "But people die every day."

Herrion's gaze shot up at the healer. "Not today," he whispered. "Not today."

Herrion scooped the boy's broken body up into his arms and struggled onto his prize black destrier horse.

"Where are you going, my lord?" the healer exclaimed. "The parents deserve the body."

Herrion ignored his cry and dashed out into the city streets. He plowed his way through the crowds and past the carts. He galloped his horse down the road and back alleys not letting up on the speed except to turn or dodge.

The horse bucked and snorted from exhaustion, but Herrion pressed it forward at full gallop. Sweat poured off its black fur as Herrion saw the City Watch headquarters ahead.

He kicked Thunder to run faster as they approached. Then, only a few hundred paces away, the horse gave out from under Herrion, sending him and the boy flying to the ground. Herrion slid into the dust. He could hear the last cries of Thunder behind him. Herrion struggled to his feet and lifted the motionless lad back into his arms. He limped past the dead horse towards the City Watch guards.

"Open the gates, in the name of the Watch commander!" Herrion yelled at them. The guards instantly obeyed.

Herrion shoved his way past them and to the door leading to the dungeon. He pried it open and stumbled down the damp stone steps.

He was drenched in sweat and covered in dust when he fell to his knees before Natalia's cell. The boy lied lifeless and cold in his arms. Natalia approached, curious at the sight of a nobleman so undignified.

"Heal him," Herrion pleaded, fighting back tears. "I know I have no favor with the Divines, but please heal him."

Natalia knelt with a smile before him. She reached between her iron bars and touched Herrion's cheek. A single tear dropped onto her fingertip.

"It is not favor but faith that heals," Natalia said laying the tear on the boy's chest. In an instant breath rushed back into the boy's lungs. His eyes shot open and his skin regained warmth and color.

"Where am I?" the lad choked out.

Herrion collapsed into a mixture of tears and laughter. He squeezed the boy tight in joy. Natalia smiled.

"Thank you," Herrion whispered. "Thank you."

"Do you know why the Divines heard you today?" she asked him.

"Because you asked them," Herrion stated.

Natalia shook her head, holding back tears of her own. "Because, for a brief moment, you were not Lord Duke Herrion, Guild Master and Watch Commander. For a moment, you gave no thought of your title or your lands but only for a boy's life. You fell before the Divines, not with a sense of entitlement, but with a selfless plea. There are more glorious things than even this, Herrion. If you would only forget the world and its failing treasures."

BROKEN DREAMS

8

Great is the man who knows his place. Great is the man who fights for a good cause. Great is the man who loves the truth and shuns evil. Great is the man who dies for the sake of others.

The First Word
   Treasures 8:19

"**W**hen I say 'forward,'" the Broken Lance trainer shouted, "you will march forward together. When I say 'halt,' you will stop together. Do you stupid green skins understand?"

The orc column stood quietly. The Broken Lance trainer shook his head in disgust.

"Maybe if you used puppets they would understand," Sir Martin taunted. He sat with James and several others at a wooden table eating a meal.

The Broken Lance trainer ignored him. "Forward," he shouted.

The orc group marched forward in the courtyard.

"One. Two. One. Two. One. Two," the Broken Lance trainer called out rhythmically while checking their footing and form. "One. Two. One. Two. One. Two. Stay. In line. Stay. In line. Pick. Up. Your feet. Stay. In line. One. Two. You. Are. Worthless. You. Are. Worthless. One. Two. Green. Skin. Bastards. Halt!"

The orc column came to a stop. One orc in the front rank stopped a step too late and stuck out like a sore thumb. The Broken Lance trainer darted to him and punched him in the gut. The orc stumbled over then forced himself to stand back up.

"When I call halt, you take one more step then halt," the Broken Lance trainer barked. "You stupid green skin. Get back in the line," he said pushing the orc back. "Forward!" he yelled again.

The orc column marched again.

"One. Two. One. Two. By. The Divines. I. Give up. One. Two. One. Two."

The orc who was punched stumbled and fell into the dirt tripping several others with him.

"Halt," the trainer shouted while he marched up to the fallen orc.

The trainer grabbed the fallen orc and smacked him across the face with his armored hand. The trainer then proceeded to punch the orc in the face multiple times until the orc stopped struggling against him.

The trainer dropped the bloodied orc and pointed at Del'Caf.

"You, take this sack of waste back to the barracks. Make sure he doesn't die."

Del'Caf nodded his understanding and scooped Kir'git up. He dragged him back to the wooden barracks while the rest of the column continued to do marching drills.

He threw Kir'git up onto his cot and found a rag to clean him with. He wiped the blood and dust off his face and out of his eyes.

"Kill me," Kir'git wept. "I am worthless, kill me."

"Stay strong Kir'git of the Urrah. This is but a drop in the moments of your life force. You must stay strong."

"I have no more strength," Kir'git muttered. "I will die here. I see my life force leaving me already. It longs to join my son in the great hills of the Urrah lands." Kir'git grabbed Del'Caf's arm. "I will challenge the Mouse man. He will kill this vessel and my life force will finally be free."

"No, you have more to do," Del'Caf asserted.

"I will not be their slave."

"Nor will I," Del'Caf stated. "We must keep ourselves. Even in this strange place."

"I am lost. I am lost," Kir'git kept repeating till he faded to sleep.

Del'Caf drew a blanket and covered his friend with it. He cracked his knuckles and walked out the barracks.

The column was still marching in circles. James and

his companions were eating and laughing. The cart, which leaves every day, was being loaded. And Mouse was sitting on a stone step, sharping his blade.

"I challenge!" Del'Caf yelled out. The whole courtyard stopped and looked to the single orc.

"I call Mouse to challenge for paper of safe travel. I challenge."

Mouse looked to James. James, chuckling, gestured towards the sparring circle. Mouse hopped up and entered the circle with a knife in hand. Del'Caf stepped into the dirt. He could feel his heart pulse in his ears. The sound was almost deafening.

A Broken Lance tossed a sword down at Del'Caf's feet. Del'Caf stepped over it and approached Mouse.

Mouse shuffled his feet effortlessly dancing around Del'Caf. Del'Caf held his arms in, ready to spring. The two opponents stared at each other for several moments as they circled the ring.

Suddenly, Mouse threw a concealed blade. Del'Caf barely noticed the movement in time but was able to dodge it. Mouse followed up with a charge. Del'Caf's instinct told him to leap back but, after seeing how human's fight, he overrode his instincts and jumped forward into the attack.

Mouse's blade missed Del'Caf's head by a hair's length. Del'Caf then grabbed the small human by the throat and squeezed with all his might. He could hear the spine bones crunch between his fingers.

Del'Caf dropped the body to the ground. James and the

others stood to their feet amazed. The trainer began to draw his sword in anger.

"Sheathe that sword," James barked. "Come here, orc."

Del'Caf approached James and bowed as they had been taught to do.

"No one has ever come so much as close to defeating Mouse," James stated. "Yet you killed him in less than a minute. How?"

"I didn't care about winning, only killing."

"Interesting," James said. "What is your name, and where are you from?"

"Sign the paper for Kir'git of the Urrah," Del'Caf stated.

James chuckled. He found pen and paper and scratched out a passport. "Here you are, Kir'git of the Urrah."

Del'Caf took the document, walked back to the barracks, lifted Kir'git onto his shoulders and walked back out into the courtyard.

He dropped Kir'git into the cart and secured him to the cart and the passport to his friend's belt.

"This is Kir'git," Del'Caf stated. "The papers are in his name, so only he can go."

The cart driver looked to James who was chuckling again. James noticed his blank stare.

"Go on," he told the driver. "You have a long trip ahead of you."

The driver mounted his cart and ordered the cart forward. Del'Caf watched as it left. Kir'git reached out a hand to Del'Caf as they exited the gate.

"Orc, come here," James said. Del'Caf obeyed. "What is your real name?"

"He is Warchief," an orc called out.

"Shut up," the trainer ordered.

"He is the spirit of our people," another shouted ignoring the trainer.

"I am Mur'grok," Del'Caf lied.

"That means 'no one' in orcish, correct?"

"Yes."

"So you are no one?"

"Here I am."

James looked to the column of orcs who are staring at Del'Caf in disbelief and pride.

"I highly doubt that," he replied.

> *Galsag had a power balance for many decades after the Great War. One scale held the Lord who was left after the slaughter of the conflict. The second scale held the guilds, which sprang from the thousands of roaming out-of-work soldiers. The third scale held the Prophets.*

> **History of the Guilds**
> **Elder Lighours**

The Guild King shifted uneasily in his chair, trying to find a comfortable position. The courtroom was filling as they waited for the prisoner, Natalia, to be brought from the City Watch.

An aide approached the king and handed him a piece of paper. The King's eyes quickly caught the Hall seal on the folded note. He broke the seal and read the note.

Red anger burned in the King's cheeks. He crushed the page in his hand. He glared up at the aide.

"Why was I not informed the Hall was taking the vote this morning?"

"A motion was passed to not wait for you, sire."

The King leapt to his feet. "Not to wait for me? I am the King, am I not? Am I not worth waiting on?"

"Yes, sire," the aide replied, lowering his head.

The Guild King returned to his seat, ashamed at his outburst. "Six votes," he muttered. "I was defeated in the hall by six votes. A single chilly night claims more than that... Six votes."

The court's side doors opened, and Natalia was brought to the center of the floor. A Prophet rose.

"Permission to begin, sire," he said.

"Go on," the King replied falling back into his chair.

"Thank you, sire." The Prophet turned to Natalia. "When did you know you were an angel?"

The crowd grew silent, wishing to hear the answers.

"I have always known," Natalia replied.

"When did you start telling people?"

"I never hid it," Natalia answered.

"If we were to cut you, would you bleed?"

"Yes."

"Why would an angel bleed?"

"This body is just a vessel, much like a clay pot. All pots are made of clay, regardless if one holds water and the other fine wine."

"So you are human?" the Prophet questioned.

"My vessel is made of clay just as yours is, but what is inside is vastly different."

"So you are different than the rest of us?" the Prophet pressed.

"Yes, very," Natalia replied.

The Prophet smiled brightly. "If it pleases the King, the court wishes to call one Thomas Smith to the witness box."

"It so pleases," the Guild King stated. The Prophet gestured and a simple-looking man, late in years, stepped up into the witness box.

"State your name for the court," the Prophet said.

"Umm, Thomas Smith, your worthiness."

"And what is your profession and home town?"

"I am a candle maker, your worthiness, from a village in Leominster."

"And do you know the accused, master candle maker?" the Prophet asked, being sure to project his voice to the whole of the courtroom.

"Yes," Thomas answered.

"And how do you know her, Mr. Smith?"

"Well," he mumbled. "She is my niece, your worthiness."

"Could you say that louder, Mr. Smith?"

"She is my niece," Thomas spoke up. Gasps spread through the crowd.

The Prophet turned towards the calm Natalia. "Who are her parents?" he asked Thomas.

"Henry Copper and my sister, Meg."

"So you have known the accused her whole life?"

"Yes," Thomas Smith answered.

"And what is her name?"

"Natalia Copper."

"Was there anything strange about your niece's birth?" the Prophet asked.

"No," Thomas answered.

"Were there any omens or prophecies about her, or that day? Any changes in the stars or sky?"

"No," Thomas insisted. "And I would have known if there was. I make candles for the Prophets in Leominster."

"What about when she was a child? Was there anything different about her childhood?"

"How so, your worthiness?"

"Did she preform any miracles or any other signs of the Divines?"

"Not that I saw," Thomas chuckled.

"Did she play with other children? Play with dolls? Get in trouble?"

"Yes, she was like any other child."

The Prophet leaned closer to Thomas. "Could you say that again?"

"She was like any other child," Thomas repeated, confused.

"Louder, sir!"

"She was like any other child," Thomas bellowed out.

The Prophet looked to the King. "Like any other child," he said in a booming voice. "Doesn't sound very angelic to me."

A silence deepened across the courtroom as the Prophet leisurely returned to the witness.

"When did she leave Leominster, Master Thomas?"

"When she was about sixteen years, I suppose."

"Did she have permission to leave?"

"No," Thomas laughed. "Most certainly not."

The Prophet turned to the crowd. "Does not the First Word say 'obey thy father in thy youth'?"

"I believe it does," Thomas responded.

"Why did she leave against her father's wishes?"

"She was pledged to marry a butcher's son."

"A butcher?" the Prophet asked nodding. "A good living for a commoner, yes?"

"Yes, your worthiness, a very good living."

"More than capable of providing a good life for her?"

"Yes," Thomas nodded. "He was quite the catch, in my mind. Her father was happy to make the deal."

"Why would the accused not wish the marriage?"

Thomas rubbed his hands trying to find his answer.

"Well, your worthiness, the butcher's son was not a pretty man, and he drank."

"Did the accused take offense to the deal?"

"Yes, she seemed upset."

"So she ran away?" the Prophet pressed.

"Yes," Thomas answered.

The Prophet turned to Natalia. "Did she ever claim to be an angel to you, Mr. Smith?"

"No," Thomas chuckled.

"So she did no healings in your village?"

"No.

The Prophet stared into Natalia's unchanged expression. "Do you deny anything your uncle has said?" he asked her.

"No," she replied softly.

"What was that?" the Prophet asked loudly. "Please speak up. They cannot hear you in the balcony."

"No," Natalia repeated louder.

The Prophet stepped back with a smug face. "So, Natalia Copper, you ran away from home. You disobeyed your parents. You didn't like the match they made for you, so you ran to Doraxe. Is that true?"

Natalia stayed silent. She looked over to her uncle. Thomas turned away from her gaze. The Prophet stepped between them shaking his head.

"Your silence answers for you," he stated. "Answer me this then, did you tell anyone you were an angel before you came to Doraxe?"

"No, I did not," Natalia answered.

"Why?"

"It was not yet my time."

"You mean you were not starving and alone; in need of a

con to trick people into feeding you."

"No, that is not..."

"Admit it," the Prophet snapped, pointing a harsh finger at her. "You are just a girl."

"No."

"A girl who was scared and lonely in a strange place."

"No," Natalia insisted.

"You are not an angel. If you were, you would have said it to your family."

"That is not how..."

"You are just a girl!" the Prophet yelled. "A girl who started telling the simple minded she was an angel so they would give her bread and shelter. Admit it. Confess your black mark!" he screamed.

Natalia flinched from the raw hate in his voice. A single tear fell from her eye.

The Prophet leaned in and shook his head. "I understand," he whispered. "Hunger is a powerful motivator. A person will say or do anything to make the hunger pains cease. You should be proud, not ashamed. Most girls in your position turn to whoring. You simply tried to give people hope. What is so wrong about that? But now it is time to confess. Tell us the truth."

Natalia lowered he head. "I pity you," she said looking up. "I pity all of you!" she yells.

"Sire, silence her," the Prophet demanded. "She is out of order."

"Your decadence has brought judgment on your own

heads," Natalia continued.

"Sire!" the Prophet protested.

"The accused will be silent," the King ordered.

"Common people," Natalia shouted. "You blind your-selves to rulers' black marks in exchange for comfort. When the judgment comes, do you believe it will fall only on some? No! All will suffer for your crimes.

"And to you nobles. You think your wealth and power was given to you for your own pleasure. But I tell you the truth, your riches and power were given to you to bless the people, not curse them. And just as the Divines have given, they can take away."

"Sire, this is an outrage!" the Prophet complained.

Natalia turned to the Prophets in their seats. "And to you false Prophets. You were charged with showing the world the Divines. But you have, instead, used your high calling as a license for gathering black marks. Therefore, the Di-vines have turned their backs on you as you have done first to them."

"Blasphemy!" Prophet Minor Thompson yelled.

"Blasphemy!" the Head Prophet joined.

"Blasphemy!" other Prophets screamed and shouted.

The crowd in the balcony erupted in protest. Guards struggled to hold them at bay. The Guild King stood to his feet. Natalia looked him in the face.

"And to you, King of the Guilds, I know your greatest secret, as does the Darkness you fear so much."

Justice is a cool drink to the righteous and bitter poison to the wicked.

The First Word
Harrowing 32:53

The road was cluttered with debris. A large wagon was flipped on its side, blocking the dirt road. The wind howled, giving life to a bonfire of supplies.

Sir Gregory rode up with twenty men. He slid off his horse and peered under a tarp covering the flipped wagon. The stench of the disemboweled guards was overwhelming.

"Damn it," Sir Gregory muttered.

Francis approached on his horse and gazed over the scene. "Are the supplies all..."

"Yes, just like the last one."

"This cannot continue," Francis declared. He pulled out his pipe and lit the bowl. "How can we rule this land if we fail to even control the roads?"

"These tracks are fresh, my lord," Gregory said. "They cannot have gone far."

"Is there not a village nearby?"

"Yes, my lord, there is."

"Well, I would wager they know something. They may even be aiding the raiders, wouldn't you say?"

"It's possible," Gregory stated. "What do you have in mind, my lord?"

Francis wiped the sweat from his brow and drew in deeply from his pipe. He blew the smoke out and sighed.

"I am thinking it is time to show these beasts who their master is."

The village was small – only a few mud huts and a pen of hogs. An old orc sprinkled bread and dry bones in the feeding trough. The hogs fought one another for the morsels.

The sound of horses galloping echoed over the horizon. The old orc looked up. A large troop of knights raced towards them.

Several children ran out to try to see the strange men in iron. A woman quickly snatched them up and hustled them back into a hut. The old orc stayed where he was as the knights entered the village.

Francis slid his horse to a stop, slinging mud up into the air around the old orc.

"I am Sir Francis Drako, steward of the orc lands. In the name of the King, the Divines, and their messengers the Prophets, tell me who attacked my caravan and murdered my men. If you tell me the truth, I will count you and your village innocent."

"There are no hunters here," the old orc stated. "We are women and young ones. I am the only hunter here, and I have not the strength to throw a spear."

Francis dismounted and walked to towards the old orc. Francis punched him in the gut. The old orc fell to his knees coughing.

"You will address me as 'my lord.'" Francis turned to his troops. "Search the huts," he ordered. The knights leapt off their horses and darted into the scattered mud houses.

The old orc struggled to his feet. The knights dragged women and young ones out into the open. They clustered them together next to the pigpen.

"The supplies aren't here," Gregory reported. "And there is no sign of the raiders."

Francis puckered his lips in annoyance. He walked past the old orc to the other villagers.

"Where are my supplies?" he yelled out. "Who killed my men?"

The orcs looked at each other confused.

"Who is attacking my caravans?" Francis screamed.

The orcs continued to stand in silence. Francis glared at them in frustration. He drew out his pipe again and lit up a fresh bowl.

Turning to his knights, he said, "Burn it down."

The old orc desperately tried to think of clever words as the knights moved to grab sticks for torches.

"My lord, please," he stammered out, using the few human words he knew. "We saw no hunters. By my life force." Francis did not so much as glance at the old orc.

His men lit torches and threw them at the huts. Flames danced from their source and soon engulfed the village. The women began to wail at the sight of their homes burning.

Francis drew in deep from his pipe and remounted his horse. His knights began to follow when Francis pointed to the hog pen.

"Sir Gregory, send a rider to fetch a cart. We are collecting these swine as restitution."

"No," the old orc cried. "We will starve!"

"You should have thought of that before you angered me," Francis barked.

The old orc grew cold. He suddenly roared and charged the unsuspecting Sir Gregory. The orc knocked him to the ground before he saw what was happening. The orc then dashed at the knights guarding the other villagers.

A crossbow dart pierced into the orc's back. He staggered before he fell into the mud. Francis held the spent crossbow. He slid back off his horse and reloaded his weapon.

"Are you alright?" he asked Sir Gregory who was recovering his footing.

"Yes, my lord."

Francis handed the crossbow to Gregory and knocked the ash out of his pipe bowl. He drew his personal dagger and caught up with the old orc who was desperately trying to crawl away.

Francis walked past him and grabbed one of the captive female orcs. She pushed and struggled, but Francis had a strong grip.

"You green skins don't understand," Francis yelled. "You are conquered. You live and die by my graces."

Francis slit the female's throat open. Blood, like red wine, spilled out of the large wound. Her eyes went wide before falling dark. She slipped to the ground dead.

The old orc clenched his teeth and buried his head in his arms as he sobbed.

"You pig whore!" a female orc screamed, charging her

guards. A knight quickly cut her down. For a moment, there was stillness. The orcs looked at their dead and dying. The knights stared at their captives.

Then in a fury of rage, the knights rushed the orcs in a chaotic brawl of sword and blood. They stabbed, cut, and strangled all in their sight. Blood and flesh sprayed up like water splashing when crossed. The sounds of the victim's cries mixed with the crushing of bones and the clashing of armor against itself. One young orc managed to escape the slaughter and run into the open prairie. Sir Gregory leveled the crossbow and ended her fanatic escape with a well-placed dart.

Francis turned to the elderly orc. He kicked him over on his back. He drew his sword as he stood over him. He pressed the tip into the orc's chest. The orc's eyes gazed at Francis as if he was dead already. Francis pushed the blade slowly down. Blood spat from the twitching body.

Francis pulled out his sword and wiped the blood off the blade. Sir Gregory leaned on a wood post to catch his breath. Francis calmly returned to his horse.

"My lord, what about the hogs?" Gregory asked.

"Leave them. No... Release them."

"Yes, my lord."

Sir Gregory went to the hog pen and kicked open the weak wooden gate. The hogs rushed out. They sniffed and snorted at the dead bodies littering the ground. They began to smell the orc's blood. Soon the drove of swine descended on the corpses. A hand was torn from its host and dragged to a corner to be feasted on. A face was gnawed on till the exposed skull was crushed between a pair of powerful jaws. One orc, still barely breathing, whimpered as the hogs ate out her intestines like a long rope of sausages.

The knights returned to their mounts and the whole company left the scene without exchanging a word about what they had just done. That eerier silence followed them all the way back to the road. Francis turned away from his knights and coughed several times. The coughs turned to dry heaves, which finished with vomit splashing the dirt.

"Are you alright?" Sir Gregory asked, riding closer.

"No, of course not," Francis spat. He gargled with some wine and spat it out. "We should send some men to clear the road."

"Yes, my lord."

"And increase guards on shipments. This shouldn't happen again."

"Yes, my lord."

"And we should..." Francis began. A knight's scream interrupted him.

Francis and Gregory both turned to look. A spear struck Francis' horse sending him to the ground before he even knew they were being attacked. Sir Gregory blocked a spear with his shield. A second tore open his horse's throat.

Francis frantically tried to get to his feet, but the dead beast had his leg pinned. He lied helplessly as a wave of charging orcs cut through his ranks. His knights attempted to fight but the hunting party was on top of them before their swords were even drawn. Francis could do nothing but watch as each one was torn from his mount and bashed, stabbed or gutted before his eyes. The whole company was wiped out in a matter of minutes.

The sharp edge of a skinning knife pressed on his neck. Francis was dragged out from under his dead horse and forced to his knees. A large orc stepped in front of him and ripped the steward sigil from his neck. Francis could hear the final scream of one of his men behind him before an orc cut his throat. The scream instantly turned into a gargling moan then silence.

"I am Oggrat," the orc before him said, "son of Sog'rim, kin of the Warchief, and I claim you, iron prince, as a hunt prize."

> *In Galsag history there have been seven assassinations of kings: one stabbing, two by arrow, three by poison, and one thrown from his window by a jealous mistress. Civil war almost always followed.*
>
> **History of the Guilds**
> **Elder Lighours**

The Guild King snored loudly. His head rested atop a stack of papers. His reading candle burned near its base. The night wind rustled the open window's curtains.

David entered the chamber. He closed and locked the door quietly behind him. David moved towards the Guild

King as silent as a whisper in the breeze. His boots gently embraced the wood planks with each step. He breathed slowly through his nose. He reached out a hand to the sleeping King. The Guild King opened his eyes.

"Sire," David said, recomposing himself.

"Trying to sneak up on me?" the King asked. "It isn't as easy as you think."

"Only checking on you, sire," David answered. "You have not slept much lately." He walked to the window and closed it.

"What time is it?" the King yawned while stretching in his chair.

"It is the third watch, sire."

"By the Divines," the Guild King grumbled. "That late?"

"I'm afraid so, sire."

"It is this damn case," the Guild King complained. "I must come to a decision, but no decision I make will be the right one. I don't know if she is an angel or not, but I know the people think she is. If I kill her, they may revolt.

"But if I do not satisfy the Prophets in this great matter, they may withdraw their support of my rein. There are still lords and guilds who would jump at such an opening. I have never been so tormented by a single girl.

"I am trying to find any break in the case. I had the Prophets send me all the testimonies of her sermons and healings. They were even so kind as to write footnotes of their personal opinions and interpretations. But as far as I can tell, she has never said anything false or heretical. Offensive, yes, but not blasphemy."

The King rubbed his forehead as David poured him a glass of wine. He approached the King with a cup in one hand and a dagger in the other.

"I have learned more theology this whole week than in my whole life," the King moaned. "The question is very simple though: is she an angel? That is the only charge with merit, but I can't prove she isn't. She said she knew my secret. But everyone has a secret, so it would not have been hard to say that to anyone with a similar effect. Yet something in her eyes told me she really knew. How is that possible?"

The King leaned back in his chair with his hand over his face in exhaustion. "I am the King, and I am afraid of a twenty-year-old girl," he laughed.

David approached closer with his knife behind him. The King took up a page and held a viewing lens to it. He strained at the small text. David stepped into arm's reach. The candle's flame flickered. The light shined on the viewing lens. The King turned it to reduce the glare. David raised the knife. The viewing lens caught the shimmer of the blade.

Without thought, the Guild King spun out of his chair and knocked the blade from David's hand. The blade flew across the room and landed by a chair.

David smashed the silver wine glass against the King's skull, knocking him to the ground. The King kicked in self-defense only to be grabbed by his attacker. David smiled before he hurled the king into the wall.

The Guild King scrambled to his feet. He grabbed a

nearby clay pot and swung it at David's head. David blocked the blow. The pot shattered on his arm.

The Guild King jabbed at David's ribs and smashed his elbow into David's nose. David stumbled back. The King then punched at David's head.

David ducked under the punch and hit the Guild King hard in the gut. The air was knocked out of his lungs instantly. The King instinctively pushed David away and wiped blood from his lips.

"What is this? Why have you betrayed me?" he asked.

David just smiled and charged the King. The Guild King jabbed and missed. David hit the King with a furious barrage of punches and strikes, finishing with an uppercut to the King's jaw.

The King was thrown off his feet and into a book self. Books fell around him. The King struggled to lift himself up but had not the strength. David calmly walked around the table towards the King.

In the corner of his eye, the King saw David's lost knife. He mustered his strength and leapt for it. Taking it in hand, the King spun up and sunk the blade deep into David's chest.

David looked down at the knife firmly in his flesh. He shook his head in disapproval. The King tried to twist the blade, but David snatched his wrist and, with a quick chop, broke the arm.

The Guild King screamed in pain. David kicked the King in the gut, shooting him back into the selves. The King gave one last attempt to stand back up but failed.

David pulled the blade from his chest and tossed it to the side. He then approached the King with a smile. The King grabbed a heavy brass candle stick holder and cracked it across David's face. The aide stumbled back a little, paused, and then twisted his head back to the King.

David's jaw was so badly dislocated the skin was stretched to the point of tearing.

"What are you?" the Guild King muttered in horror.

David casually reset his jaw with a firm push of the hand. He shifted it around a bit to test if it found the right placing. David's eyes turned blood red.

"Your reckoning," he stated.

"By the Divines," the King stammered, "you're a demon."

"In the flesh," David said with a bow, "so to speak."

"Monster," the King muttered. "Monster!"

David laughed and stepped forward. A loud knock from the door echoed in the room. David looked to the entrance, annoyed at the interruption. He strolled over to the bloody knife and took it in hand.

"It seems our time together has come to an end," he commented with what sounded like remorse.

"Sire," the guards outside shouted. "Are you alright? Let us in!"

David leaned over the wounded King, letting his face come near to his. "Time to die," he muttered.

The door flew open with a ball of fire. David leapt back in

surprise. Philipus walked in, an unnatural glow surrounded him. David, or at least the creature in him, growled and hissed at the Head Prophet. Philipus stood firm.

"You will not succeed here, demon!" Philipus yelled as flames formed around his fingers.

Philipus threw the fireball at David. Smoke and debris shot out from the impact. The heat was overwhelming.

Philipus looked for his target, but as the smoke cleared, he was not to be found. Philipus scanned the room with a calm expression. Several guards rushed to the King's side.

"Fetch the healer!" a guard screamed. "Hold on, sire, you are fine, quite safe now."

"It is still here," Philipus stated.

"What?" the guard asked standing. "Where?" A blade shot out of the guard's face. Philipus' eyes darted to the ceiling. The demon crawled across the marble roof like a spider. His skin was peeling off the bone from the fire blast.

"Mor tumtak spkinze tas griladabe," it hissed.

"Kilu timena," Philipus replied.

A stream of fire shot from Philipus' hands at the demon. The King cringed under the heat and flames. The demon's screams were deafening as it was consumed in flames. The entire room filled with the aroma of baked poultry.

> *Orcs were often misunderstood by the humans. Their ways seemed strange to them. Orcs eat what they kill. So when a trader saw an orc accidently kill a fellow orc, then proceed to eat him, it began the rumors of orc barbarity.*

History of the Guilds
Elder Lighours

Francis awoke to the wails of a man in the deep darkness. The moon hid behind thick racing clouds. The only light came from a large bonfire in the distance.

Francis pulled on his ropes. The bonds were tied to a post stuck in the ground. Not with three horses could he have broken them.

"My lord steward," the familiar voice of Sir Gregory whispered. "Are you alright?"

"Sir Gregory?" Francis muttered.

"It is me, my lord."

"Where are we?"

"I don't rightly know. The orcs carried us deep into the plains. No patrols venture out this far," he whimpered.

"How many of us are left?" Francis asked struggling against his ropes again.

"They took five alive, but they have already come for two and... they..." Gregory's voice broke, unable to finish. He took in a deep breath. "They did things to them, my lord. Things even the most twisted of murderers would never consider."

Francis strained his neck to look past Sir Gregory. There were four other posts in the ground; two were now empty. Francis laid his head on the wooden post and tried to think.

Three or four orcs emerged from the darkness. The knight next to Sir Gregory screamed and kicked at them as they cut his bonds. Francis could hear Gregory fight back tears as the orcs dragged the knight away. A blood-chilling scream resounded across the plain then the slam of an axe against a wood block. It was followed with silence. Francis could barely hear the other chops of the axe. It sounded as if they were cutting thin branches from a tree then twisting them free.

Silhouettes of orcs appeared around the bonfire. They were holding chunks of meat to the flames. Francis could just make out what looked like a turkey leg roasting over the fire, except this turkey leg had five fingers.

"By the Divines," Francis muttered.

"I'm going to die," Sir Gregory wailed.

"We are not going to die," Francis answered.

"We are going to die!" Gregory repeated, sobbing. "Death in battle is one thing, but no man should die like this, not like this."

"Get ahold of yourself, sir," Francis ordered in a harsh whisper.

Sir Gregory began to pray through his tears. "Father Divine, please kill me now. Spare me this pain. No man should be... eaten."

"Sir Gregory," Francis snapped. "We are getting out of

here. I promise you."

Gregory turned and stared at him blankly.

"How, my lord?" he asked. Francis lifted up his right leg and shook it until a knife fell from his boot. Gregory instantly sat up and stopped weeping.

Francis tried to use his foot to drag the knife closer but had little success. Gregory, with effort, turned his body and stretched out his leg. The edge of his heel hit the blade. After a few tries, he slid it behind Francis.

Francis gripped the knife handle and wiggled it out of its case. Spinning it in his palm, he started to cut through his ropes. Sir Gregory wrenched himself so he could see. Francis continued to wear on the ropes while watching the bonfire for movement.

One orc tossed a bone away and began to walk towards them. Francis held a stoic expression as the orc drew close. He could feel the ropes come loose as he worked through them.

"Iron prince in the flesh," the orc chuckled. He leaned down close to Francis' face. His hot breath steamed Francis' skin.

"You killed my kin, iron prince. Cut him down outside your stone house. Even after both his sons stained the dry grass in the valley. You took his life force. I will take yours." The orc smiled wide, showing bits of human flesh stuck in his teeth.

Francis drove the knife blade into the side of the orc's neck. The beast's eyes went wide as Francis twisted the blade and ripped it out. The orc fell over with a small fountain of blood following him.

Francis stayed still and waited for signs of movement from the camp. Francis rolled over to Gregory quickly and cut his ropes. Once free, Gregory checked the dead orc for weapons and found a small, bloody skinning knife.

The orc's fire faded into the night as the two humans frantically ran across the plains. Francis looked for any sign of their location, but the terrain merged into one formless prairie. Gregory fell to the dirt in exhaustion.

Francis stopped. "On your feet, Sir Gregory," he ordered. "We cannot stop here."

"I can't. I think my foot is broken."

"And my ribs are crushed, but we must go on."

"No, leave me," Gregory pleaded.

Francis grabbed Gregory and lifted him up. "I will not leave you," he said. "I will not."

Gregory looked up at his lord and nodded his head. He struggled up and tried to walk. He began to speak when a spear flew into his chest. His eyes grew dark, and he fell without a sound.

Dozens of orcs come from the darkness and surrounded him. Francis drew his knives and readied for battle. Oggrat stepped forward.

"Give up, iron prince," he said. "Fighting gains you nothing; not even a good death."

Francis grinned. "I may die here today," he replied. "But so will you."

With artistic grace, Francis threw his knife. The blade spun through the air like a falling autumn leaf. It struck Ograt in the chest. Blood barely had time to spray before the stunned face of the dying orc met the ground. The other orcs sprung forward. Francis leapt at them with a desperate cry.

Men of honor are few to find. Who can know the truth?

The First Word
Treasures 23:74

The Guild King cried out in agony as the healer pulled the sticky bandage from his pus-filled wound. The King bit down on a closed fist as the sores were drained into a pan.

Philipus stood watching over the healers. He waved them away once their work was done. He poured the King a glass and dropped in some medicine. The King saw him add things to his wine.

"What is that?" the King asked.

"Medicine, sire," Philipus explained.

"No, dump it out. I want wine. Plain wine. You," he said pointing to a random healer. "You will test it in my presence before I drink."

"Sire, all here are your friends," Philipus explained.

"No," the King interrupted. "Do as I say."

"As you wish." Philipus poured the wine out in the pan

and filled up a clean glass. He handed it to the healer. The healer looked at the cup confused.

"Go on," Philipus said. The healer took a sip from the drink.

"Drink more," the King ordered. The healer did so and began to hand it to the King. "No, wait. I want you to wait."

The healer held the glass out for several moments while nothing happened. The King then gestured that he would receive the glass. He took the wine and drank it in a single gulp.

"What attacked me, Philipus? Tell me true."

"It was a demon, sire."

"So they are real..."

"Yes, sire, very real."

"How did this happen? How could I have not seen David was a demon?"

"I don't believe he always was," Philipus explained. "Someone must have possessed him. Someone close to you."

"Who?"

"I don't know, but I will find out."

"Why would they attack me? Why now?"

"You have their leader in chains," Philipus said. "It is natural for them to attempt this."

"Leader? You mean Natalia?"

"Yes, sire."

"Call in Lord Duke Herrion," the Guild King commanded. An aide rushed into the waiting room filled with anxious

Guild Masters and other members of court.

Lord Beritor and Sir Snaca stood in a corner out of ear-shot.

"This is a disaster," Beritor whispered.

"Stay calm, my lord. No one knows anything as of yet, and if we are careful, no one will."

"You promised to make me king. How can that happen if the King still lives?"

"My master has a plan," Snaca stated. "I do not always know the details of it."

"Oh yes, I forgot, you are a dark lord's lackey. Nothing more!"

Snaca grabbed Beritor by the testicles. "Ease yourself, my lord," he said as he squeezed slowly. "We do not wish to make a scene." Lord Beritor clenched under the pain, slowly slumping over. He nodded his head in agreement and Sir Snaca released him.

"Lord Duke Herrion," the aide cried out. "Lord Duke, the king wishes to see you."

Herrion stepped out of the crowd and followed the aide back into the King's chamber. He bowed low before approaching.

"Yes, my king?" he asked.

"I have made my decision on the Natalia case. She is clearly guilty of blasphemy and fraud. She used her innocent appearance to trick the common man and has even, at times, tried to seduce her betters."

"Yes, sire," Herrion said mournfully.

"She will be burned," the King stated with a labored breath. "But I fear what the peasants will do when the flames touch her. Therefore you will expose her true nature so the commoners can see her as we educated men see her. You will purify her until she confesses her black marks. As Watch Commander, you have the resources in your dungeon."

"Sire," Herrion started nervously. "It is illegal to purify a woman in the way you are implying."

"She is no woman!" the King spat. "Have you not heard her? She is a worshiper of demons and a teller of lies. She is a witch, and she has just made an attempt on my life. She possessed my dear David and turned him against me. Who else has she possessed, Herrion? Who are my friends, now?"

"I am your friend, sire," Herrion assured. "I swear to you this will be done."

Herrion stood and left back into the waiting room. Umbra stopped him mid-way.

"How is the King?" he asked.

"He will live, I think," Herrion muttered. "That girl in my prison will not though. Excuse me, baron. I have unsettling work to do."

Umbra stepped aside and worked to conceal the rush of emotions Herrion's words caused. A hand pulled on Umbra's coat. Umbra turned, annoyed. Charles bowed politely.

"What do you want, Mesmer?" Umbra hissed.

"A word, my lord."

"I don't have time or desire to speak with the likes of you."

Charles nodded and stepped closer. "I know the plot against the King," he whispered.

"Who?" Umbra replied.

"Not here."

Charles drew back and motioned to the hallway. Umbra carefully followed the Mesmer. They walked out of the palace and into the garden. Scattered snowflakes fell on their heads.

"What is this?" Umbra asked. "What do you know?"

"A few days ago, Hall Master Frederick asked me to kill Guild Master Duncan. It may surprise you to know this, but I am not merely the King's artist, I am..."

"Yes, you are his token Mesmer killer. I know. What of it?"

"The King never ordered Duncan's death. Frederick was acting alone... in the King's name."

"Perhaps he does not like Duncan. I know more than a few who would agree."

"He wanted him silenced before the vote," Charles explained. "Someone is trying to set themselves up as regent. Someone who wanted to make the guilds see him as their protector, then kill the King and be voted in."

"Lord Beritor?" Umbra asked in a mumble.

"I fear so."

Umbra smashed his fist into his palm. "I'll kill him. I'll smash his head in with my bare hands."

"Noble of you, but you need proof, my lord. Proof from someone who is not close to Beritor."

"You believe Beritor is blackmailing Frederick?"

"I am betting his life on it," Charles said. "I know enough of his secrets to know it is possible. With his kill order on the bill's biggest supporter, I am certain of it."

Umbra weighed the facts quickly. "Repeat this to no one," Umbra commanded with a stern finger.

"As you wish, my lord."

TRUTH SPEAKS
9

There are many legends about the fighting skill of Sir Francis Drako. It is true most of them did not crop up until after his death, but even during his life, he was a hero of the blade.

History of the Guilds
Elder Lighours

Jayden wiped the sweat from his brow with a piece of cloth. The sun beat down on him and the large search party as they rode deeper and deeper into the endless plains. Jayden popped the cork from his wine sack and took a drink.

"Not so much, your worthiness," a sergeant with a scarred faced warned. He pointed a disfigured hand to the hot sun. "It is not yet midday, and you risk finishing our supply."

"Why is it so damn hot?" Jayden grumbled wiping his

brow again. "Is it not supposed to be nearing winter? Yet the chickens could lay boiled eggs in this heat."

"This is not Galsag, your worthiness. And it is certainly not North Galsag where soft skin daisies pretend to be men. Here the sun is hot, and the moon is cold."

Jayden glanced around the blank terrain. "How long have you been in the orc lands, sergeant?"

"This will be my third winter. I came here with the advance scouts before the army. I lived in Longlast before that; in the service of the Mead family."

"I hear Longlast is a hard place to live," Jayden commented. "I only passed through, but it left an impression."

The sergeant pulled on his reins and spat a brown spit in the grass. "Longlast is not a place for the meek or soft. Its people and lords are stubborn and short tempered. That's probably why Castle Hightower was the only castle never to fall to the Guild King in the North Wars."

The sergeant grabbed his wine sack and took a brief drink. He then tossed the sack over to Jayden who took another long drink.

"What are your impressions of the orcs, sergeant?" Jayden asked.

The sergeant wiped the remaining wine from his chin. "You mean what I think of them?"

"Yes," Jayden confirmed. "Your thoughts."

"They are capable enough. Hell of good scouts. We hired some when we first beat feet here. They know how to approach a position unseen, circle it and leave without a trace."

"And what of our search? Do you see hope for our Steward?"

"I'll find him; that I promise. What condition he is in when I do... I won't make claims on that."

"So you believe him dead?" Jayden asked in dread.

The sergeant scratched his nose in thought. "Well, it has been three days, and we are not sure where on their patrol they disappeared. In fact, no trace of any of them has been found yet. That means one of two things. They are lost, or ambushed... or both."

"Wouldn't we have found bodies if they were attacked?"

The sergeant shook his head. "No."

"Why? Are the orcs so respectful they would bury the dead?"

"Orcs believe one should eat what he kills."

Jayden's skin paled at the thought. "That's barbaric."

The sergeant shrugged. "Maybe, but it is their way."

"We found something!" a scout called out in the distance. Jayden bucked his horse and hurried to the source of the announcement.

The dismounted scout was squatted by the dying embers of a great fire. Bones and torn patches of clothes and chainmail were scattered in the grass. The decapitated heads of the missing knights lied in a single grotesque pile.

Jayden slid off his horse and half walked, half staggered to the scout. He felt something soft crunch under foot. He glanced down, raised his food, and saw the remains of a half-eaten hand.

Jayden rushed back to his horse and quickly vomited up all the wine he had drank.

"By the Divines," Jayden stammered out.

The rest of the party caught up to him. The hardy sergeant shook his head in disgust. The others looked away in nausea.

"What?" the sergeant barked. "You've never seen brutality before? Spread out! I want a full account of the dead and the missing. And find the steward!"

The men-at-arms snapped to their duty and began to search through the chaos. Jayden stumbled away, unable to bare the scene. He soon came across a line of wooden posts stuck in the ground. A single dead orc lied before one.

Jayden grasped the closest post to catch his breath and curse away his nausea. He felt his stomach turn again, and he prepared himself for more heaves of vomit.

While staring at the ground, Jayden noticed cut ropes in the dirt. He immediately looked up to the horizon. Dozens of scavenger birds were circling an area not far off.

Jayden moved towards it not sure if he wanted to know what he would find. As he approached, the scavenger birds swooped down and picked at the multitude of orc corpses lying in the grass.

In the center of the fray was Francis, covered in blood, holding a broken dagger.

Jayden approached carefully. He slowly reached out a hand to the motionless steward. Francis did not respond to

Jayden's presence.

"My lord," Jayden whispered. Francis remained motionless. Jayden moved to the front of Francis and slowly lowered himself to his knees.

"My lord, are you hurt?"

"They ate them," Francis muttered.

"I know, I saw," Jayden said glancing back towards the orc camp.

Francis lunged at Jayden and grabbed him by the sides of his face.

"You did not see," Francis stated with wide eyes. "You did not see. I saw."

Jayden struggled under Francis' grip. "Yes, my lord," Jayden managed out. "I understand."

Francis loosened his hold, and Jayden slipped out. "I killed them," Francis muttered.

"All of them?" Jayden asked looking to the orc corpses. "By yourself?"

"Fifty seven," Francis said. "There were fifty seven. It took me nearly six hours."

"My lord... I..."

"I killed them," Francis repeated. "And I enjoyed doing it."

> Great are the black marks on the man's soul. Who can bare them? Many are his evil thoughts, and horrid their effects.

The First Word
Treasures 163:3

"Herrion, I protest this violently," Sir Edward stated, walking next to the somber lord. "She has never done anything wrong."

"The King would disagree. He feels she was behind the plot to assassinate his person."

"I cannot state as to what the King does or does not know, but I know she is innocent. She had nothing to do with the assassination attempt. She is an angel of the Divines."

Herrion stopped abruptly and faced his friend. "Sir Edward, as a man who cares for your well-being, I will advise you to put such thoughts behind you. For my part, I will forget you uttered such treason."

"Don't do this Harry," Edward whispered. "This is the kind of black mark a man can never wash off – no matter what the Prophets say."

Herrion sighed. "You have not called me Harry since we were children."

"I have not felt such an urgent need to since we were children."

Herrion leaned upon the wall and grabbed his friend's arm for support. "I confess I stand at a crossroads," he said. "One path angers gods I am not sure exist. The other angers a king, whose wrath I know full well."

"Don't worry about the Divines, or the King's wrath," Edward continued. "Don't do it because it is wrong to do. Walk away, Harry. Walk away for your own benefit; for if you don't, your conscience will never give you a full night's rest again."

"If I do not do as my king wishes," Herrion sighed. "I will never see another night's rest."

Herrion pushed past Edward and traveled down the stairs to Natalia's cell. Two guards were waiting with chains.

Natalia rose to her feet when she saw him. "You are playing the Lord Duke again," she said staring at him.

"It is my rightful role," Herrion replied.

"I hope you find it worth it."

"I am here to oversee your examination," Herrion stated flatly. "The King of the Guilds, long may he reign, has found you guilty of blasphemy and fraud."

"And on what evidence does he present his case?"

Herrion pulled out a document, ignoring her question completely. "This is a confession of your many crimes. Sign it and you will receive a quick death. Refuse and you will be examined further. This is the best I can offer you. I plead with you to accept it."

Natalia smiled softly. "You are the second person this week to offer me a document full of lies to sign. The other promised to save my life with a stroke of the pen. If I would refuse it, why would I accept this?"

Herrion nodded. "I am humbled by your integrity. I wish more in this world were like you."

"You would only kill them as well," Natalia giggled.

"It would seem so," Herrion admitted. "Take her below," he ordered.

The guards opened the cell and escorted Natalia out. She did not resist or fight even as they led her into the dark torture chamber. The guards strapped her to a wooden table with iron chains.

Herrion took a small knife and gently cut open her dress to expose the skin. With his free hand, he brushed the hair out of her face.

"Sign the paper," he whispered. She shook her head.

Herrion stepped back and allowed a guard to approach with a hot poker. He hovered it above her face so she could see the glowing red tip and feel the intense heat.

"Sign the paper," Herrion said again, coldly.

"I will not," she replied.

Herrion nodded to the guard. The guard touched the poker on Natalia's inner thigh. She screamed and contorted in pain. Herrion suddenly pressed down on her and drew close to her face.

"You feel that?" he asked. "Did you feel how that was? I want you to remember this moment, because this is the best it will be. That was the kindest I get. It will only get worse from here... Will you sign?"

Natalia sniffed back her tears. "I will not." Herrion nodded to the guard again. He pressed the poker on her skin harder. Her screams could be heard down the halls. Herrion let her scream and the skin boil and burst off her leg before ordering the poker off and back into the fire.

"This ends when you choose it to," Herrion said. Natalia remained silent. He turned to the other guard in the room and nodded. The guard pulled down on a wheel and suddenly the chains locked to Natalia's limbs grew taut. He pulled down on it again and Natalia cried in pain as her joints were strained on the rake.

"Sign the paper," Herrion repeated.

"No," Natalia muttered. The guard tightened the rack again.

"Sign the paper."

"No."

The rack was tightened again.

"Sign the paper."

"I will not!"

The poker was pressed into her leg. She screamed with all her might. The rocks shook from its echo.

"Sign the paper."

Natalia could only manage the strength to barely shake her head. Herrion pounded his fists on the table.

"Sign the paper," he demanded. Natalia gave him no response. "Why won't you sign?"

Natalia turned towards Herrion with great effort. She moved her lips as if to speak. Herrion leaned in to hear. A brush of hope filled him that she had broken. That this would end before it became truly ugly.

"Tighter," she whispered into his ear.

> *The Master of the Hall should be a man of great integrity. He should guard the guild's right with his life and protect them always, as his solemn duty.*
>
> **The Guild Compact**

Frederick stuffed another shirt into a trunk and closed the lid. He rolled up his traveling blanket and ordered a servant to saddle his horse. The food on his table was quickly becoming cold, but he did not dare stop packing to eat it.

He heated a stick of red wax with a candle's flame. Blood like drops fell onto the folded pieces of parchment, pooling on the crease. He pressed his Hall Master ring into the cooling seals and sat them on his writing table for his successor to read.

He headed towards his door when he remembered something he wished to bring. He returned to his desk and looked for the ring the king gave all veterans of the Vycesie Expedition. He knew he would never be accepted in the Vycesie's court without it.

He jostled through the draws and cabinets, knocking his fresh letters to the floor. He looked under the stacks of papers he had long ignored, hoping he would rediscover his forgotten trinket.

Revealing nothing, he turned to the chest he was leaving behind and rummaged through it. As he searched through old clothes, he felt his finger hit a solid object. He slid it out on his finger and gazed at the simple gold ring with the king's mark flanking the engraving, 'Long into Night We Came, to Bury our Foes in the Dawn.'

Fredrick looked over the old ring with a smile. He slid it onto his right ring finger and knelt down to gather up his knocked-over papers and letters.

The door to his room was suddenly kicked in with a bang. Frederick jumped in surprise and tripped on his own feet, falling hard to the ground. Umbra entered wearing his armor, hammer in hand, and with Koll behind him.

Frederick quickly recomposed himself. "Baron Umbra, to what do I owe the honor?"

"No honor here, my friend," Umbra replied glancing at Frederick's packed trunks. "Planning a journey?" he asked.

Frederick nervously cleared his throat. "Yes, I am."

"To where, might I ask? And on whose authority?"

"The King wished me to visit the Vycesie. He has been pushing me to do so for months."

"Those plans are canceled," Umbra stated.

"Canceled? Why?"

"You bloody know why!" Umbra snapped.

Frederick loosened his collar. "I simply thought now would be an ideal time for a visit. To assure the Vycesie that nothing has changed, despite this tragic incident."

"I know who told you to do it," Umbra said coldly. "I don't know why, and I don't know who else."

"I really don't know what you are..." Frederick began. Umbra interrupted him with a backhand to the jaw.

"Who else was involved?" he shouted.

Frederick wiped the blood from his lip. "I don't know what you are..." Umbra smacked him again.

"Do not lie to me, Frederick. Our friendship buys me at least that. So don't lie to me."

"Umbra, I don't know what poison has been poured in

your ears but..."

"Why did you order Duncan murdered?"

"What?" Frederick coughed out. "I never did such a thing. Duncan is alive and well, last I heard."

"Yes, because the man you ordered to kill him came to me instead."

"And you would trust a Mesmer's word over mine?" Frederick shouted, infuriated. "They murdered your brothers. They are evil to the core. They corrupt everything they touch. How could you even listen to such lies?"

"Usually I would agree," Umbra said with a shake of his head. "But how did you know it was the Mesmer, Frederick? Lest you truly hired him."

The color drained out of Frederick's face. "Please don't torture me," he begged. "Anything but torture, I beg you."

"Names, Frederick. I need names."

"And I would give them to you, if I was not so afraid of the cost of doing so."

"Frederick, you have nothing more to lose. You only get to choose the amount of pain you suffer before death."

"They forced my hand, Umbra. They found things that would have lost me the King's love. You must understand – I hold nothing but care for the King."

"Names, Frederick."

"Promise me my family will be taken care of."

"You tell me the truth, and I will see to it your family is not stripped of land and assets."

"Give me your word," Frederick pleaded grasping hold

of Umbra's black cape. "Your word, sir."

"I give you my word."

"Lord Beritor."

Umbra nodded. "I knew his ambition knew no bonds. Who else?"

"I dare not say."

"You dare not hide it, sir. Your family's maintenance hangs in the balance."

"He is not a normal man, Baron," Frederick cried with tears rolling down his cheeks.

"Who? Not normal how?"

"He serves a darker master than either you or I could imagine. He has powers I could not dream of. I fear for your safety if you confront him."

"Who, man!?" Umbra barked.

"Sir Snaca."

Snaca knelt before the dark mirror and chanted his phrase again and again. The parts of small animals lined a triangle drawn in chalk with blood sprinkled in a circle. Snaca's chant grew more and more intense and frantic until the image of a figure began to appear.

Why do you call on me? It asked.

"Master," Snaca replied. "The King still lives."

Yes, the voice muttered.

"Master, if the King still lives, how can Beritor take the throne and offer you the proper sacrifice?"

He cannot.

"Master, I do not understand. I have done all that you have asked of me. Master, I need your guidance. The King is suspicious. He will see Beritor behind this. Beritor is no man of honor. He will give me up to ease his suffering. Master, I beg you to give me clarity."

Has Charles grown fond of the Mesmer girl? It asked.

Snaca was taken aback. Confusion brushed against his face. "Master?"

Has he grown fond of her? Has she grown fond of him?

Snaca thought for a moment. "Yes, master. I see them together often. Master, please. Give me your strength. They will come for me; do not let me be taken!"

No, the voice said. *You have served me well, Snaca. You have done all I require.*

"Master?" Snaca muttered, confused. The dark figure began to fade back into the mirror. Snaca, filled with panic, leapt to his feet and took hold of the mirror's frame.

"Master, don't leave me," he cried. "I have never questioned you. Don't abandon me here! Master!"

"I'm right here, Sir Snaca," Umbra said from behind him. "There was a time when I was your master, or so I thought."

Snaca turned and glared at Umbra unpleasantly. "You are not worthy to be my true master."

Snaca pointed his fingers at Umbra as if he expected something to shoot out of them. Umbra raised an eyebrow at the odd display. Snaca chanted something in a bizarre language and tried again – once more, nothing happened.

"My master has abandoned me," Snaca lamented, falling to the floor. "I am lost."

"Who is your master?" Umbra asked.

"I cannot tell you," Snaca stated indifferently.

"It will go better for you if you do," Umbra explained.

"I cannot," Snaca said. "For despite all the pain I am sure you will cause me, the torment my master could bring is far greater."

"Give me his name," Umbra ordered. "Or you will find out if our torment is comparable."

"You make a mistake to think of my master in terms like man or woman. He is neither and both equally. He is a darkness you cannot suppress. He is coming, and he will have what he desires."

"And what does he desire?" Umbra asked.

"Everything," Snaca replied. "He wants everything. And he will have it."

Some hold to the belief that orcs are somehow less mentally capable than humans. Of course, elves hold similar views of humans. And the gods, whoever they are, probably hold similar views of elves.

The History of the Guilds
Elder Lighours

"Humans are not the biggest or the strongest," James explained to Del'Caf while sitting next to a fire. James leaned over a map table and whirled the wine in his cup. "And we know it. So we use tactics and specialization of skills to augment our weakness."

"That is how you won in the valley?" Del'Caf asked peering at the maps. This was the third time Del'Caf had dined with the Master Trainer over the last month.

"Yes, exactly," James continued. "Your tribes have power and fight like devils, but you had little in the way of tactics or order. Your lines were not used to fighting horses so, instead of standing your ground and halting them, you let the cavalry in among you.

"Also, your people have little armor and no shields, which made you easy prey for the archers. Remember- no matter how strong you are, an arrow will still kill you if it strikes flesh."

"Cowardly way to fight," Del'Caf scoffed.

"Perhaps, Mur'grok, but victory has its own honor."

"Why do humans build stone homes?" Del'Caf asked. "And why must they be so tall?"

"You mean castles?"

"Yes."

James pulled a chart out of his desk and unfolded it on the table. A drawing of a castle's structure filled the page.

"Castles serve as choke holds. They also serve as secure supply depots and command posts. If one places a castle near a bridge, for instant- the bridge on a wide river, the enemy must cross his whole army there. Now you know where your enemy will be and can prepare. Half the battle is already won at that point.

"If an enemy is foolish enough to advance on a castle, you will have archers on the walls, stone drops on the gate and boiling oil near the ramp. Thus a much smaller force can defeat a greater force with ease."

"So how does one take a castle?" Del'Caf asked looking over the diagrams.

"There are only two practical ways to take a castle. The first is by siege." Del'Caf looked puzzled by the word, so James explained. "That is where you surround the castle with your men and cut off supplies. After a few months, the defenders will starve out and surrender."

"Do humans not believe in combat?" Del'Caf asked.

James laughed. "Not if we can avoid it."

"And the second way?"

"Tunnel under the wall and collapse it out from under them."

"Why not tunnel under and pour in behind the wall?"

"Because, it is not easy or safe to move large numbers through a tunnel."

"Then have them open the door."

"Yes, as long as the way to the gate is not too defended. You could rush your cavalry in and win a quick victory."

"Orcs would be good fighters in a castle," Del'Caf said. "Don't have to worry about marching or forming in line."

"Ha, orcs eat too much to survive a siege," James pointed out.

"Has your castle been sieged?"

"Castle Pearl? No, Castle Pearl never has been sieged. It hasn't held strategic value in centuries. It is the most out-of-the-way castle in Galsag."

"Then why build here?" Del'Caf asked.

"Well, back in the ancient times, this was the home of many slaves who mined the pearls in the cliff caves. You see, when the tide comes in, it fills the caverns that dot the cliffs. Then when the tide rolls out, it leaves hundreds of oysters and clams. You pop open these oysters and sometimes find a pearl in them. Thus how our castle got its name.

"The castle is still littered with hidden passages dug by slavers to reach the caverns faster. Now local workers come down from the beach and do the work."

"Pearl?" Del'Caf formed the word in his mouth.

"A pearl is white ball, considered beautiful and valuable. They are sold as jewelry."

"Ah, so they please your gods."

"I doubt the Divines care about our jewelry," James explained.

"Are they good omens? Do they protect you from spirits?"

"I doubt it."

Del'Caf shook his head. "Then why wear them?" he asked. "What purpose do they serve? Are oysters hard to kill?"

"No, they are little shells you pop open with a knife."

"Do they attract females?"

"In a way, females tend to wear them."

"I do not understand," Del'Caf stated.

James laughed. "Honestly, neither do I," he admitted. "Humans are strange. We place value on what is rare and lovely to the eye. If one human has more of what is rare and lovely to the eye, he is seen as higher than those with less. It is the way of things."

"Why do you teach me these things?" Del'Caf asked. "How do you gain by me knowing what a siege is?"

James scratched the back of his neck. "I must admit, my benevolence is purely selfish. I have been charged with training up a people I hold no fondness for into a fighting force worthy of the King. I have quickly realized I cannot do it without help.

"And in you I see a spark – a light, if you will. I see the potential for greatness that I do not see in other orcs. There is greatness to be had, Mur'grok, in this new world you have been thrust into. There is even a place for the orcs, if they take it.

"Whether our invasion was right or wrong is no longer an issue, the ways of your fathers are gone. I hope you understand that. Here, you must learn new ways and use them to gain favor and success.

"Only by pleasing the King will the orcs gain a future, and orc units who cannot even march have no future. I wish to teach you how to succeed, Mur'grok, so then you may lead the orcs here into success as well. Do you want that?"

Del'Caf pondered for a moment then nodded his head.

"Yes," he said. "I wish to find my place here, and then maybe one day I will live in my own stone house."

James laughed loudly. "Maybe, maybe, my friend, but first we need to talk about logistics and force marches."

ENDLESS PAIN

10

And the Divines poured out blessings on man, because of the great love they had for their creation. They showed them how to work the land and how to spread the seed. They gave them all they needed and more.

The First Word
   Summerset 42:28

"Dreams are funny things. They show us who we are when you strip away the lies. You are completely natural in a dream because you are not aware you are not supposed to be."

Jayden opened his eyes. The blurry image of his dead father drifted from memory. Jayden sat up in his large bed and shook the sleep off. He lit a candle and drew back his bed's curtain.

He was startled instantly by Francis sitting in a chair by

his door. Francis stared at him with empty eyes.

Jayden, recomposed, sat the candle down and cleared his throat. "Can I help you, my lord?"

"Sleep avoids me," Francis explained. He lit his pipe and drew in. The blue smoke floated to the top of the wooden hut.

"My lord, how much peace grass are you smoking?" Jayden asked.

"Too much, I know. It calms my nerves."

"Perhaps it is why you cannot sleep," Jayden suggested.

"No," Francis quickly dismissed. "It helps sometimes."

"Let me call the healer, my lord. Maybe he has a remedy not involving the pipe."

"Do the Divines love us?" Francis asked blankly.

Jayden struggled for words, not sure what to make of the question.

"My lord?" he forced out.

"That question has kept me up every night for three weeks. Do the Divines love us? I know they made us, and I even see how they work to bless us, but do they truly hold affection for us, or is it more a general hope for the best? Have we convinced ourselves they love us so we can hold on to hopeless faith that things will grow better if given time?"

Jayden recalled his lessons in the Academy. "The First Word tells us consentingly of the Divines' great love for man. It says, 'man was made just below the Divines and given their face.'"

"What of my knights," Francis asked leaning forward in

his chair. "I doubt they felt the Divines' love when the orcs were chopping them apart and feeding on the remains. If we are slightly less than gods, why are we so helpless?"

"They were knights, my lord. There is risk in such a profession."

"But why did those knights who prayed die, and I, who refused to pray, live?"

"Perhaps the Divines have a plan for your life. The Divines work in strange ways, my lord."

"Why would I be worthy of saving? I am a murderer, a coward and a thief. I did not deserve their favor. Only the Divines' love could have saved me, but why me and not those who loved the Divines? Do the Divines enjoy affectionless relationships with their creation?"

Jayden sighed. "My lord, I must admit I don't know. I know what Prophetic law teaches me to say to these questions but if pushed, I must admit, I don't believe a word of it.

"What I do know is that there is darkness in this world. Evil, some would call it. Others call it black marks. But whatever you call it, it exists. And when darkness dives into someone or something, it twists it. And what it was meant to be, it is no longer. It turns it into darkness, and the Divines are the cure.

"I am not the purest man alive, nor the most corrupt, but I know darkness. And I know all men have it in them just waiting to surface. My lord, with all due respect, I think your true question is not, 'do the Divines love us,' but is, instead, 'why is there evil in this world?'

"Personally, I believe this to be a foolish question. The world and all things in it are naturally evil. We fell from the Divines' good graces long ago. The crimes committed during the Great War prove it. The more interesting question is, if this world is fallen and hopelessly evil, why is there any good in it at all?"

Francis chuckled, amused at how his Prophet had turned the question on him. "Why?" he asked.

"Because the Divines love us," Jayden stated.

Francis laughed and drew in on his pipe. "You would make a better Prophet than you think."

"I had a wise teacher," Jayden said.

"And who was that?"

"Prophet Elder Lighours. Many call him radical, but I found his teaching moving somehow. I don't think I could follow his path. He angered so within the Prophets that they exiled him to Tilton. I think he works as a scribe now."

Francis stood to his feet and knocked out his pipe bowl. "I cannot bring myself to hate them," he stated. "The orcs, I mean. I want to hate them, but I don't. I felt pity on that chief I killed. Pity. Umbra would have felt none. He would do his duty without question or regret." Francis hanged his head in shame.

Jayden thought of comforting words. "I also pity them, my lord. Just as one feels pity for wild horses being tamed. But it is much better for us all if they are tamed. Imagine the chaos of thousands of wild dogs running about. It is time for change to come to these people."

Francis slowly nodded his head and filled another bowl of peace grass. "I will be leaving tomorrow. You will take command in my absence."

"Where are you going, my lord?"

"That orc chieftain who wants to eat our horses has found a whole field of peace grass. I am leading a team tomorrow to survey and harvest it. If the orc is telling the truth, I could retire on the profit." He paused as he walked towards the door and muttered, "And I just might."

> *I don't believe the Guild King was a harsh man. I believe he was a strong man in a harsh time. The crown is easy to judge with a pen, but fair harder to wear.*

> **The History of the Guilds**
> **Elder Lighours**

The Guild King, leaning heavily on his cane, limped on down the hallway. His heavy armor did not make the journey easier on his hurting body. His right arm still rested in a sling, and his leg still ached from the infected gash.

Lord Duke Herrion hurried to the King and bowed deeply.

"Is it time?" The Guild King asked.

"Yes, sire. The stakes are ready and covered in oil."

"Replace Frederick's wood with dry timber. I want him

to roast slowly. Beritor never hid his ambition, and for that I can at least respect him. But Frederick played my friend."

The Guild King stumbled slightly as he attempted a step. Herrion caught him and helped steady him.

"He was my friend for twenty years, Lord Duke. His betrayal hurts me more than any blow or wound. I elevated that man from nothing. I brought him into my household. I fought with him, Lord Duke. I fought with him. He has been my Hall Master for fifteen years; the only hall master we ever had. How could he do this?"

Herrion dropped again to one knee and lowered his head. "Sire, I must ask forgiveness for having relationship, sometimes close relationship, with these most horrid of traitors."

The Guild King smiled and gently touched the top of Herrion's head. "You and Beritor grew up together, did you not?"

"Now to my shame, yes, sire. We did."

"There is no shame in honoring lifelong friends, Lord Duke. It seems we have the distinction of being brothers in betrayal. Both of us have had dear friends backstab us. Your loyalty is not in question. I assure you. If there was any evidence against you, Umbra would have... Let us just say he never misses a chance to burn a highborn. You are forgiven, Lord Duke. Rise, you are embarrassing me."

"You are most kind, sire, but I'm afraid I must ask for forgiveness from his majesty again," Herrion stated. "I have failed to persuade the witch Natalia to sign her confession."

"After all this time?" the King exclaimed. "Have you used the proper methods?"

"Sire, I have examined and purified her with all the methods of man, elf, and Mesmer. Yet her resolve is still strong and shows no signs of breaking."

"Truly if there was any more need of evidence to witch-craft, this provides it."

"Yes, sire."

"Do you have the confession with you?" the King asked.

"I do, sire. I had hoped a public display would sway her."

"No, nothing will sway that witch. I see that now. Give me the document." Herrion drew the paper from his coat and handed it to the King. The King called an aide over and signed an X on the accused line.

"There, now it is signed. Burn her with the rest."

"Yes, sire," Herrion replied taking the page back.

The Guild King started to walk forward but struggled.

"Sire," Herrion began. "Is it wise to wear full armor while you are still injured?"

"The real question, Lord Duke, is would it be wise to not wear full armor while I am still injured. If this sad plot has shown me anything, it is that assassin's blades can be any-where. I must remain vigilant."

"Yes, sire."

The town square was filled with people. It was quite an event for Lords to be burned with a witch. The Guild King limped up the platform's steps refusing help from his aides.

Baron Umbra was waiting for him. The Guild King slid into his seat and caught his breath. Umbra sat in the much smaller chair to his left.

"How are you, sire?" Umbra asked.

"Healing, my friend. I am healing."

"It delights me to know. Will the Queen not be joining us?" Umbra asked glancing at the empty seat to the King's right.

"She abhors violence, burnings more so. Umbra, I owe you more than I can repay."

"For what, my king?"

"You uncovered this plot and exposed all its members before my bandages needed changing. You are a true friend."

"My only regret is that I failed to protect you from this malicious deed in the first place."

"None could have foreseen such black magic. We attacked the orcs to cleanse the south of demon worshippers. It seems to me now; we should have started in Doraxe first."

"Yes, sire."

"Umbra, I have been thinking."

"Yes, sire?"

"This will be the first time the Hall will be without a Hall Master."

"Yes, sire. According to the Guild Compact, the King must nominate a new one."

"And who would you suggest?" the Guild King asked.

"He must be impartial, to start. He cannot be of noble blood for the guildsmen would never accept him, but he must have a title, else the noble Guild Masters will reject him. He must be seen to be honorable but have your best interests at heart."

"I agree," the Guild King noted. "But he also must be a man who will take the duty seriously. The Hall Master is meant to protect the rights of the guilds after all. It is important the guilds feel protected. They are my base of power, always have been."

"I agree completely, sire."

"Which is why I am nominating you," the Guild King stated.

Umbra's face drained of color from shock. "Sire, no. I..."

"You are the natural choice, Umbra. Accept it."

"Sire, I would be seen as too much your supporter. They would never accept me."

"Anyone who has campaigned with us knows you are more than willing to correct me when I am wrong. You would fulfill your duty."

"Sire, I plead with you to not do this," Umbra stammered. "I am your man, you know this..."

"All the more reason to nominate you. My friend, with your every word you convince me you are right for the job."

"Sire, I plead with you..."

"Enough," the Guild King harshly stated. "It is done. It will be put before the Hall tomorrow. You will be accepted. I made sure of it."

Umbra lowered his head. "Yes, sire," he whispered.

"And the first order of business in your new office will be to present my tax bill to the hall again. It is obvious to me Lord Beritor poisoned the Guild Masters against their conscience to oppose it. I need that bill passed, Umbra. For the sake of the kingdom."

"I understand, sire."

The crowds roared as the prisoners were dragged out into the streets. Guards pulled each prisoner by chains clasped to their wrists. All except Natalia, who was carried in a simple chair, having had her limbs all pulled from their sockets on the rake.

Frederick wept aloud as they went. Beritor cursed at the crowds as they flung rotten food and mud at him. Snaca walked lost in himself, oblivious to his surroundings. The guards led them up the stone steps and latched each to their own post.

Frederick looked to the King. "Forgive me!" he yelled out.

"Die like a man, you fool," Beritor snapped back before turning to the crowd. "I am Lord Beritor, and I spit on all of you! Your blood is not worthy of my dogs. You and your king can go to hell!"

Herrion walked up the steps and unrolled a scroll. "Lord Beritor, Sir Snaca, Hall Master Frederick and Natalia Copper; you are hereby found guilty of high treason, of witchcraft, and of conspiracy and envisioning the King's death. For these crimes, you will burn until dead. Your ashes will then be buried and laid with salt, so your spirits will trouble us no more."

"Divines protect the King!" Natalia blurted out. "And long may he reign."

"Long may he reign," Umbra muttered to himself.

Head Prophet Philipus blessed each of the accused and prayed for their black marks. Then, with a nod from Herrion, the guards lit the wood piles under each prisoner. The crowd cheered as the flames caught onto their clothing. Beritor let out a horrid scream. The fire grabbed at his hair and face, eating away at it.

Frederick's wood burned slow and the heat rose on him more and more. The crowd watched as his face drew pale with fear, and then his eyes bulged and his head dropped from his heart stopping suddenly. Neither Snaca nor Natalia made a sound as the flames consumed them.

Lord Victor Drako sat on a padded chair on a separate platform away from the king and crowd. He watched with a smile as his rivals burned.

Charles came near him and bowed graciously. Victor beckoned him up and offered him a seat.

"Sit, my friend. You have done better than I could have hoped. Perhaps now the fools will think twice about questioning our authority. My family will be royal for a thousand years. That is assured now."

"My lord," Charles muttered so no other could hear, "you know I am completely loyal to you and your family. The blessings they have placed on me since you brought me in from the streets of the Free City..."

"You have more than repaid my kindness today, Charles. More than repaid."

"My lord," Charles said with a tremble in his voice. "I..."

"What is it?" Victor asked, turning his attention to him.

Charles drew a folded scroll from his coat. "I was given this document, my lord. I bring it to you now only because I have confirmed its truth in the royal records. Please do not turn your kindness to wrath on the simple messenger."

"What are you talking about? Give me the note," Victor demanded taking the paper from him. He opened it and quickly read it. His cheeks turned red in anger.

"My lord, I..." Charles began.

"Leave me," Victor ordered. "Leave me to think on this."

"Yes, my lord," Charles said slipping down the steps and back into the crowd. A man in a black cloak and a large hat handed Charles a purse of gold as he passed.

> *If a man has a child with a woman, not his wife, that child is forfeit of all rights under the father. He is a disgrace to the man's rightful wife and a dishonor on the father.*
>
> ***The First Word***
> ***Harrowed 7:25***

The Guild King fell into his sitting room couch. The Queen washed a towel in cold water and touched it to his forehead.

"I told you not to wear your armor to the execution. You are burning up, husband."

"It is important people see me as strong," the King counted. "Besides, I have no desire to be in public without protection."

"A company of royal guards was with you."

"That is not enough," the King declared slapping his wife's hand away from his forehead. The cool towel fell to the floor. "I will not be outside my chamber without armor on. And I will have a different aide help me every day. I will not suffer another attempt on my life."

"Husband, you are not being..."

"I am the King! Not just your husband. You will call me sire, or your majesty. I am the state, and the state is I. I speak for the state and lead it."

"As you wish, your majesty," the Queen stated rising to her feet.

The sound of arguing voices rang out from beyond the closed door. The door flew open and a furious Victor marched in with a nervous aide behind him.

"Sire, I tried to stop him, but..."

"It is alright, we will see him," the King stated.

"We?" Victor scoffed. "How appropriate you would now refer to yourself in the royal form as the old kings did." Victor tossed a leather bond book onto the table. The ancient royal seal was pressed into its cover. The Guild King and Queen recognized it instantly. Victor noticed their reaction.

"Good, you know it. Then we can skip the lies and dive

to the truth."

"I don't know what you are talking about father," the Queen protested.

"Of course you do, my dear. You know damn well what I mean. This document is the report of four different healers. It was written in the years after your wedding to our most 'noble' king. You used the old seal so it would not be noticed. I thank the Divines the plotters did not kill you. It leaves me the privilege."

"I will not be spoken to..." the Guild King began.

"I will speak to you however I please!" Victor screamed, his face so red the Queen thought he might exploded.

"Guards!" the King yelled.

"No!" the Queen pleaded. "Majesty, please."

"What?" Victor asked. "Are you offended? Good, then you can grasp at how I felt when I read the report that my daughter's womb is as barren as the desert and always has been!"

"Father, stop."

"When I agreed to marry my daughter to you, it was on the promise my grandchildren would be the royalty they rightly deserve."

"They are," the Queen cried.

"I have no grandchildren!" Victor snapped. He shook his head at his daughter as tears began to roll down her face.

"You knew about this." he stated. "You condoned your king and husband lying with loose women and then present-ed his bastards as your own? How could you? Do you have no shame?"

"The balance of power in Galsag has always been delicate," the Guild King explained. "Without an heir, the guilds would have fractured. We made a decision for the betterment of the whole."

"What of my heirs?" Victor barked. "What of this kingdom? Do you have so little honor that you would put a bastard with no royal blood on the throne?"

"Father, we did what was necessary. Difficult, but necessary."

"You, my daughter, are the worst kind of woman," Victor spat. "I cannot even conceive how you... I wish I could call you a whore, but at least whores have offspring! Bastards though they be!"

The Guild King struggled to his feet. "That is enough, Lord Drako. I understand your anger. What was done was done for the sake of peace. I hold no regrets."

"No regret?" Victor asked chewing on the words. "I will make you regret this insult. For twenty years we have been allies by the marriage of my daughter. But since you have made no heir with her, I consider all agreements between us void."

"Father, you are talking about war!"

"I'm not talking about it! I'm declaring it," Victor snapped.

The Guild King grew silent and cold. "Sir," he said in a whisper, "you are beginning something you do not understand. I am a warrior king with many campaigns to my name. If you wish for war, I will give it to you. But be warned, money will not save you from my swords."

"Sir, you may not think highly of my martial skills, but I assure you, this war will be your end."

Victor stormed out of the room pushing aides out of the way as he went.

The Guild King fell back into the couch and sighed. "How I longed to have peace in the twilight of my years, but when I start to rest and feel the comfort of my own bed, the Divines remind me I am a man of war and always shall be. Aide!" he yelled out.

A young man rushed into the chamber. "Majesty?"

"Call what is left of my inner council, and call the Hall together. I must ask them to declare war."

The winds of change turn on a man as fast as fortune leaves him.

The First Word
Treasures 41:36

Raven brushed her hair with a fine comb. Her days in the palace had become increasingly boring after the assassination attempt on the King. Raven's mother had ordered a double guard on her and regular checkups during the night. She said it was in the name of security, but Raven suspected someone had told her mother about her outings.

The entire city was abuzz after Victor's sudden departure and the calling up of volunteers for the King's army. There was also talk that the guilds would all be assembling at the city soon, something that has not happened since the North Wars.

It is said that soldiers make for poor neighbors, and Doraxe was about to have one hundred thousand of them at their door. A disquieting thought. War, it seemed, was inevitable, and yet all Raven could think of while she combed her hair was the site of Charles gazing at her exposed skin while he painted her.

It had been weeks since she had last seen Charles.

The doors to Raven's chambers opened and several servants entered with boxes and flowers. Lady Edoweyhn was close behind them with an impeccable grin upon her face. The servants laid the boxes on the table and left the room closing the door behind them.

"What are these?" Raven asked gesturing to the boxes.

"Gifts," Edoweyhn explained. "I can't imagine you have been living pleasantly of late and thought these could be a small step in apologizing."

Raven approached the boxes and opened a few. They were filled with fine dresses and jewelry. Raven lifted one beautiful gown from the box with a giggle.

"Oh mother, this is gorgeous."

"The finest craftsmen used the finest silk to form it," Edoweyhn explained.

"I can tell," Raven said holding it against her body and viewing herself in a mirror. "It feels perfect against my skin.

Oh mother, thank you."

"I am happy you like them," Edoweyhn said with small laugh of pleasure at her daughter's delight.

Suddenly Raven stopped and sat the dress down. "You pledged me to the prince, didn't you?"

"You say that as if it is a bad thing," Edoweyhn laughed. "The Guild King sent over the signed contract a few hours ago. He even conceded to all our demands. He must have become desperate. I know not else why he would agree to pay the dowry I asked for."

"What did you get for me?" Raven muttered somberly.

"Don't be like that," Edoweyhn scolded. "This is a happy day. I doubled the Free City's holdings today. The King promised me all of Eye and Chimgham, plus a sum of fifty thousand gold coins. He even added the trade city Anchor to the North. Can you imagine? The riches of that town alone are more than measure."

"Eye? Anchor?" Raven mumbled. "Mother, those are Lord Victor's lands."

"Yes, I know. But it seems the Guild King plans to confiscate them soon. The King and his father-in-law seem to have had a falling out."

"That will mean war!" Raven exclaimed.

"Almost certainly," Edoweyhn stated flatly. "All the more reason to finalize your wedding."

"Mother, Victor's armies are only a few days march from Mesmer City."

Edoweyhn laughed. "My sweet, if there is anything I

know about Lord Drako, it is that he will never attack the Free City. He depends on our trade too much. Plus, I intend to strike first. I have already sent orders for the fourth army to march on Anchor. It is the prize, after all."

"Does this mean conscriptions will be announced?"

"Almost certainly, we will want to defend our new holdings. Power is vital in this changing world, my love. And territory and money are power. So I intend to grab as much of it for the Mesmers as I can."

Raven sat back down and started to brush her hair again. Edoweyhn fiddled with the jewels her daughter no longer showed interest in.

"I will be leaving tonight for the Free City, to prepare for the campaigns and any assistance the King requires."

"You are making our people servants of the Guild King," Raven stated harshly.

"I am preserving our future. The Free City has always survived by good political policy."

"Then why tie us to a kingdom always at war?" Raven shot back. "How is that good political policy? How does that preserve our future? The Guild King will drag us into this destruction. We should have nothing to do with it."

"We cannot live on an island any longer," Edoweyhn explained, annoyed. "Playing both sides no longer works when there is a clear winner."

"Is there a clear winner?"

"The Guild King has the support of the guilds. He massively outnumbers Lord Drako. Victor is being a fool to fight him."

"And what if you are wrong?" Raven asked. "What if the guilds stop supporting the King? What if Victor is not as much a fool as you think?"

"Stop this," Edoweyhn exclaimed. "It is a pointless debate. I have decided. You will stay here with your future husband. I love you. I will see you in a few months for the wedding."

Raven laughed. "Is the prince even old enough to have an erection?" Raven mocked.

"He soon will be," Edoweyhn stated. "And you will bear him many sons and join our peoples forever. Then there will be peace, forever peace."

"You are wrong, mother. As long as lords and kings rule there can be no peace. And you are a fool to corrupt our republic by allying yourself with them."

Edoweyhn shook her head. "How many times do I have to explain this? The Guild King's legitimacy comes from victory in war. The young prince will need legitimacy. How long can he hold the strong-willed guilds together without an enemy to unite them? The young prince will betray an ally when he comes to power. I aim for it not to be us."

"Sell me off like a whore if you want, mother," Raven scowled. "But it will still be us."

Friendship is such a vital thing. There is no doubt in my mind that the strength of the guilds in the North Wars was the friendship between Umbra and the Guild King. There is no greater commodity to a King than trust, and the Guild King trusted Umbra. I believe he trusted and loved Umbra above all others, right up until the end.

History of the Guilds
Elder Lighours

Umbra walked down the hall of the palace. The guards escorting him broke away as they neared the King's chamber. Umbra opened the door himself. The Guild King raised a firm hand at him to stop him where he was. The King walked to his armor stand and strapped on his chest plate before approaching Umbra and sitting at a large table. Umbra followed.

"Is the armor really necessary?" Umbra asked.

"Victor's spies are everywhere," the Guild King said. "I cannot be too careful."

"But surely when it is only me in the room," Umbra began.

"David showed me that even my trusted friends can be turned, against their will or not. I have had too many betrayals of late to drop my guard. Now, how is my new Hall Master this fine day?"

"Overwhelmed," Umbra admitted. "I have been doing my best to coordinate with the guilds to raise a force against

Victor. I have accepted Sir Conner as Lord Beritor's replacement and I have set up the vote on the tax bill for tomorrow."

"You gave Sir Conner the Sword Brethren? Why did you not confiscate the lands for the war effort?"

"The Guilds have the right to vote for a Guild Master's successor. Having found no evidence of knowledge or involvement in Beritor's plot, I saw no reason to block his installment."

"You could have found evidence, or made it," the King growled. "The taxes from those lands could have kept an army fed and paid for a year, and you gave it over to a man who may try to pick up where his master left off."

"Sire, I highly doubt..."

"Oh, forget it," the Guild King dismissed. "It won't matter after the vote tomorrow anyway. I will gain rights over the taxes and be able to raise the needed fund that way."

"Sire, about the vote," Umbra started carefully. "I am not convinced it will hold."

"It had better hold," the King exclaimed. "Without those powers, we cannot wage effective war against Victor. The Guild Masters will see that, you will see."

"I pray it so, sire, but I cannot see this bill being popular even after the treasonous plot was washed out."

"Selfish fools," the King grumbled. "I should throw them all in jail. What kind of world is it when half the Hall was shaking hands and being friends with a traitor? No, they will not vote against this bill out of fear."

"Fear of what, sire?"

"Fear of seeming disloyal," the King explained. "It is the duty of every guild to support the kingdom and their king. A vote against this bill is a vote in favor of Victor, and I will treat any who vote against it in such a way."

"Sire, it is the right of the guilds to vote without fear of reprisal."

"Don't preach to me on guild rights," The Guild King demanded. "I am tired of everyone complaining about their rights. The only rights they have are the ones I gave them. Before me, the only rights a man had was won by his sword."

"And if the Hall does vote down the bill, sire?"

"They won't."

"Yes, but if they do?"

"I am the King. I will do what is necessary to protect this kingdom from any and all threats."

"Even at the cost of our honor?" Umbra pressed. "We made a compact, a covenant with the guilds, guarantying their rights and privileges. Sire, it is the solemn duty of the Hall Master to protect the guilds."

"It is your solemn duty to serve your king," the Guild King corrected, harshly.

"Sire, I pray the bill passes, but if it does not, you must obey the law. The law is what took us out of chaos. It lifted us up and made us a nation. No person, even the king, is above our law. That is how it was designed. Not even the Divines go against their own law."

"The Divines never had to rule a kingdom," the Guild King scoffed. "All that I do, I do for the betterment of the people. Anyone who cannot see that is my enemy. I have worked too hard and too long to have my kingdom undercut by traitors, and selfish rebels, who want nothing but to destroy all order and justice in this realm. The Guild Masters will support me because my cause is right, and they have always put the kingdom first. Tomorrow, they will do so again."

"I will pray for your success then," Umbra stated standing.

"Hold your prayers, dispense some money instead."

"Are you suggesting I bribe Guild Masters, my king?"

"Of course not, I am suggesting you reward them for their loyalty to the crown."

"Yes, my king." Umbra replied somberly. He closed the door behind him and headed down the steps when he was blocked by Philipus.

"My lord," the Head Prophet said.

"Your worthiness," Umbra replied trying to walk past. Philipus pushed closer to stop him.

"I want to congratulate you on your new position."

"Thank you, your worthiness."

Philipus looked at Umbra coldly. "And remind you of your duty."

"I need no reminder," Umbra hissed back.

"Good," Philipus stated. "Because if it were to ever be revealed that you were in fact a member of the Divinities, a follower of the witch Natalia, it would not be good for you. But I am sure after the bill is passed tomorrow, all will be forgotten."

"Is that a threat, Head Prophet?"

"No, Hall Master. It is a statement of simple fact."

RIGHTS
OF KINGS

11

One hunt is enough. Two hunts are plenty. Three hunts is greed.

Orc Proverb

here was no wind on the prairie. The former night's frost clung to the grass like dying hands. The hills glittered like broken mirrors scattered on the ground.

Francis rode on his horse with little appreciation of the wondrous view. A lit pipe was firmly held between his lips. Chieftain Mur'kog walked beside the steward with a smug certainly.

"How much further?" Francis asked.

"Not far," the orc replied.

"Why did you not find this field before?"

"It is not in our hunting path. My scouts never walked

there till now."

"I see."

"Why do the iron men want peace grass?" Mur'kog asked.

"What did the orcs use it for?" Francis asked drawing in on his pipe.

"Only a Shaman would smoke as much as I see iron men smoke."

"And why would they smoke it?"

"Hard to know Shaman's thoughts. They are not normal orcs. They are the orcs who have found truth in life. They call the stars friend and the ground mother. They know the deep caves and eat raw flesh without growing ill. They mastered all but lead none."

Francis nodded. "I have been curious on this issue, and since all the Shamans are now without a tongue, I will ask you. What do they do in your culture?"

"They guide."

"Guide how? You said they didn't lead."

"They guide the tribes to understanding. They hold the stories of the tribes. All life force comes from Shaman."

"If the Shamans were the keepers of your history, why would the Warchief agree to the peace settlement? Have you not lost your history now?"

The orc shook his head slightly. "Every generation has a Shaman who rises above his beginnings. He becomes more than a guide. He becomes the soul of the tribes. He becomes the heart of our people. As long as he lives, our history is safe."

"And did this Shaman already present himself to our knives?" Francis asked.

"No," the chieftain stated flatly. "Nor will he. He will die first."

Francis laughed. "That can be arranged."

"It is just over the ridge," the orc chieftain pointed. Francis bucked his horse and sped ahead. He came over the ridge and halted his mount.

Terror filled his veins.

The field was filled with orc hunters. The old Warchief stood by a large pit.

The cries of Francis' men rung out as they were ambushed and destroyed behind him. Francis dared not look or turn to help. He knew they were doomed, and so was he. He would not be as lucky as the last time he was in the orc's company.

Those of his men, who were not killed, ran off into the open plains with orcs chasing after them. They would not get far.

Francis tossed his pipe aside and drew his sword. "Just you and me, Warchief? Good! I have always wanted to see you fight."

The Warchief slowly tore open his shirt to expose the distinct tattoo pattern of a Shaman. "Today my people will be free from you, iron prince. Today I will reclaim my right as spirit of the tribes. Today I avenge all you have killed."

"Today you die!" Francis yelled charging his horse at the

Warchief.

The Warchief rushed towards Francis and his mount. He reached out, grabbed the horse's head, and twisted it until the neck snapped. The horse collapsed under Francis, sending him flying to the ground.

Before Francis could return to his feet, the Warchief took hold of him and threw him like a stick. Francis landed in the dirt with a crunch. He fought to push himself up. Blood dripped from his nose and mouth.

The Warchief brushed his white hair from his face and approached. Francis struggled to his feet and struck at the Warchief with all his remaining might.

The Warchief took the blow to the face, but his head barely moved from the impact. The Warchief grabbed Francis' head and drove his face into the ground. Francis let out a pain-filled grunt.

The Warchief stepped away from Francis and watched the proud steward try to crawl away. After a few moments, the Warchief took Francis by the leg and dragged him towards the pit.

Francis kicked frantically with no effect. The Warchief lifted Francis up by the neck and hung him over the dark hole.

Francis began to laugh hysterically. The Warchief raised a confused eyebrow.

"What amuses you, iron prince? Do you find death funny?"

"No," Francis forced out from under the Warchief's grip.

"It is just that I don't trust orcs."

The Warchief shook his head, not understanding. He began to loosen his grip on Francis when an arrow pierced into his ribs. The Warchief looked to the smiling Francis in surprise. More arrows flew across the plain as a second company of mounted knights rushed to their steward's rescue.

The Warchief stumbled from his wound and lost his footing on the pit's edge. He slipped and fell into the hole with Francis still in his grip. The sounds of battle echoed above them as they fell into eternal darkness.

Right is it to stand by the Divines against an unjust case. Good is the man who dies on principle.

The First Word
Treasure 43:87

Umbra stood nervously before the assembled Hall. The sigil of Hall Master felt strange on his neck even after wearing it for weeks. Koll sat in the Broken Lance's chair acting as his guild's voice in his stead. The Guild King rested in his place of honor waiting eagerly.

"Guild Masters," Umbra called out with as much confidence as he could muster, "I call the Hall to order and recognize the King of the Guilds." Umbra gestured to the King. "Sire."

The Guild King rose with the help of his cane and cleared

his throat. "Guildsmen, our most honorable father-in-law has betrayed us. He has betrayed you. He has gone back on his word. His pride led him to defy us and, we believe, even plot to kill us."

The Hall filled with whispers and murmurs.

"Furthermore, he has declared our reign illegitimate, and our princes bastards."

"How dare he!" a Guild Master called out.

"He wants war; he has it," another shouted.

"Yes, my friends. It pains me to think of our most beloved ally has turned against us. But we will not allow such affronts to our person and issue to go unanswered. Therefore, I call Lord Drako to be declared rouge, stripped of title and land."

The Hall stomped its approval.

"We also move for all the guilds to be gathered with post haste so we may march against him and defeat him before he draws this country into war yet again."

The Hall continued to stomp.

"We also move that the tax bill, which was so foolishly and deceitfully discarded, be passed to assist in this war effort."

The stomping stopped. Guild Master Duncan rose.

"Majesty," he began. "That bill has already been voted on and decided."

"That was when this Hall was lead and filled with traitors and sorcerers," the King explained.

"Yes, but your majesty, it is not proper to propose a bill

that has already been voted on."

"These are extraordinary times, my friend. Proper protocol is not as vital."

"We will bring the issue to a vote," Umbra declared. "Which is allowed if there is reason to believe the first vote was somehow corrupted. Having several members of the Hall found guilty of high treason constitutes corruption, would you not say Master Duncan?"

The Hall laughed.

"Yes, Hall Master Umbra. I will agree that constitutes corruption."

"Very well, the bill is to the Hall. All in favor of the King's tax bill?"

Hands went up and were counted. The Guild King limped to the table were the bill laid ready to be signed by him upon approval. He released a sigh of relief, feeling confident he would carry the day.

"All opposed?"

Again hands rose and where counted. After a few moments, the aide handed Umbra the result. The Guild King looked to him and smiled. Umbra struggled to find his voice.

"The bill is rejected by a margin of ten," he said.

The Guild King's face dropped. His skin became pale, and he was forced to lean on his cane for support.

"Idiots," he muttered forcing himself to Umbra. He snatched the count from him and looked it over to make sure.

His face grew red with rage. "You are all idiots!" he yelled. "I made you all rich. I made you all powerful. You were nothing before me! You are nothing without me! How can we defend these lands when your stupidity ties my hands behind my back and gags my throat?"

"The Hall has spoken, sire," Umbra stated. "The bill has been…"

"The Hall does not have power over me!" the King shouted. "Guards!"

The Royal Guards poured into the Hall and lined the center. The Guild Masters rushed off their seats and onto the floor. The guards quickly formed a line with their spears leveled and dared anyone to test them. The unarmed Guild Masters decided to not.

"Sire, you can't do this!" Umbra exclaimed running to his side.

"I cannot fight a war with an empty coffer," the King stated. "You of all people should know that."

"Then call for a loan from the Vycesie, or the Mesmers even, but not this."

"No, we are in debt enough as it is. I will not leave such burdens on my son!"

"Sire, you are destroying your kingdom. You're undoing everything we have done."

"I am protecting the kingdom!" the King barked. "Why can you not see that? Hard measures are needed. Do you not understand?"

"Sire, you formed the Hall of Guilds. You promised the

Guild Masters veto power. You cannot go back on your word now and still be king."

The Guild King glared at Umbra. "How dare you," he hissed. "How dare you question me. All I do, I do for the good of the nation. I am the nation!"

"No sire, you are not!" Umbra screamed. "And if you touch that pen to paper, you will become a tyrant and a usurper."

"Watch your tongue," the Guild King spat. "I raised you above your station. I can lower you as well." The Guild King grabbed the quill and dipped it in ink.

Umbra slammed his hands on the table and leaned in close to the King. "If you sign that paper, you make yourself an enemy of the guilds. Thus making yourself an enemy of me. For as Hall Master, it is my sworn duty to defend the guilds: a duty you gave to me!"

The Guild King paused with the pen hovering above the document. "Umbra, please do not betray me too," he whispered sorrowfully.

"Arthur, don't make me your enemy," Umbra whispered back.

"I have no choice," the King muttered as he signed the bottom of the page.

Umbra stood up straight. A tear formed in his eye as he pointed a firm finger at the king. "Because you have broken your lawful compact with this Hall of Guilds, I, Hall Master, declare you no more the King of the Guilds! I dissolve your reign and strip you of all power!"

"Guards, arrest him," the King ordered.

"No!" Koll shouted, charging forward. The royal guards grabbed the young man and pushed him to the ground.

"I release all Guilds of their obligation and loyalty to the usurper." Umbra yelled as the guards wrestled him to the floor and began to carry him away. "I also call on all true subjects to rise up and oppose him with rightful arms!"

"This will mean war!" Koll yelled. "My father will never let this stand!"

"Take him away," the King demanded. "Arrest any that resist. I am the law now. I am the state! I am the King."

> *The first man came not from the sky*
> *but from the ground. The earth was his*
> *skin, the rocks his bones, and the water his*
> *blood.*
>
> **The First Word**
> **Summerset 1:32**

Francis awoke with a labored breath. The sound of dripping water mixed with the crackle of a fire. Francis brushed dirt from his face and tried to sit up. Pain shot up his leg forcing him back down. Francis carefully reached down and felt a sturdy branch latched with cloth to his limb.

"You broke it when you fell," the Warchief said out of his sight.

Francis gently worked his way onto some rocks so he

could sit up. The old Warchief was kneeling in front of a fire with an arrow still embedded in his side.

"Why help me?" Francis managed to ask.

The old Warchief tore a strip of cloth and took hold of the arrow's shaft. With slow determination, the old Warchief pulled the arrow out of his flesh inch by inch. Blood spilled from the wound. The Warchief's face wrenched in pain.

Finally, the arrowhead emerged from the skin and came free. The old Warchief let out several labored breaths before he plunged the iron arrowhead into his small fire. He waited until it grew red hot then he jammed it into the open wound. The sound of the skin sizzling made Francis cringe.

The Warchief held the arrow tip against his skin as long as he could bare it, then he dropped it and fell back against the rocks. Not once did he cry out from the pain.

"Why did you save me?" Francis asked again.

"None survive the caverns alone," the Warchief answered.

He lifted himself up and wrapped his side with the cloth he tore earlier. After tying it, he pulled himself to his feet and picked up a branch. He held the branch's end over the flames until they turned to embers. He then held the embers close to the walls.

Hundreds of runic carvings covered the stone walls. Francis could not read them, but he knew they were not orcish.

"We knew your gods long before you did," the Warchief explained. "We were their children before man even saw light of the sun and stars." The Warchief reached out and touched the runes nostalgically. "The Shamans have remembered the former things for centuries. The things you have forgotten."

"What do they say?"

"Your tongue could not utter them," the Warchief explained. "They tell the story of your people... and of mine."

"I don't understa..." Francis began to say. A sharp pain grabbed his chest then his head grew dizzy and his vision blurred. He fell back into the dust.

The Warchief rushed to his side and touched his feverish forehead. Francis began to shake and sweat uncontrollably.

"What... is happening... to... me," he managed.

"How much peace grass have you smoked?" the Warchief asked.

"I don't... I don't... I don't know."

The Warchief touched Francis' cheek and neck. He sighed in dismay.

"We must go," he stated. "If we wait, you will die."

"My... leg... I..."

The Warchief lifted Francis up onto his shoulder and together they limped into the darkness. Francis' body went from blistering hot to freezing cold then back to blistering. His head felt as if it would split open and his brains would pour out. His wrenched from what seemed to be his rips crushing his spine.

"Where..." he struggled. "Where are... we... going?"

"There is a fountain deeper in the caves. It may save you.

It may not."

"Don't... don't we need... torch?"

"No," the Warchief answered. "There are things here you don't wish to attract."

"How do... you... know... these things?"

"All Shamans come here," the Warchief explained. "It is the place where we find ourselves."

"Why... don't you... leave me?"

The Warchief grunted. "You will live, or you will not. If you live, you will see your crimes for what they are. If you do not, your gods will show them to you. Either way, the price will be paid."

"I..." Francis tried to say. Tears flowed from his eyes as he clenched his side in pain. He felt his vision go dark and his life slipped away.

The Warchief shook Francis awake. Francis coughed and cried in pain.

"Do not die yet," the Warchief said. "It is not yet time to die."

> *Love is a fire in a furnace. The more the wind blows and the coals are stirred, the hotter the fire will burn. And if not controlled, a single coal can melt iron into nothing. Such is love uncontrolled.*
>
> **Mesmer saying**

aven stood in her window and stared at the path where a few hours earlier she had seen Umbra and Koll dragged away by Royal Guards. She clenched the railing of her balcony and breathed the night air in terror.

"What have you left me to, mother?" she muttered to herself.

There was a loud thud from outside her door followed by another thud. Raven ran to her closet and drew her rapier. The door opened slowly to expose Charles standing over two unconscious guards.

"Charles!" she exclaimed dropping her sword and rushing into his arms. He embraced her and kissed her passionately. "What are you doing here?" she asked.

"I am getting you out of Doraxe," he explained. "It is no longer safe for you here."

"But I am pledged to the prince. I cannot leave."

"Raven, the coming war will be ugly – uglier than all believe. The King could use you to control your mother. I will not see that. The thought of you a prisoner or worse, it..." Charles struggled on his own words.

"Where will I go?" Raven asked saving him.

"I have a carriage waiting for you. It will take you to my master. You will be safe there until he can arrange for your return to the Free City."

"Will you be coming with me?"

Charles shook his head. "No, I have duties to attend to, but I promise I will see you soon."

Raven pulled Charles in again and kissed him deeply.

"Do not let this be goodbye," she stated.

"I will not, but we must go."

They went down the halls quietly but quickly, being careful to pause for guards to pass. Soon Raven could see the carriage Charles spoke of and found herself reluctant to leave.

"Here is some gold for the journey, and papers for any check points," Charles said. "It is a royal carriage so there should be no problems, but..."

"I love you," Raven blurted out. Her face went red with embarrassment. Charles smiled.

"And I love you," he replied. "Now go."

Raven ran down the steps and climbed into the carriage. Charles waved to the driver who flicked the whip on the horses and sped off into the night.

Charles collected himself and sneaked out of the citadel and into the city. The City Watch building was covered with men fearing a rescue attempt on their two newest guests.

Charles hid in the alleyway and threw a rock at one standing on the edge of the perimeter. The rock hit his helmet and, annoyed, he came into the alley to investigate.

Charles stabbed him in the throat with a needle-thin knife, which drew little blood. He tore the clothes off him and quickly put them on. He was out into the street before any other watchmen noticed their comrade was even missing.

Slowly, Charles stepped closer to the gate until the guards at it were used to his presence. Then he discreetly tossed another rock away from him. The guards instinctively looked towards the sound, and Charles walked on behind them.

He made his way up into the tower where the noble prisoners were kept. The torches lit his way all the way to the top. A guard was standing in front of Umbra and Koll's cell door. Moon light poured in by a small window at the top of the stairs.

Charles approached casually as if he was there to take the next watch. The guard noticed him and turned to address him. Charles stepped in close then rushed forward, pushing the unsuspecting guard through the window. He barely had time to scream before he hit the cobblestones below.

Charles removed his stolen guard helmet and opened the cell door. Umbra and Koll stood amazed and confused.

"My lords." Charles bowed.

"What are you doing here?" Umbra asked, annoyed.

"I am here to deliver you from your bondage, my good lords."

"You are lying," Umbra spat. "You are the King's man."

"It is true the King has been a great friend to the arts. But Lord Victor has been my patron for many years."

"Mesmer trickery," Umbra scoffed. "Leave me be and let me die in peace. I am nothing now."

"I'm afraid I cannot do that, my lord. For you are, in fact, everything. My master, Victor, knows he cannot win this coming war alone. He needs the support of the guilds, and you, Baron Umbra, can give it to him."

"And why would I help Victor fight my king?" Umbra

asked.

"Your king has you locked in a tower, likely to be beheaded. You have little choice."

"There is always a choice," Umbra stated sitting back on his hay cot.

"My lord," Koll said. "If we do not go with him now, we are surely dead men."

"I am already dead," Umbra stated. "All I have worked for is dead. The guilds are dead, stripped of rights and power. I am lost."

"My lord," Charles started. "If you help Lord Victor, he promises to allow the guilds to continue as they are."

"I do not believe you."

"My lord," Koll said. "We can make an alliance with my father to guarantee his word. Victor will not fight Northrim and Galsag."

"He is right, my baron. Victor only wants his heirs on the throne, as is his right according to the agreement he made with the Guild King. Your friend, I am afraid, is the only man whose word is questionable."

"And who would he put forward as King?" Umbra asked

"I believe his son Maxwell was his choice."

"No," Umbra stated flatly. "He puts Francis as king or I will not help him. At least Francis can be called a true guildsman."

"I believe he will agree to those terms."

"I want to hear it from his lips."

"That will not be possible in this cell," Charles explained.

"You are right," Umbra said standing to his feet. "So how will we escape?"

Charles pulled out a rune-covered stone and whispered into it. The rock began to glow as bright as any star.

"Come my lords and touch it."

Umbra and Koll reluctantly did as they were told. They reached out, and as soon as they touched the stone, they found themselves in a cut wheat field. The lights of the city were far behind them, and the road sat empty before them.

"Mesmer magic?" Koll asked.

"No," Umbra said. "Something darker, I think. No matter, come. We have a long road ahead and much to do."

"Where are we going?"

"To Castle Pearl to gather the Broken Lances," Umbra replied heading towards the road in the moonlight. "And then to war."

The world will always remember the great heroes of time. But they rarely remember the true one.

History of the Guilds
Elder Lighours

Lady Edoweyhn tried to relax in her carriage, but the bumps and jostles of the road made rest impossible. Her trusted man sat across from her with a pleasant expression.

"Raven will make an excellent Queen," he said.

"She would make an excellent Mayor," Edoweyhn replied. "Which is why I am glad to be rid of her. The last thing I need is someone competing for the title in the next election."

"My lady, you have won three times, I doubt anyone would challenge you now."

"Never underestimate the underdogs," Edoweyhn advised. "If left unchecked, they will bite your legs out from under you."

The aide nodded politely. "The fourth army reports they are moving towards Castle Pearl. They will arrive before the winter comes in full force, but they will not be able to move to Anchor till the spring."

"Fine, fine," Edoweyhn dismissed. "Only make sure the Guild King understands it is my army, not his. I want Anchor. I don't care about anything else."

"Yes, my lady," the aide stated.

The carriage rolled to a stop. "What is this?" Edoweyhn asked.

"I will see," the aide said stepping out of the carriage.

"What is it?" Edoweyhn repeated leaning her head out the door.

"It's some traveler blocking the road."

"Well, move him!" Edoweyhn shouted.

"Yes, mistress," the aide said approaching Charles. "Sir, you need to move this cart off the road. By order of Lady Edoweyhn of Mesmer City."

"Is Lady Edoweyhn in the carriage with you, or are you only acting in her name?" Charles asked.

"She rides with us," the aide stated confused. "Sir, I really must insist."

"No, I understand," Charles said drawing a pistol and shooting the aid at point blank range. The guards on horseback moved to act, but Charles killed them both with two throwing knives. They fell into the mud without a chance to cry.

The coach driver reached for his sword, but Charles leapt up onto the coach and ran the driver threw with his rapier. Lady Edoweyhn jumped from the door and ran into the woods terrified. Charles calmly followed.

Edoweyhn pushed her way through branches and over roots. She sprinted as hard as she could, losing her wig and much of her fine dress to the forest's outreached limbs. Her foot finally caught on a root, and she tripped into the dead leaves. She struggled to get back up.

"It was clever to send your entourage on a different route," Charles said walking up from behind her. "Almost fell for it myself, but my task is too important to fail."

"I can pay you!" Edoweyhn offered. "Whatever your employer paid plus double."

"I don't need money," Charles replied.

"What do you need? Power? Position? Women?" she asked franticly then raised an eyebrow. "Men?"

Charles pressed the tip of his rapier against Edoweyhn's neck. "All I need is right here."

He raised his blade. Edoweyhn screamed. The scream was cut short.

> *The First Word tells us little about our origins. Summerset has some cryptic lines about being made from the earth; rocks are our bones and the like, which has led to wild speculation. I believe our ancestors wanted us to forget where we came from. I believe they knew it would somehow twist us to know.*

> **History of the Guilds**
> **Elder Lighours**

The Warchief felt the cavern wall with his hand. Francis' breathing became more labored with each passing moment. A gentle stream of water touched the Warchief's foot. He hurried down the turn, following the flowing water.

The cavern opened up into a large cave then into a huge open area. Small bits of light escaped through cracks in the ceiling, revealing what looked like structures and ruins.

The Warchief sat Francis down and used a piece of flint to light a scrap of wool. He tossed the small burning cloth into a trench near him. The trench caught fire and ran out across the open area, illuminating an ancient underground city. Francis, even through his shivers and dry heaves, was stunned by what he saw. The Warchief lifted Francis back onto his shoulders and carried him into the ruins.

They passed buildings that looked like houses with water troughs and waste buckets. They passed by a shop with stone-cut jewelry hanging on display. But as they neared the center of the city, they then began to pass bones. First, it was the remains of soldiers clad in armor. But as they went, the bones became smaller and more innocent in their pose. Francis saw one skeleton with its arms wrapped in protection of a much smaller skeleton. They passed piles of such bones.

They reached a fountain with what looked like moldy water in it. The Warchief sat Francis by it and scooped his hand in the murky sea. He offered the water to Francis.

"Drink," the Warchief said. Francis shook his head in refusal looking to the sickening lake. "Drink," the Warchief ordered holding open Francis' mouth and pouring the water down his throat.

Francis immediately vomited and spat. The water was the foulest thing he had ever tasted. Darkness overcame him.

"You have killed me," he muttered as he lost consciousness.

Francis saw himself in the distance. He saw torches being burned around him. He saw children run past him. Fire began to burn the ground. He moved to flee, but his legs were grabbed suddenly by snakes. Then there was darkness and a quiet whisper in his ear.

His eyes opened to a woman he did not know. Her black

hair fell on her shoulders. Her eyes made one smile. Francis sat up.

"Who are you?"

"You don't know me," she said in a gentle voice.

"Where am I? Am I dead?"

"Not yet," she replied. "Not for many many years."

"What is going on?"

"You are awaking."

"From what?"

"From a spiritual sleep. You are not allowed to be asleep anymore."

"Are you from the Divines?" Francis asked, terrified he knew the answer.

"Yes, I am an angel. Their voice and will."

"I have many black marks," Francis confessed.

"Yes, and the Divines know them all."

"Will I burn?"

"We will see..." she replied.

Francis awoke with a jolt. The Warchief was roasting a few rat-like creatures over a fire. Francis sat up and felt his forehead. His fever was gone, so were the chills and shivers. He felt his broken leg and found the bone completely healed and the muscles reformed.

"What was in that water?" he asked.

"Old medicine," the Warchief commented. "In the ancient times, people would travel far to drink from it."

Francis looked about him at the ruined city. "What is this place?" he asked.

"The place our peoples first met."

"What do you mean?" Francis asked.

"As I said, we knew your gods before you did." The War-chief offered Francis one of the roasted rats. "Eat," he said.

"Starvation would be preferable."

"The cave spiders will kill you before hunger comes," the Warchief stated. "Eat. You need strength."

Francis took the meal from the orc's hand and tore into the tasteless flesh. "Why are you helping me?"

"I said once already- can't survive caverns alone."

"But I have been no use to you; in fact I have been a burden. So why go to the trouble?"

The Warchief sighed heavily. "Among my people, when a hunter goes mad from heat and kills his brother, he is not held guilty for his crime. He instead must balance the scale of his evil deed. You were mad with peace grass, iron prince. I cannot punish you for your crimes."

"What crimes?" Francis laughed. "That chief I killed? The Shaman's tongues I cut out? The books I burned? I did what my king demanded, nothing more. I hold your people no ill will."

"You cut down females and young ones," the Warchief muttered. "You cut them down out of anger and let the hogs eat them. You went mad, iron prince."

"I..." Francis began. "It was for..." Tears rolled down Francis' face. "Oh Divines, what have I done?"

"You must balance the scale," the Warchief stated. "You must for the sake of your life force. You must balance the scale."

"Tell me what to do," Francis pled crawling towards the orc. "How can I make this right?"

"The gods will decide," the Warchief stated standing to his feet. "But first, we must leave."

"How? There is no way out."

"There is a tunnel and a hole. It is where the air comes from. I will show you."

Francis stood to his feet and stretched his sore muscles. The Warchief went out ahead beckoning Francis to follow. Francis caught up quickly and followed the Warchief through abandoned streets till they came to a pile of rocks.

"This was not here before," the Warchief explained.

"When was the last time you were here?"

"Two hundred winters."

Francis sighed. "Is there no way around?"

"No," the Warchief stated. "The hole is on the other side."

"Well, great. Now we are trapped."

"So it seems," the Warchief said sitting down in front of the rock pile.

"What are you doing?" Francis asked. "We will never find a way out sitting here."

"I am thinking," the Warchief replied. "Perhaps iron men would have fewer problems if they did more of it before acting."

Francis moaned in annoyance. He paced about anxiously then sat next to the orc. There was silence between them for several moments.

"There must be another air vent," Francis stated. "Some-where."

"You are right," the Warchief said. "But I know not where they are, and so they might as well not be there."

Francis climbed to his feet again and began to pace about annoyed. He came up to the pile of boulders and kicked one out of frustration. The rock moved slightly. Francis shot a look to the Warchief who stood to his feet.

"Run," the Warchief muttered.

"What?"

"Run!" he shouted.

The boulders suddenly rose to life and towered over them. Francis and the Warchief sprinted off down the alley-ways of the lost city. The giant rock creature charged after them, crushing homes and bones as he went.

Francis saw the Warchief dash under and outcropping and soon followed after him. He dove into the blackness and rolled when he hit.

"What is that thing?" he asked in a whisper.

"A monster of old," the Warchief explained. "The vent should now be clear. Run to it, escape, balance your scales."

"What about you?"

"I will draw it."

"No, let me die. Let me balance my scales with my life."

"Your life force has many more journeys till it rests," the Warchief stated. "It is time for mine to join my son."

The old Warchief shot out back into the city streets. The rock monster noticed him and slammed its fist on the ground near him. The Warchief was sent flying but landed on his feet.

"Go, iron prince!" he shouted while running deeper into the city. "Balance your scales!"

Francis waited until the rock monster followed after the orc before he crawled out of the outcropping and made his way towards the vent. He could see a small hole in the stone within arm's reach of the ground where the boulders once slept.

He reached it and jumped to grab the edge. With effort, he pulled himself up into the hole and started to crawl in the dark dirt. A blood-curdling scream rang out behind him followed by silence.

Francis hung his head in respect then pushed on. The soil was wet and mushy. He began to feel bugs crawl along his skin. He was forcing his way through roots and grass.

A glimmer of light peeked through the haze of debris. Francis pushed on towards it. Soon he could smell fresh air and even feel cool water drip on his face. He continued to claw his way up till he burst out of the ground and into open prairie. Tears of joy suddenly began to roll down his face as he dragged himself away from the hole. The sun beat his face. The clouds never looked so welcoming. Francis stood to his feet and began to walk.

About the Author

Max Cooper was born in Illinois, went to college in Kansas, and went to Germany to find his wife. He served briefly in the army and is now a full time writer and artist in Wichita, Ks with his wife and son.

Visit www.candersonpublishing.co
for more about Max's works and other great authors.